"Who's t

"Tinsley, really! Delores patted her white hair nervously as she looked at her niece in horror.

"Well, they are. And their owner was young, kind of good-looking. He came late and didn't stay for tea."

"Oh, that was just Alex Berringer."

Tinsley waited, curious.

But Delores changed the subject. "I must say I was a bit surprised at your behavior this afternoon."

"Why? You've known me all my life. You know I get excited about things. What's wrong with that? You know I love nothing more than a good fight."

"We were at a literary meeting, for heaven's sake."

Tinsley smiled. She was in too good a mood to let her aunt's words bother her. Her mind returned to the man who'd been in the audience. Alex, her aunt had said. Alex Berringer.

Books by Sharon Brondos

Southern Reason, Western Rhyme

Sharon Brondos

Harlequin Books

TORONTO • NEW YORK • LONDON
AMSTERDAM • PARIS • SYDNEY • HAMBURG
STOCKHOLM • ATHENS • TOKYO • MILAN
MADRID • WARSAW • BUDAPEST • AUCKLAND

Published December 1992

ISBN 0-373-70527-1

SOUTHERN REASON, WESTERN RHYME

Dedicated to my mother, Elaine F. Hardy,
who is, to some degree,
all of the women in this book.
Thanks, Mom!

The cowboy poetry herein is written by Terry Henderson of Douglas, WY. Thanks, Terry, for introducing me to and educating me about this remarkable folk art.

ACKNOWLEDGMENT

Special thanks and acknowledgment to Terry Henderson for permission to quote from her poems: "Camp Coffee" (1991), "The Lonesome Close of Day" (1987, revised 1991) and "In My Mind" (1987, revised 1991).

CHAPTER ONE

THE POET WILL READ FROM HER WORK, the carefully lettered sign stated. It sat on an easel, right in front of a potted palm, in full view of every single person in the room. Tinsley Cole stared at it. She was going to die. It was that simple.

"I did not agree to read my own material," she whispered to her aunt. "I'm not prepared, for goodness sake! I'm not really a poet, just a lawyer. I'll fall flat!"

"Oh, don't be silly." Delores Bishop patted her niece's hand. "You don't need to prepare. You're a natural. They'll love it! You'll have them all in stitches in minutes." Her tone was so reassuring, it had just the opposite effect. Tinsley felt worse.

"Delores, I write *cowboy* poetry! I talk about horse manure and spittin' tobacco. Half these ladies are wearing white gloves and hats! With veils!"

Delores just smiled serenely.

Tinsley looked out at the audience and her nervousness level rose to new heights. She was dead meat. A week ago, when she had agreed to give a lecture to Delores's literary society, she had no idea her aunt would put her on the spot like this by asking her to read from her own writings. Although her poems had been published—mostly in cowboy magazines—her stuff was not appropriate for this audience. She was definitely going to bomb.

And, she had a vested interest in success here. She was not just doing Delores a favor, she was trying to work on her own future. She needed to fit in with South Carolina ways. Not an easy task for a person who had been born and raised on a ranch in Wyoming.

She searched inside for the courage she knew lurked just out of reach. In the past, she could call it up on demand. These days, it came when it wanted to. She was older and wiser now. Less willing to take chances. Despite the room being air-conditioned, sweat was beading along her hairline and trickling down her sides.

The room was beautiful. Gracious, really. Gracious, in the sense of style she had become familiar with during the time she had lived with Delores. A style she was growing to appreciate, even though it was vastly different from what she was used to. Here everything seemed in soft focus. Southern sunlight, mild and gentle, filtered in through the wide French windows, illuminating the terrazzo floor, white walls and the rows of chairs on which the elegantly dressed audience was seated.

That audience was mostly women, though a few men were scattered about. The males were of the older variety, displaying white hair or tanned baldness, dressed only slightly less elegantly than the women, with tweedy sports coats and ascots instead of ties. Stylish, subtle and aristocratic. Definitely not a cowboy crowd. Not by the wildest stretch of anyone's imagination.

But she had agreed to read and give a lecture on regional poetry, and a bargain was a bargain. The only part she hadn't banked on was presenting her own work. Delores had assured her they were interested and enthusiastic to learn.

Tinsley sighed and stared down at her hands. The creases in her palms were glistening with nervous sweat.

Stage fright. More of the painful legacy she was apparently going to carry with her for the rest of her life. Before the accident, she had never had butterflies or stage fright over public speaking. Never. And she had read her material to far more critical audiences than this on more than one occasion. Audiences that understood her poetry because they lived it. Never had she been so worried before.

Well, there were a lot of nevers in her life now. And she was dealing with them, one or two at a time. She reached under her legal pad and pressed a damp tissue against the wetness on her hands. She straightened in her chair, ignoring the twinge in her back. She looked out at the audience and smiled. At least she still had her pride. Not one of them would know she was turning to jelly inside.

Delores Bishop noted that most of the members were in place and waiting. She glanced over at Tinsley and saw her niece struggling for control of her nerves. A twitching had developed beneath Tinsley's left eye, making the smooth, pale skin jump slightly, and tiny beads of perspiration glowed above her upper lip. Tinsley's long, graceful hands disappeared underneath the note-covered legal pad, and Delores knew she was wiping her palms dry. She saw the small, pinched expression of pain cross the young woman's face. Back trouble? Now?

For a moment, she experienced a horrible wave of doubt. Perhaps Tinsley really wasn't ready for this. Perhaps she was making a terrible mistake, exposing her niece to public speaking too soon, even though she trusted her literary group to be kind and gentle.

But none of her friends, not even the closest, knew how fragile Tinsley might be. She certainly didn't look fragile. Not with that mane of healthy, thick, platinum blond hair, blue eyes that could warm to deep indigo or freeze to an icy gray and a figure that was, to say the least, robust and statuesque. Then she saw Tinsley smile, saw the old fire and courage shining through her eyes and knew it was going to be all right. Delores smiled herself, rose to her feet, walked over to the podium and opened the meeting.

"Ladies and gentlemen," Delores began, surveying the group. "Today we have a special treat in store for us. My niece, Miss Tinsley Cole..." She broke off for a moment as a latecomer made his way to one of the few remaining seats.

Typical of the man, Delores thought. Rather than sitting in the back, inconspicuously, he did have to blunder up front, distracting everyone. She waited until he was settled, trying not to give him the satisfaction of glaring at him, but failing. She glared, hoping he felt her withering gaze. She then continued, addressing the entire membership once more.

Alex Berringer sat down in his chair, well aware his entrance had annoyed the regal Mrs. Bishop. He was embarrassed about it, as he always was when he breached social protocol—behaving properly had been drilled into his very marrow. Brainwashed since the moment of his birth. Which was why, he believed, he tended to overreact when he was in the wrong.

Certainly, it had not been his intention to be rude, but some little imp had perched on his shoulder and whispered that, as long as he was late, he might as well make an effort to be conspicuous. It went with the territory he'd staked out for himself years ago, after all. Slouching even more carelessly, he rubbed a hand across the stubble of beard on his face and looked up at Delores.

Delores wasn't looking at him. She was glancing and gesturing at the young woman seated on the speakers' dais. Evidently she was a poet. The program placard declared she planned on reading some of her stuff this afternoon. A newcomer to the area, she was also a relative of Delores's, judging from what he'd heard on his way in. Alex let his gaze drift over to the new woman, who was this month's Literary Society's sacrificial victim.

His eyes widened. She surely didn't look like his idea of a female poet! He sat up and wished fervently that he had taken the time to shave. Made himself more presentable. He felt his mouth still smiling, but now he knew it was just a foolish twist of his lips. All he could do was stare at her and grin like an idiot.

Tinsley saw the latecomer looking at her with a friendly smile on his face and wished she felt more like smiling back at him. Of all the people watching her as if she were an insect in a jar, he was the only one who seemed even remotely likely to appreciate the earthiness of her poetry. Although he was dressed formally enough to get in the front door of the exclusive clubhouse, it was a studied parody of sartorial elegance that he wore.

His sports coat was light, linen or maybe silk, but it hung on his broad shoulders like a garment that had spent most of its life slung across the foot of a bed, or even crumpled on the floor. His shirt was open, with neither tie nor ascot at the throat, and she could see black chest hair at the low point of the vee. She also noted the tail of a wrinkled tie sticking out of his coat pocket—worn to get past the eagle-eyed manager of the club, then removed. She felt the corners of her lips move upwards. She approved of this kind of defiant behavior in this world where so many rules of dress and action seemed to be the norm.

Her gaze moved on. Ah, he was wearing jeans. They fit him like a second skin, just as they were supposed to. Long legs and old, worn jeans. She felt a warm rush of homesickness. He had on deck shoes instead of boots, but those legs looked like Wyoming. Tinsley smiled now, noting the lean thighs. She looked back up and saw he was still staring right at her. He was dark haired and deeply tanned, with radiating squint—or smile—lines leading out from the corners of his eyes. She decided they must be smile lines, because of the laughter she thought she saw in his light green eyes. She stared back, letting her eyes lock with his. When she heard Delores finally finish introducing her, she had trouble pulling away.

But she managed. As she stood, the twinge hit her back again, and she almost forgot the man in her effort to keep from grimacing. She straightened her shoulders and walked to the podium, more conscious of controlling her gait to accommodate the pain than of the people watching her. By the time she set her pad of notes on the lectern, she had dismissed him from her mind and was ready to launch into her presentation.

She had also forgotten the pain, her butterflies, and furthermore, the palms of her hands were dry.

"Cowboy poetry," she said, "comes out of the everyday experience of ranch workers, male and female. It's authentic—written by someone who's actually lived the life—it tells a story."

She paused, giving the audience time to digest what she had said and to anticipate what she was about to say. "It is not about pretty or high-flown things," she warned, deliberately widening her eyes and leaning forward. The right moves were coming back with the courage, she realized with joy. She was cooking!

Alex sat, entranced. She was no great beauty, as he understood and appreciated feminine charm. All the goods were there, some in generous proportions, and she certainly had a face that would make him look more than once.

But she was...big. Her face was broad, her cheekbones prominent. Her nose looked a little crooked, as if it had been broken once and reset off-center. Her lips were full, sensuous and wide...

She had a big mouth, plainly speaking. Wide shoulders, too, and he could tell the silky shirt she wore had no shoulder pads. Didn't need them. Her bosom strained the front, and though she had a relatively narrow waist, her hips were flared and giving the material of her skirt some work, as well. She had a big rear, plainly speaking. Generous hips and thighs...

Big woman...

Sexy woman...

He sat back and folded his arms across his chest. Strange. All his sexually aware life, he had preferred the delicate, magnolia blossom type of woman. They liked him, too. So why this inexplicable reaction to Juno? Maybe it was the fantastic hair. She had a wild mane of white-blond that reminded him of palomino horses, rushing across a wide, western prairie... No wonder he'd stared. She surely called up all sorts of images.

And it hadn't been one-sided, either. She had stared back at him. He felt a glow inside at the memory of her steady, blue gaze. Nothing sexual in her stare, nothing flirtatious. She'd just *looked* at him.

That was odd. He blinked, bringing himself back to the immediate moment. He listened and began blinking harder.

She was reading from some of her own poetry, Alex realized. Had been for a while, while he had been assessing her physical attributes. He felt like shaking his head to clear his ears and mind. She could not possibly be read-

ing a poem about a cowboy with an urgent, no, *desperate*
call of nature and a bedroll zipper that wouldn't open!
   She was.

   "The cowboy took a final cup
   and drained the campfire pot.
   That extra drink he didn't need
   but it was steaming hot.

   The night stars shone upon his camp.
   It'd been a long hard day.
   Unknowing as he crawled in bed,
   by morning he would pay.

   It was the middle of the night
   when nature made her call.
   The cowboy hurried to get out,
   confined by a zippered wall.

   His bedroll wrapped around him tight,
   bound him from head to toe.
   Desper't'ly he clawed his way,
   but he just moved to slow.

   The zipper wouldn't budge an inch,
   the bag became a noose.
   The struggle didn't help him now
   as nature turned him loose.

   The moral of this story is
   before you make your camp,
   throw out that extra coffee
   or by morning you'll be damp."

   The finish nearly finished Alex. It was the pause that
made it ambiguous enough to cause doubt about the

quality of that "dampness." Since he was seated in the front row, he couldn't see the reactions of his fellow Literary Society members, but he could certainly hear the indrawn breaths and the smothered gasps. He could imagine the looks on most faces. Alex put his hand over his mouth. It was going to take everything he had to keep from laughing out loud. She was good! *Very* good.

Tinsley knew she had everyone's rapt, if horrified, attention, now. Even the guy in the wrinkled jacket and tight jeans was watching closely and seemingly hanging on every word. She was no longer concerned about what anyone thought. She was stating her case, giving her argument, presenting her evidence for cowboy poetry. Just as if she were in a courtroom again.

"Now. Bodily functions may seem an inappropriate topic for poetry," she said, addressing herself directly to a woman in the fourth row who looked as if she were about to stand and walk out. "But to the men and women of the frontier, then and now, a slug of strongly alkaline water can result in an unforgettable case of the trots. It's real and the memory is unerasable. An existential moment, if you will, and I believe, one that deserves mention in the annals of American poetic literature." She paused to let the point sink, and noted that the woman settled back, her eyebrows quirking as if she were considering the matter.

"Frontier experiences," Tinsley added, "especially physical ones, tend to fit the universal mode of human experiences. Read a poem about unrequited love to a person from another culture, say, one that doesn't hold with the concept of romantic love, and you've lost your audience. But *everyone* has had...um...digestive upsets from time to time. The whole human race can relate to poor old Sam."

"But... but it's not *poetry!*" The woman in the fourth row sputtered the accusation. She had pale blond hair like Tinsley's, but it was cut in a short style, framing her narrow face, and was too dull to be a natural color. Her skin was deeply tanned, and she had the thin, muscled arms of an avid golfer.

Tinsley looked at her and smiled. "That is your opinion. Your are entitled to it."

"Mine, as well," added the man sitting next to the woman. His face, with its smug, superior expression, was red from overexposure to the sun, and she saw a stickpin in the shape of a golf tee jammed into his ascot. The unlit pipe stuck between his lips bobbed as he spoke. "I personally find the subject matter of your poetry quite disgusting. Young lady, your lecture has been interesting, but nothing you've said induces me to become a devotee of drivel dealing with dead horses and human, ah, waste..."

"Sanford!" His companion put her hand gently on his arm. "Be careful of your language."

Tinsley leaned her elbows on the lectern. She was ready to take on the man. "Sanford," she said, taking advantage of knowing his first name and using it to bring him down a peg. "I wouldn't dream of forcing devotion on you or anyone else. But I have to ask, when you blow a golf shot, are you inclined to recite romantic poetry to express your immediate emotional feelings or do you just say...ah...a word that describes human waste, such as...?"

She didn't finish the sentence, but let the deleted word hang unspoken. The group was dead silent for a moment, absorbing the impact of her suggestion. Then, snickers started. Sanford turned purple, and the pipe bobbed so fast it fell out of his mouth. She knew he couldn't talk back. He was too close to screaming at her.

So Tinsley just nodded, knowing she had made her point and defeated the competition. She went on. "Shakespeare was considered quite crude by many of his contemporaries. We've accepted his language as among the finest produced by an English speaker. Consider this: out there on the vast Wyoming prairie, the Shakespeare of the twenty-first century is riding on his horse, thinking up poems about common human experiences. Or, maybe *she's* piling her kids in the back of a pickup truck for a ride into town, and all the while, an epic about being a ranch wife is building up in her mind. And I guarantee she isn't composing sonnets about spring flowers and undying love!" She stepped back a fraction. "I invite debate on this."

Debate came. Alex listened, astonished, as the usually quiet, tame Literary Society launched its collective self into the fray. Miss Cowboy Poetry set herself squarely in the center of the hurricane and looked like she was having the time of her life. At first, she had remained protectively behind the podium and lectern, holding on as if she were supporting herself. But soon she was out front, using a voice that carried without the aid of any microphone, waving her arms to emphasize her points. She and Sanford Taylor got into a shouting match, and she won. Not, however, without acquiring some scars from Taylor's agile verbal swords.

Alex watched, turning his head from one combatant to the other, as if at a tennis match. But he didn't say a word. By now the other members of the audience had entered the fray, some siding with Tinsley, others with Sanford. The longer the conflict went on, the more uncomfortable he felt. This was just the sort of situation he hated. A little gentle teasing was one thing, but yelling and accusations of intellectual fraud were quite another. Neither side attempted to be polite, and it was getting hot. Alex wanted out.

Delores Bishop sat rooted to her chair, also observing the action with disbelief. This could not be her calm, pensive Tinsley. Nor could this angry, loud-voiced mob be the sophisticated, polite members of her adored Literary Society! What demons were possessing everyone? She looked out at the crowd. Only young Alex Berringer was sitting in his place, an expression of extreme embarrassment on his tanned, unshaven face. And Alex was usually the troublemaker, injecting a word of disagreement here, giving a shrug of disapproval there. But never, never, *yelling*. Not even Alex would dare. One just didn't. Until today. Her friends! So many of them were actually *yelling*. Had everyone lost their minds?

Finally, Tinsley brought it all to a halt. "I think," she said, in a voice that carried over all else, "that we've had an exciting discussion here today." As she spoke, she gradually lowered her tone. Delores watched, amazed, as the others stopped shouting and talking and slowly settled back into their seats. Tinsley was working them, Delores realized, playing them just like an instrument. Why, she'd had no idea the girl was so gifted. And she looked as if she were having a fabulous time. So excited, her skin was flushed with color, and her hair almost stood out straight from her head.

Tinsley moved back behind the podium. She felt wonderful! "We've disagreed on some important issues," she said. "And I am delighted." She grinned, hoping they could understand the affection she had for each and every one of them, now. "Thank you all for letting me speak to you. I hope to have the honor again sometime."

She picked up her notes. Applause started spatteringly, then it grew. Then, as she walked back to her seat, several women stood, applauding loudly, and calling, "Brava!" Soon, the majority of the Carleton Cay Literary Society was on its feet, applauding. Only Sanford Taylor remained seated, muttering to his thin, agitated wife.

Alex Berringer stood, too. Then he walked out.

"So, TELL ME, Delores. Who was the guy in the blue jeans?" Tinsley asked as she and her aunt drove home later. The club was only a few blocks from the Bishop mansion, and Delores had chosen to chauffeur them herself. April afternoon sunlight slanted dustily through the live oak trees lining the road, giving the air a golden glow. Spanish moss hung from the huge branches. Tinsley watched the shadows of the trees as they passed. She was counting them. One...two...three...twenty, twenty-five... So many trees. So much light and shadow here. Even the moss cast lacy shadows....

"Jeans?" Delores's hands still quivered a bit. She hadn't quite recovered yet from the shock of Tinsley's performance and, more, from the aberrant behavior of her trusted friends. The very ones she had counted on to ease Tinsley gently back into society. Gently! "Someone had on blue jeans?"

"Yeah." Tinsley leaned her head back against the headrest. She still felt great, better than she had in a long time, but she was tired. "Young. Kind of good-looking. He hadn't shaved, but he had terrific thighs."

"Tinsley!"

"Well, he did. He came in late. Clumped all the way up front. Like he owned the place, and didn't care what anyone else thought of him. And he left right after I spoke. Didn't stay for the tea and informal talk."

"Oh. That was just Alex Berringer." Her tone indicated dislike.

Tinsley waited, curious.

But Delores changed the subject. "You..." her aunt said. "Your behavior this afternoon..."

Tinsley said nothing.

"Well, I must say, I was a bit surprised."

"Why?" Tinsley turned her head to look at her aunt. Delores's profile told her only that the woman was upset. "You've known me all my life. I get excited about things. What's wrong with that? You know I love nothing more than a good fight."

"This was a *literary* gathering." Delores's lower lip tucked under. "Not a courtroom, for goodness sake."

Tinsley chuckled. "I know. But that Sanford guy is pretty game in a squabble. I'd sure love to argue a case against him, sometime. He isn't a lawyer, is he?" she asked, hopefully.

"He is not." Delores turned the wheel, guiding the long, lean Lincoln carefully up the slope of her driveway. The sight of Sanford Taylor, screaming at her niece, had shaken her badly. "He's a retired bank president." She cocked one eyebrow. "I do believe, however, that young Berringer studied law for a while. Not that it's likely he ever passed the bar." Again, that tone of disapproval.

Tinsley sat up. "What was he doing at a Literary Society meeting in the middle of a weekday afternoon? He didn't go into practice? What's he do, then? Doesn't he have a job?"

"He writes a bit." Delores pulled in front of her home. The white columns lining the front porch gleamed in the late afternoon sunlight. "Nonfiction. Historical articles about the coastal area. I hear he's quite good, though controversial in his conclusions. I haven't read anything of his, myself. And he doesn't read to us.''

''Maybe he's shy. He didn't utter a peep this afternoon. That's for sure. And I think he was the only one besides you who didn't.'' Tinsley got out as soon as the vehicle stopped. She grinned in triumph at Jason Turner, Delores's butler, chauffeur and general factotum, who was just coming out the front door. She and Jason engaged in this duel every time the car stopped. It had been weeks since she'd still been slow enough to allow Jason the chance to open her door for her and help her out. The man gave her a pained look and hurried around to assist Delores, who accepted his service graciously.

''Thank you, Jason,'' Delores said. ''Go ahead and park in the garage. We won't be going out tonight. I'm sure Tinsley has tired herself all out, behaving as she did this afternoon.''

''Miss Tinsley.'' Jason glared across the roof of the car at her. ''Did you do something to upset your aunt?''

''No, I did not.'' She looked closely at Delores. ''Or maybe I did. I kind of got wound up, Jason. See, there was a difference of opinion...''

''She certainly did get wound up,'' Delores interrupted. ''She actually instigated a fight. A verbal one, of course, but a fight, nevertheless.'' She, too, glared at Tinsley, but her niece could see the love beneath the anger. ''And I doubt it did your condition any good at all. Now, off to bed with you. You should rest before dinner.'' She waved her hands toward the door.

Tinsley felt her euphoria eroding. ''I don't need to rest,'' she said, thinking how like a child she sounded. ''My back hurts a little, but otherwise, I...''

"Miss Tinsley." Silvie, Jason's wife, appeared at the front door. "There's a phone call for you, child. It's your momma."

"I'm coming." Tinsley turned and started up the steps. She was thirty-one years old, and still called a child around here. She smiled wryly as she crossed the gleaming black-and-white tile of the foyer. Well, being treated as tenderly as a child had been exactly what she'd needed for a while. She didn't need it now, but wasn't sure how to get out of this soft, safe nest she'd made. Being protected by love was sometimes a pain. Delores certainly wouldn't let her move out without a fuss, even if she could afford to.

Which she couldn't. The months of medical treatment after the accident had taken up most of her savings, even though the insurance had helped with the hospital bills. She needed to get back into the work force and earn some cash. The sooner the better.

Tinsley went into the drawing room and picked up the phone. "Hi, Mom," she said. "What's up?"

"Hi, darlin'," Ellen Cole said. "How are you doin'?"

"Fine." Tinsley tensed. "I'm just fine. How're you?" Whenever her mother was upset, she slipped back into the Southern drawl of her childhood, reverting from the flat, open sounds of the Wyoming tongue. Her drawl was pronounced now. Something was wrong.

"Oh." Ellen started crying.

"Mom!" Tinsley gripped the receiver. "What is it? Is Dad...?"

"Tinsley, baby." Her mother sniffed, getting control. "It's not us. Darlin', it's Brad. He..."

"He what?" Tinsley straightened. The pain in her back was suddenly sharp. She pressed her hand against the scar, feeling the long, rough line of it through her shirt. "Come on, out with it, Mom."

"He's getting married." Ellen sniffed again. "The snake!"

ALEX PARKED HIS JEEP by the dock and sat in his seat, staring out at the bay. The sun was low, and his island looked like a jewel way out there in the water, the light turning the green into gold. His island. Alex frowned and squinted until the view blurred. It was all he wanted out of life. All he needed. There, he had achieved the sense of peace and tranquility he had yearned for, and nothing could take that away. Not now.

Why then, he wondered, had he let that woman bother him so much this afternoon? She certainly wasn't peaceful or tranquil. But that wasn't his problem. It was hers. If she liked rabble-rousing, so be it.

Alex sighed and stretched. Had to admit it had been funny, though. The way she'd gotten Sandy Taylor's goat like that. It had been great theater. Alex grinned. She'd needled the old boy right where he lived—his golf game. His overblown pride.

He got out of the Jeep and locked it. He tossed the keys into the air and then dropped them into the pocket of his jeans. Belatedly, he remembered the silk sports coat he'd shed earlier, but decided to leave it on the passenger seat where he'd tossed it. He wouldn't need it again for a while, anyhow.

His deck shoes scrunching on the shell walkway, he went down the path to the dock. She was something. Up there, reciting those strange poems. He'd heard of cowboy poetry before, he supposed. Just never heard it spoken, or rather, read aloud. He grinned. No wonder, given the subject matter and style. It was crude. Far too real and earthy for the kind of literary company he was used to keeping.

But she'd carried it off. Alex waved to Timothy Blane, the dock guard. The tall man grinned and waved back, calling something Alex couldn't hear over the sound of the water lapping the pilings and the gentle roar of a fishing boat passing by. The waves grew after the boat was gone, then receded to normal size. Alex stood by his taxi. The little motorboat bobbed on the waves.

Yessiree. She had carried it off. He put his hands in his pockets and gazed out over the water. Standing up there, big, no, *bigger* than life, and reading her own poem about that poor sap with the defective sleeping bag and the severe case of the trots.

Alex chuckled and bent to release the bowline. Took nerve to do that. Nerve and a lot of skill to run that verbal free-for-all. More nerve than he cared to expend, as a rule. Alex straightened. The scene had made him a little uneasy, he had to admit to himself. He didn't mind fighting for what he believed in, of course, but he preferred doing it a good deal less publicly. After all the years of emotional hurt and then healing, he still hated being at the center of any controversy. Clearly, that woman did not. She seemed to love it.

What did she do for a living? He tossed the line into the boat and went down to release the stern line. An actress? She certainly had the presence, if not the beauty. But sometimes the camera was particularly good to a woman with unusual looks. He stepped into the boat, adjusting his weight without thinking about it. Yes, she might be a stage actress, too. With her size and the power of that voice, she could project to the last row with no trouble. No trouble at all.

He sat and started the engine. The machine rumbled gently, purring for him. He patted it and headed out to the channel. The wind whipped his hair and caressed his skin with a swift, rough touch. The salt water smelled fresh, cleaning the odors of the mainland out of his head. The island glowed. It beckoned.

Alex felt his muscles relax. The water moved under him like a wild animal, willing for the moment to be ridden quietly. He adjusted, feeling its mood and swell. In a little bit, he'd be home. Home and alone, where he could think and make sense out of what he had been feeling today.

Where was Delores's niece's home? Out West somewhere, obviously. Alex leaned back, controlling the tiller with his fingertips. He was going to have to find out. Call Delores next time he was back on the mainland. Hell, he couldn't even remember the niece's name. Something like...a salad vegetable. Lettuce? Lettice? No, that wasn't it. Damn it, he just couldn't remember.

It was funny, since he couldn't seem to get her face and body out of his mind.

CHAPTER TWO

"TINSLEY. Telephone again." Silvie's voice belled up the stairway, down the hall and into Tinsley's room. Tins pushed back from the desk and faced the doorway.

"I hear you," she called, amazed as always at the strange acoustics in Delores's home. You could whisper secrets to a lover behind closed doors and not another soul on earth would hear you. But open those doors, and a mouse's burp would be audible all the way down in the kitchen.

"I'm getting it," she added, unnecessarily. Silvie would already assume her message was received and go on about her business. Tinsley went for the phone.

The only upstairs phone was out in the hallway on a special table. Delores had not seen fit to place phone jacks in the bedrooms. It was uncivilized, she told Tinsley more than once, to be sleeping and have something right by your ear that just anyone in the world could use to invade your rest and privacy. If a call was a true emergency or otherwise vitally important, the caller would manage somehow, to get in touch with you.

Tinsley had to admit that, although the setup was inconvenient, Delores did have a point. Living graciously was an art form to her aunt. Tinsley approved when it also included convenience and common sense. This thing with the phone rated somewhere in between.

She reached for the receiver of the old-fashioned dial phone. "Hello," she said, leaning back against the wall, her bare feet planted on the thick carpet. "Tinsley Cole. Who's this?"

There was silence on the line.

She looked at the receiver in annoyance and started to hang up. She didn't have time for this. Her hand was an inch from the cradle when a squawking noise that sounded like a wounded chicken emitted from the mouthpiece. Annoyance passed and curiosity bloomed. Tinsley lifted the receiver back to her ear. A man spoke to her immediately.

"Sorry, I almost dropped the phone. A gull just dive-bombed me." The speaker laughed, then turned formal. "Miss Cole?" The voice on the line was deep and masculine. "Am I speaking to Miss Tinsley Cole?"

"Yes." Tinsley straightened, her hand on her hip, easing the tension in her back. "Who is this?"

"Um, Miss Cole, you don't know me. I'm Alex Berringer. I, that is, we haven't exactly been introduced, but I feel as if I—"

"Oh, sure. The guy at the meeting yesterday with the jeans." She smiled, remembering. The guy Delores thought was a bit unorthodox or something. Strange, anyway.

"Jeans?"

"You wore jeans. I liked that. Made me feel more at home."

"It did? I did?"

"Yes." She pictured the strong, lean length of his thighs and the color of his green eyes. She remembered the amusement and then the confusion he'd seemed to show when she had argued with that Taylor guy. An interesting, contradictory combination that intrigued her. She felt very friendly toward this man. "You did. I was on the verge of a wild case of stage fright, and you helped pull me out of it. I appreciate that. Thanks."

"I... You're welcome."

"It's okay. What did you want?"

Silence.

"Alex?"

"Sorry. I was just thinking. You had stage fright?" He sounded as if he couldn't believe her.

"Sure did. I was nervous as a cat in a room full of rocking chairs." She twisted the telephone cord on her fingers. Intriguing or not, this conversational dance was taking too long. She had things to do and wished he'd get to the point of his call. Back home in Wyoming, a call from a man, a social call as this one seemed to be, was limited to a few sentences and an agreement on a meeting place. Long, meaningful conversations usually took place in person, not over a wire.

Laughter over the line. Surprised laughter. "A cat! In a room full of rockers? Miss Cole, you do have a way with words and..."

"Call me Tinsley, Alex. What's on your mind?"

"Um." He sounded hesitant, or perhaps just surprised. Tinsley waited.

She had noted she had a way of making folks around here seem surprised and even nervous when she talked to them. She was just too abrupt, her aunt told her. Too blunt and direct. She didn't take enough time for the amenities of polite social exchange, Delores said. Maybe she'd managed to offend this Alex.

A moment later, he continued, however, and didn't sound offended at all. In fact, he sounded quite the opposite. "I enjoyed your reading and was impressed. I'd like to see you, Tinsley. I'd like..."

"Well, come on over. I was busy, but it wasn't anything really important. Just writing some letters. It can wait. I could use a break."

A pause. Then: "Now?"

"Sure." Tinsley frowned. This was an odd reaction. Why had he called now if he didn't want to get together right away? He sounded so hesitant, she regretted her impulsive response to him. As usual, her curiosity had set her up. "Unless it's inconvenient, of course," she added, hoping to cover the embarrassment she suddenly felt. It rose up from some place deep within her and made her face hot.

"Well... No, it isn't." he replied after another pause. "I just... Well, you have caught me a bit unprepared." His voice was deep and soft as a lover's caress, but she thought she heard a chiding tone underlying the sweetness.

Tinsley gripped the receiver. She had committed some sort of social faux pas with her words. Exactly what, she wasn't sure, but instinctively, she knew it. She was in an emotional state now, unreasonably embarrassed at doing something that came naturally to her. Why in the world was she reacting like this?

It was unsettling. She felt as if she were slipping on ice, slugging through mud, aiming at an unseen target. She felt as *awkward* as a teenager. Why? Time to step back a few paces! Give herself a chance to collect her feelings and figure them out. "Look, Alex," she said. "It was nice of you to call, but if you..."

"Tinsley, don't hang up! I'll be there as soon as I can." The words came out in a rush. "I just didn't expect you to jump on my invitation so quickly. Most women... I mean, it is unusual around here to respond so directly."

"Oh?" Was that *all?* She *jumped* on his invitation too quickly? Good grief!

"It'll take me an hour or so to get to the mainland," he went on, speaking rapidly, his southern accent making his words sound slurred to her ear. "I can be at Delores's in, say, an hour and forty-five minutes. Will that be all right?"

"Mainland?" She listened, hearing in the background that strange chicken-screaming noise, feeling certain she must have misunderstood him. "Where are you?"

He laughed. "Out on the dock. I'm using a portable phone. Can't you hear the sea gulls? I'm feeding them, and they're raising a real ruckus. Yelling and cussing in sea gull language and fighting over the scraps. They're devils with each other when it comes to food. It's quite a sight. I'd like to show it to you. Maybe you could write a poem about that."

Now she laughed, relieved of oppressive, awkward feelings. Feeling only good things again. Friendly emotions. Warmth. Something about his voice... The sound of his laugh... "Maybe I could. You know, we have gulls in Wyoming. Sea gulls that have never seen the sea." She gave the idea a mental double take. "You're right. I might be able to whip something together using that. Never crossed my mind before."

"I like your poetry." His tone was almost intimate, as if he were complimenting a physical attribute, rather than a literary one.

"Thanks." She felt heat in her face again, but this time it wasn't from embarrassment.

"It's unique."

"I'm looking forward to talking to you, Alex. See you in a bit. Goodbye." She hung the phone up quickly, astonished at the variety of emotions she had experienced because...

Because of Alex Berringer's voice.

How silly!

This was not like her at all. Shaking her head at herself, Tinsley went back into her room. She sat down at her desk. One thing was for sure, if she reacted so strongly to a strange man's voice, it was certainly time she got back into some social activity. High time! She thought about her mother's phone call.

The news that Brad was finally marrying Millie was not a shock, although it could be considered a slap in the face, nevertheless. Brad had been cheating on her with Millie for well over a year, anyway. And, since the night of the accident, any attention he paid her was purely political in nature. For show, only. Maybe that's why it had hurt so much. She hated lies, no matter how they were packaged. Truth was almost like religion with her, to the point where even her father had commented on her fanaticism unfavorably. And he rarely found anything wrong with either her or her mother.

Well, one thing was for sure; she was never going to get involved romantically and emotionally again, unless the man's honesty and loyalty were as clear to her as the glass in the window, if not clearer!

Tinsley looked down at the letter she was writing to her mother. "I am truly relieved," she had written, "to hear Brad has finally made his big move with Millie. It's a chapter in my life that's done with. Time for me to move on, too."

That's right! She was moving on, growing away from the pain of the past and feeling darn good about it all, thank you very much. She picked up her pen and wrote.

You'll be pleased to hear I'm going out this afternoon with a guy I met at Delores's literary group.
Don't get the wrong idea. He's no pale poet type.
Actually, he does write, Delores says, but he looks
more like a guy who works outdoors with his hands
for a living. Tough and self-assured, you know. He's
young, about my age, athletic, good-looking and...

And what? She didn't know anything else about this
Alex Berringer except that Delores thought he was
strange. Hmm. Wouldn't do to tell her mother that. Not
right now. Not while residual anxieties about her daughter's physical and emotional well-being still lingered in
Ellen Cole's mind and heart. So, Tinsley finished up the
description by saying merely that he was from an old, established family. That ought to soothe any worries her
mom might have. Ellen was still Southern enough to be
impressed with "family." Tinsley added a few more chatty
comments about life at Delores's and signed her name
with love.

A soft rap on the doorframe interrupted her thoughts.
"Who was that on the phone?" Delores asked. "Not your
mother this time of day, surely?"

Tinsley turned and smiled. Delores stood, framed in the
doorway, slender and regal with her silver hair shining like
her own special aura. The older woman was completely
unaware of the beautiful picture she made. "No," Tinsley said. "It wasn't Mom. Alex called and said he'd like
to get together this afternoon."

"Alex?" Delores's eyebrows rose. "Alex Berringer? He
called you?"

"Mmm-hmm."

"Dear, I..."

"Listen." Tinsley stood up. "Unless he's got a wife locked up in a tower or something really horrible like that, I'm not concerned with his private life, his personality or his intimate secrets." She went over and patted her aunt's arm lovingly. "I'm just going to spend a little time with him, that's all."

Delores looked away, not meeting her gaze directly. "Well, I just worry about you. You're such a wonderful girl, I feel you should have the opportunity to spend your life with someone who deserves you."

Tinsley blushed, feeling anger as well as discomfort. "For goodness sake, I'm not going to marry this Berringer person. I'm just seeing him for a while this afternoon." *And I'm hardly a girl, anymore,* she thought, a little hurt at the unintentional put-down. It was just a word, of course, but it never failed to act like a red flag. Women were *women* where she came from. Not "girls" or "ladies" like most people called women around here.

Besides, Tinsley wasn't so sure spending a lifetime with someone who "deserved" her was such a great fate. She wanted a life with someone who wanted and needed her. Someone who was hungry for her, for crying out loud! She made a small, rude noise, indicating her feelings.

Now, Delores did look straight at her. "If you're really ready to date, I can arrange for you to meet some very nice young men."

"No!" Tinsley nearly grimaced at the notion of the kind of "nice man" Delores would have in mind. He would probably be pale, blond, well groomed, so polite, she'd nearly scream with frustration at his smooth ways, his pleasant lies. And he would be as sexually appealing as a glass of warm milk. "Thanks, but no thanks. I'm not dating Alex. I'm just, well, I don't know. He said he wanted to see me. And he's coming by."

"That," Delores said, darkly, "is a date."

"Not in my book." Tinsley felt the rise of hot defiance. She didn't feel this way with her aunt as often as she had when she was small, but her temper did surface occasionally when Delores pulled her chains hard enough. Tinsley's father referred to it as "Western grit." Delores and Tinsley's mother called it "mulish stubbornness." Whatever it was, Tinsley could recognize it. She knew she was now operating on emotion, not logic. "And I plan to go as I am," she added, making an effort not to sound too belligerent.

Delores's gaze took in the T-shirt, jeans and bare feet. "No makeup," she said, not asking it as a question. "No special dress, either, I take it." She touched Tinsley's cheek gently, as if patting a wayward and incorrigible child, then turned and left the room. The soft sound of a suppressed sigh trailed after her. Tinsley watched until her aunt was out of sight, then closed the door. She leaned her forehead against the cool wood until the throb of tension in her back eased.

At least, Tinsley thought, Delores had accepted the situation with her usual grace. Of course, that made *her* feel guilty for having been so rude. Rude by Delores's gentle standards, that is, not Tinsleys's. Southerners and Westerners were different enough to have come from different planets in many ways, she had long since decided. So, calm down, she told herself. She was trying to be Southern now.

She went back to the desk, picked up the letter to her mother and placed it in an envelope. As she licked the stamp, she thought of Alex Berringer and wondered if he used Delores-style standards of behavior and if he thought she was rude.

Not that it really mattered one bit if he did. But she wondered.

ALEX SET the cordless phone handset down beside him on the dock and considered the odd conversation he'd just had. He'd made the call on impulse, pure and simple. Even though that impulse was backed up by thoughts of Tinsley Cole that had been on his mind ever since he'd laid eyes on her yesterday afternoon. Impulse, after all, was still impulse.

Wasn't it?

High above his head, the gulls flew, squawking and screaming, furiously demanding he pay attention to them again. Alex tossed out the rest of the bread and let them fight over the treasure while he continued to muse on what he had done.

He'd committed himself to taking the boat to the mainland. Now. Not later this afternoon or evening, or even tomorrow. No, he'd told Miss Tinsley Cole he'd be there as soon as possible.

Why had he done that? Alex leaned forward and looked down into the water. It lapped softly at the pilings of the pier. He had planned to spend the day sitting out here, thinking and making notes about his new book. Something he needed to do alone, sitting still. In peace. Not charging across the sound to a rendezvous that held little promise of anything but amusement at best, aggravation at worst.

He took a deep breath, smelling the salt and sweetish rotting scent on the tide. Better than the finest perfume. It meant life! He stared down at the water, seeing his reflection as a vague shadow. Seeing another shadow near his ...

Her hair would look like gold underwater. Gold with a faint, fine, green patina. It would swirl and whirl like a fire around her face, making her look like a mermaid from an ancient fable. Or a siren from ...

Alex sat up, slamming his palms down on the dock. This was just the kind of useless daydreaming he'd been doing ever since he set eyes on her. Wasting his valuable time on fantasies that had no roots in reality. He hit the dock again, this time with his fist. The telephone handset jumped and bounced, scaring a curious sea gull that had waddled too close. He started to reach for the handset. He'd just have to call her back and explain he hadn't meant he wanted to see her right now. He'd explain ...

But she expected him to be on his way already. She'd be preparing, taking time out of her own day just for him. He certainly had heard enthusiasm in her tone. She had told him she was busy, hadn't she? But she was willing to take a break to see him.

A break. A change in her plans just because he had called. Alex smiled, in spite of his annoyance at having to restructure his plans for the day. He loved women for that extra effort they put forth for men. For their willingness to adjust to a man's plans. They spent hours, sometimes, just picking out the right dress to wear. More hours fixing their hair and putting on makeup. He liked women and was extremely happy to be a man most women liked, as well. Maybe that was egotistical, but he preferred to think of it as enjoying the way life set him up.

Okay. So there had been a crimp in his plans, a matter of misunderstanding over the phone with her. Big deal. He asked to see her, she had agreed, and he owed her the simple courtesy of showing up when he said he would. Alex slapped his palms on his thighs, grabbed the phone and stood up. The gulls hollered at him, then sailed away on the breeze. They were accustomed to his departure being the signal that no more goodies were available. Predictable birds. He had them well trained.

He walked down the length of the pier to his house. The sun beat hard and hot on his back, warming and loosening the muscles that had tightened while he was deliberating his situation. Alex felt good.

The interior of his home was cool, making his skin tingle when he first entered. He put the handset back on the phone base and went into the bathroom to shower. He would certainly raise another good sweat taking the boat across, but it pleased his sense of order to wash off the old before getting the new. He also decided to dress with a little more than his normal casual attention to style.

He shaved again, scraping away at the bluish black stubble that always appeared less than an hour after his morning toilet. Usually, he let it grow and didn't bother with touch-ups during the day.

But this day, he was calling on a lady. She would expect and deserve that he look his best.

THE LADY SAT OUT on the front steps of her aunt's home, a writing pad in her lap and a pencil in her hand. Kicking off her sandals, she stretched, enjoying the feel of her muscles moving. She checked the soles of her feet before propping them against the white columns holding up the roof of the front porch. Her feet were clean. Not like when she was a child and had made footprints all up and down the pristine whiteness. Then, she had been mad about something. Now, she was happy. No need to smudge the paint, just because she wanted to be comfortable. Tinsley sighed, contentedly.

Things were looking up for her. She'd made a public speaking appearance and had survived. Had fun, in point of fact. And she apparently had also netted the interest of an interesting man.

Alex Berringer. She wrote his name down and then erased it. Nice name. Had a ring to it. A rhythm. Da-da *Da* da-da. She smiled. Always had to be poetry when she wrote for herself.

So what? Nothing wrong with that. Poetry had helped keep her mind off the extreme pain when she was healing, hadn't it? Some people sang or played music or read or even watched TV to take their thoughts off their problems. She wrote verse.

Everyone had their own temporary way out of reality, didn't they? Everyone was entitled to that. She wondered what Alex Berringer's way was.

Well, it hardly mattered. Most folks liked to keep things like that secret. Not broadcast them to the world.

She sighed again, this time remembering the poem she had read at the national festival of cowboy poetry a few years ago. It had been so funny, deliberately so, that it had brought the house down, but she had composed it out of a private pain she scarcely remembered now. The topic had been a romance between a cowboy and a city girl and was based on a failed relationship of her own from her senior year in high school. Success out of disaster. She tapped the eraser of her pencil on the pad of paper. Another poem began forming... About a cowboy facing the end of a hard day... of a hard life...

It comes down to that time of day.
Loneliness grips him all the way.
The emptiness when the sun goes down
is echoing silently all around.

The fields are bleak with snow and ice.
He has no mate, he pays the price.

A cowboy's job of solitaire
will make him yearn for loving care.

The rest of the day is fairly fleeting
but evening comes, a sting, sleeting.
He needs someone to tell his woes.
When no one's there his mind can close.

A rugged individual shrugs.
Just one more night without those hugs.
A tough exterior shell by day
at night will fall to bits of clay.

Though lean and lined, his face will tell
how many times his soul he'd sell
for companionship at the close of day
to field that lonesome haunt away.

She looked at the work, then made some changes, here and there. Sad stuff. Loneliness.

Failed relationships. Funny, she hadn't really thought about it this way before, but it seemed that right after a love affair went wrong, she experienced a kind of life-changing event. Not always a good one like having her poetry honored, but life-changing, nevertheless. Her mother's call informing her of Brad's marriage could be considered the termination of that particular relationship. Was she in for something earth-shattering, now? Headed for a fresh success? Or the opposite? Doomed to deal with some new turmoil?

Lord, she hoped not! Tinsley shifted position until she was resting with her back flat and comfortable on the top step and her feet still on the pillar. She relaxed and closed her eyes. The last thing in the world she wanted right now was a crisis, good *or* bad.

All she wanted was peace and quiet and time to find out where she wanted to go with her life. That wasn't too much to ask, was it?

She relaxed more, breathing in the soft scents of springtime in the South. The air was heavy here, so much thicker than back home in the high plains of Wyoming. Heavier and stronger. It could carry more aromas, more smells, it seemed. Pine from the long-needled Carolina pines that made up a small, shady forest over in the corner of the lot. Sweet perfumes from the last of the perennial spring flowers. The rich, earthy odor of the soil, and the ever-present, illusive smell of water.

That was one of the biggest differences between South Carolina and Wyoming. Water was everywhere. Even the air was saturated with it, so much so that at times she felt like she was swimming, rather than walking. Humidity always registered well above fifty percent. Stifling to her. At home, if it topped twenty percent, you felt like you were drowning.

Yes, water made the area alien to her, in many ways. She was used to seas of grass, not H_2O! A sharp pang of homesickness hit her. She opened her eyes and saw the trees. They loomed everywhere. The trees were another problem. They got in the way.

At home, she could remember the horizon going on forever. It was normal to see for miles on end, sometimes viewing mountains located over a hundred miles away. Here, if you saw ten feet without having a tree block your line of sight, you were doing well.

But the trees were so... majestic. Like the high mountains at home. They lined the quiet residential streets like sentinels, Spanish moss dripping from low-hanging branches. They crowded together to make dark, cool forests. And they lived far longer than the humans who admired and tended them. Trees here were entities to be reckoned with. Beings with real personalities. At home, they were even more precious, but they rarely reached appreciable size and certainly didn't last all that long.

Exceptions existed, of course, she mused. There was that old cottonwood down by the creek in the back part of the upper pasture. She really loved that tree. Climbed it often when she was a kid....

In my mind I'm sittin' in
the ideal place to be:
Up there on that mountain side,
beneath an old pine tree.

Listenin' to the whisperin' winds
tellin' me their tales,
Far off—hear a coyote cry,
listenin' to his wails.

She drifted, dreaming and dozing, the Carolina sun warm on her face and arms. She felt the heat, but was only vaguely aware of it. She was far more aware of her daydream and the memories that started to rise in her mind because of it. She was home, in Wyoming, driving.... Driving toward home.

The day was sunny, as usual. So sunny and bright, in fact, that she had to squint behind the dark lenses of her sunglasses. The road stretched forever, a bright, glaring arrow point in the direction of home. Tinsley felt the tingle of excitement that hit her every time she headed back to the ranch.

But this time, the tingle was tainted with the anxiety of knowing she was going to have to tell her parents her wedding plans with Brad were off. Plans she should never have made, given the personality of the man she had *thought* she'd loved! And furthermore...

And as she let her mind deal with arguments about Brad, she scarcely noticed the pickup truck heading toward her. Didn't notice the driver was weaving.... Didn't notice until the glare on the surface of the road blinded her like sudden, bright headlights for a moment and...

She heard the screech of brakes and screamed, throwing herself to one side. Pain knifed into her back, and suddenly she found herself falling down the stone steps of her aunt's South Carolina mansion instead of into the dark terror of an automobile crash. She yelled again in anger, ready this time to take action to save herself. Tinsley threw out her arms in an effort to stop her body from crashing to the ground, but...

Other arms caught her. She clung to her savior, crying out at the pain in her back. It wasn't as agonizing as in the dream, but it hurt badly enough to bring tears to her eyes.

She was embraced, pulled against a man's body, protectively, not sexually. Tinsley panted, trying to catch her breath, trying to override the pain. Groaning aloud with the effort. Someone said her name, gently, soothingly. Gradually, she began to feel better.

Then she looked up and saw who was holding her.

CHAPTER THREE

"DON'T MOVE," Alex Berringer said, holding her tightly against his chest. So tightly, she could feel his heart beating. So close she could smell the scent of the soap and shampoo he used. Even the salt spray and sunlight in his hair and on his skin. Clean, fresh.

"Are you hurt? Does it feel like you broke anything?" he asked.

"No." Tinsley stared up at him. "Where'd you come from?" she asked, her voice shaking. She was disastrously close to tears.

He loosened his grip on her slightly, though his worried gaze seemed to hold her even more tightly. His feelings showed in his words, too. His Southern accent thickened and sounded almost like a foreign language to her ears. He actually came close to babbling like Delores did when she was upset.

"Why, I thought you heard me," he said. "I pulled in by the magnolias over there and my brakes caught on me. Made an awful noise. Squalling like those gulls I told you about. I thought that startled you. I'm really sorry to have disturbed you like that. It certainly must have given you a fright to make you lose your balance and..."

She straightened, wincing with the pain, and pushed away from him. "Your brakes squealed?" she asked, just to shut him up for second.

He nodded, silent, apparently out of things to say.

"That must have been what triggered my dream, and..." She rubbed her eyes. "You must think I'm really nuts," she said, noting that her voice sounded quite normal once more. At least, she no longer felt like she was going to burst out crying in front of a stranger.

"No," he said in a gentle tone. "I don't think that at all."

She blinked, focusing on him.

He looked gorgeous. Close up, his eyes, which were still regarding her with an expression of serious concern, seemed greener than emeralds and were fringed with thick, black lashes. Sunlight made them sparkle like gems, and she knew it wouldn't take much to be drawn right into the dreams she imagined she could see in their depths. She moved farther away from him, feeling just about as awkward as she could remember. "I must have fallen asleep, waiting for you," she said. "The sun was so warm, and it's so peaceful out here, I guess I just dozed off."

"And had a nightmare?" His hand still rested on her shoulder, his palm warm and his touch somehow comforting. "Miss Cole, you bellowed out like an angry bull alligator just before you started tumbling. Then you yelled again. You sounded really mad! That must have been one heck of a dream."

Tinsley pushed her hair back. It had come loose from the ponytail and was hanging around her face, tickling and annoying. "It wasn't really a dream," she explained. "Most of my dreams are good. I was reliving an accident. It was a bad experience. The sound of your car must have set it off, like I said."

"Must have been some experience," he said. "Car wreck?"

"Mmm-hmm." she continued to gather up her hair, not willing to lie, but also unwilling to go into detail. She hoped he wouldn't ask any more questions. He said nothing, but he watched her like a hawk, as if the sight of her struggling to get her ponytail back in place was the most fascinating thing he'd seen in ages.

Maybe it was. If he liked slapstick comedy, anyway. She was sure putting on a show! Her dark hair was so thick and fluffy from the humidity that she couldn't get it under control. She stretched the band as wide as possible, but it wouldn't fit. She stretched it a tiny bit farther.

She swore as the elastic broke, the ends snapping and stinging her fingers. Her hair fell back down onto her neck and shoulders. She gathered it up, let out a small yowl of frustration and let it all fall again. Then she smiled at Alex. "Hi," she said. "Pretend nothing of the last few minutes ever happened, please! I'm embarrassed enough. So what's up? What did you have planned for us to do this afternoon?"

Alex laughed and made himself look away. His fantasies about her spending hours fixing herself up for him were certainly just that—fantasies. But it didn't matter. She was so utterly appealing and charmingly disheveled it was all he could do to keep from embracing her again. If he allowed himself to continue looking, he realized, he would very likely lose control of what good sense he had left.

Pretend the last few minutes never happened? No chance! She'd fallen down the stairs right into his arms and snuggled there finding sanctuary while she fought with the demons of her dream. It was a special, supremely intimate experience for him.

He liked the feeling. Liked it much too much, given the fact he'd just met this woman. "Well," he said, slowly getting hold of his thoughts. "I don't really have anything particular in mind." That was a big lie. The longer he stood near enough to smell her sultry, natural scent and sense her body's warmth on his own skin, the more something very specific was developing in his mind. This was one sexy woman. He was, therefore, responding, accordingly.

Apparently, she was totally unaware of it, too. He noted again that his earlier egotistical fantasies of her were hardly prophetic. Probably, everything he had imagined about her, based on his past experience of women, was less than accurate, he decided. He had to remind himself that he was drawn to her because she was so unique.

She wore no makeup that he could see and her clothing was strictly grabbed-from-the-drawer. He saw nothing at all in her eyes or the expression on her face to indicate she was making any effort whatsoever to be alluring. Her charm was in her complete naturalness. And that, he reflected, was far more exciting than any reality he'd experienced over the years or any fantasy he had entertained of late. He saw a shadow of a frown appear between her tawny eyebrows and realized she was waiting for an answer to her question.

"I didn't have anything specific planned," he repeated, realizing all he wanted was a chance to be with her and to check out his feelings. "What would you like to do? Besides taking a fall down the stairs, that is," he asked, hoping to lighten the mood and his own emotions, hoping she didn't mind a little teasing.

Tinsley didn't mind. "Let me think about it a minute," she said, grinning at him as she sat back down on the step. There was a tenderness underlying his words that she liked. She studied him, her nerves back to normal now. He sat on the step beside her, regarding her, but not staring, and patiently waiting for her to make up her mind.

He looked different from her memory of him. Unlike the casual way he'd presented himself at the meeting, today he was dressed to the nines. Though he wore sports clothes, they were sharp and elegant. A white polo shirt, so clean it gleamed. His muscled shoulders and upper arms stretched the material nicely. Khaki pants. Top-siders. Even his face was freshly shaved. He looked younger and smoother, more sure of himself.

Tinsley decided she liked him better the other way—scruffy, a little flustered about being late for the Literary Society meeting, but plain and honest. That was the Alex Berringer who had attracted her attention. This one was certainly okay, however. He looked . . . well . . . clean-cut and nice. Delores would surely approve, if she saw him. Funny thought. Clothing really didn't make the man any different inside but around here, it was important to make a good surface showing. Tinsley made a decision.

"Let's take a walk, then, if you really didn't have specific plans," she said. "I kind of kinked my back when I fell, and I'd like to work it out. Walking always seems to help." She had another reason for her suggestion, but she didn't mention it. Walking aimlessly with a new acquaintance, she had learned long ago, was also a way to get some insight into how that person ticked. She was curious enough about this man to want a little more of that kind of knowledge.

"A walk it is." He seemed relieved and pleased at her suggestion. He stood and offered his hand to help her up, but she had already scrambled to her feet. "Where would you like to go?" he asked.

Tinsley shrugged. "Right here, I guess." She arched her back, testing for pain and found only a slight twinge. "Around the block, maybe. I've been running it in the early mornings. Be interesting to see it in slow motion for a change." She bent over gingerly, her hand pressing the scar on her back. It didn't hurt much. Hardly at all, in fact. "Ah," she said. "Think I'll live." She walked down the driveway, setting a brisk pace.

Alex followed more slowly. He felt downright lecherous because of his sexual reaction to her body. When she bent and twisted, clearly intent only on checking the damage to her back, she had elicited some powerful erotic responses in him. She might be big, but she was supple and moved in the most interesting ways. Again, all unaware, he was sure. He was both pleased and annoyed. He started to analyze that strange combination in himself, when he noticed something strange about her.

"Say, Tinsley?" he called.

She stopped and looked back at him.

Alex pointed. "Your feet. Shouldn't you have on shoes?"

DELORES WATCHED the two young people from the window of the living room. She didn't like to snoop, didn't approve of eavesdropping and certainly wouldn't observe others without their knowledge under normal conditions. But she did not regard what she was doing right now as any sort of invasion of Tinsley's privacy. She realized that Tinsley might not agree, of course, but this was a special situation as far as Delores was concerned.

She'd been alerted to it, heart pounding, by her niece's cry of fear and pain a few minutes before. She had been on the verge of rushing out the front door to Tinsley's aid, when she'd seen Alex Berringer through the beveled glass panel beside the door.

She had paused, sure that no matter how odd young Berringer might be, he would not deliberately hurt Tinsley. She was right and was glad she had stopped herself

from interfering. It was clear to her that Tinsley neither
needed nor would welcome her help right at that moment. My goodness, no! She had clung to the man as if he
were an angel rescuing her. Delores backed away and
moved into the living room, where she could watch the
events more discreetly. Jason and Silvie had appeared
briefly, looking to help, but she waved them away. She
wanted to be alone. She sought comfort in the most familiar piece of furniture in the room. The one Ben had
bought for her first Christmas they were together as
husband and wife.

Delores Bishop sat in her special chair by the big fireplace and let her gaze drift to the scene on the front porch.
She could see Tinsley and Alex talking. She tried to
imagine what they were saying and how they felt from
their movements and expressions. It wasn't too difficult.
Since living alone, Delores had spent a lot of time observing others and drawing conclusions.

She saw how concerned the young man seemed to be.
She could tell Tinsley was brushing off the incident,
whatever it was, and barreling on with her plans. Pretending nothing had happened. Business as usual. She led,
Alex Berringer followed. Delores saw something and sat
up straight. She frowned. Tinsley was still barefoot.

Then, Delores had to smile. Apparently Alex said
something about it, because Tinsley turned around, a look
of embarrassment on her face. She grinned sheepishly, ran
back to the porch and grabbed her sandals. Delores
watched as her niece braced herself against the young
man's arm while she slipped the shoes onto her feet.
Hopping around awkwardly like a little child. No attempt at dignity whatsoever.

Oh, Tinsley, her aunt thought. *I surely would have died before behaving so casually in front of a new beau! Why, I...*

Delores shut her eyes and felt tears stinging behind the closed lids. She remembered how carefully she had conducted herself while Ben Bishop had courted her those long decades ago. Her fingers gripped the armrests of her chair so hard she felt physical pain. The tears broke and rolled down her cheeks. She still missed him terribly even after all this time.

She knew her grief was affecting everything she did in a negative way. And that, Delores knew, was wrong. Very wrong. Ben would be the first to say so! Be the first to tell her to get off her... derriere and do something about it.

But, she knew there was no one else she could ever love as she had loved her late husband. No one who could touch her heart in the same way. No one else to "do something about it" with.

So Delores Bishop sat, silent and solitary, long after Tinsley and Alex left the grounds of her home. She knew it was wrong to be so self-indulgent, but she could not bring herself to get out of her beloved chair. There were so many memories. Memories she was not prepared to turn from. Memories that she knew were holding her hostage against her future life. But what did the future hold for her without Ben? Nothing that she could think of. So she sat recalling the past, reveling in the good memories, aching over the bad.

TINSLEY WALKED, her hands jammed into the pockets of her jeans and her attention directed to the cracked, mossy brick sidewalk. She was aware of Alex, but only peripherally. It was a comfortable awareness and not intrusive.

Oh, he'd made her uncomfortable and a little angry when he reminded her to get her shoes on, sure. Would it have been so terrible if she'd gone barefoot? But it wasn't really him she was angry with, she realized.

She was annoyed at herself. So she'd covered her feelings with a cute act of guilty forgetfulness. "Oh, my," she had chirped, idiotically. "How *silly* of me to go off without protecting my feet. Thanks so much for reminding me." Blah, blah, blither, blither. She wasn't acting like herself at all then. Tinsley kicked a pebble off the sidewalk. It bounced into the gutter, splashing as it hit the narrow stream of dirty water that always seemed to flow along the roadside.

"Care to share?" Alex's voice almost startled her. "Or do you kick little rocks around for the simple pleasure of it?"

She turned and looked up at him. She was tall, but she had to tilt her head to look into his eyes. He was a big man, she realized. Bigger than he seemed at first. "I was just ruminating," she confessed. "Kind of sourly, actually."

"You could have fooled me."

His smile and gentle tone brought an answering smile to her face. A big, strong guy, but more than that. A man of some sensitivity, she decided. He certainly deserved more of her attention than she was giving.

"I'm afraid I'm not much good company right now," she said. "I tend to get real quiet when something's bothering me, and I have to tell you, I'm still bothered about falling down the stairs right into you."

"I didn't mind. You were graceful, at least."

Tinsley laughed. "I guess it was like an old-fashioned Southern belle swoon, wasn't it? How corny can I get!"

He grinned now. "Pretty corny, judging from some of the poetry you read the other day. It's not exactly Southern and definitely not graceful. But it fits you and has a dignity all its own. The poetry, I mean. Not the fall."

"Thanks, again." She looked at him for a moment. "Alex, I'm glad you called me. I like you." She touched his arm, then put her hand back in her pocket and walked on.

Alex nearly missed his next step. She liked him? It was nice to know that, but he just wasn't used to being told so soon in a relationship. Relationship? Relationship! He nearly misstepped again. What was he thinking? He'd just come over for the afternoon, for crying out loud! A few hours to spend with her. That was all.

He worked on getting control of his feet for the next few minutes.

Tinsley didn't notice. She strolled along, unaware of much else except her surroundings. She did jog through this neighborhood just after dawn almost every morning. But then she missed the riches of the place while concentrating on her body and its "sacred rhythms" of breath and heart rate and muscle burn. Now, with Alex at her side, keeping quiet and thoughtful company, she could see clearly and in detail.

See and hear and smell and, at times, feel. The neighborhood was an old one with homes that dated back in some cases well over one hundred years. The town had been leveled during the Civil War and rebuilt on the foundations of that ruin.

Tinsley knew this from stories about Yankee aggression against the South she'd been hearing since she was a tiny girl. Stories that came mostly from her now-deceased maternal grandparents but also occasionally from Delores. And even Ellen, Tinsley's mother, shared the prejudice of her generation, whose roots went deep into the rich, southern soil. Walking by these homes now, Tinsley could almost feel the old agonies. But she could also appreciate newer the beauty that had emerged from the devastation.

She could learn from this place. If only she could get quiet enough inside to pay attention to what was being said. Inner peace had never been her strong point.

She paused, listening, as piano music tinkled in the air, drifting out of an open parlor window. The music was simple, halting, and probably played by a kid who was enduring enforced lessons. But it sounded sweet. She smiled.

Alex saw the expression. "Do you play?" he asked as they walked on past the home. "You have a look of sympathy on your face. Makes me think you might have taken lessons as a little girl."

"No," Her smile spread into a grin and she looked at him. "Not like that." She indicated the house with a tilt of her head. She laughed, softly, almost mockingly, to herself.

He waited for more. She was silent, keeping her secrets. Alex felt his curiosity level rise, teased as if it were an erotic emotion rather than an intellectual one. He wanted to know, but acknowledged her right to silence. They continued to walk.

They reached a property bordered by a high stone wall. Tinsley paused to watch a small lizard dart along a thin ledge of mortar and disappear into a dark crack. She sensed Alex move closer to her. He poked at the crack with a finger, teasing the lizard.

"It's a skink. Actually it's full name is Six-lined Racerunner," he said, answering the question she did not ask.

"Blue-bellied. Their undersides are bright blue. Like sapphires. They're really beautiful, you know."

"Oh? Right." She glanced at him. "A lizard's a lizard in my book. Not a work of art."

"Think so?" Alex took a small twig and very gently provoked the little reptile until it burst out of his shelter. It scooted along the stones and he ran after it, capturing it in his cupped hand just before the wall turned the corner of the lot. Sweat trickled down the side of his face, tickling, but he ignored it. He covered the lizard with his other hand, turned around and held it out to her.

From a distance of almost half a block, she looked at him. She hadn't followed in the chase, but had stood and watched him. Alex suddenly felt like a little boy, holding a frog or a spider, knowing that the little girl he was trying to impress was going to scream in horror at his prized offering. Then, Tinsley Cole turned on the sunniest smile he had ever seen.

"You *caught* it!" She came running up to him. "Just so I could see the color!" She tried to pry open his hand. "Oh, Alex. Don't hurt it, but don't let it get away. I want to see! Then let it loose!"

He laughed, holding the tiny animal up out of her reach. She danced on her toes, just like a kid, full of excitement. He brought his hands down, drawing her closer to him, enchanted by the expression on her face. They were inches apart. "Shh," he whispered. Then he flipped his hands so the lizard lay upside down. He lifted one hand and uncovered it.

Tinsley gasped. The little animal lay still and quiet, but it was alive. She could see the beat of life on its bright blue chest and belly. "Beautiful," she said, sighing the word. "But is it all right?"

Alex slipped a finger under the lizard and gave it a gentle push. The lizard turned over, stood still for a second on his palm, testing its surroundings with its senses. It puffed itself up, defensively. Then it jumped off and scurried for the stone wall and safety.

"It's fine," he said. "Has enough sense to run away, and not to try fighting me."

"You mean, *biting* you? I'm surprised it didn't."

He shrugged. "Any wild creature will, if you corner it and hurt it. The secret to keeping teeth out of your skin is all in the way you handle the animal."

Tinsley decided right then that this man was a person she wanted to know better. "Who are you, Alex?" she asked, looking at him directly. "Delores says you studied law and that you write nonfiction, but that you never read your material to the literary group."

His handsome features tightened. "I have a law degree," he said. "My family insisted I get one. It was expected of me. But I never practiced. Not to say I won't ever, of course. I can't predict the future."

"That's the truth!" She turned and started walking again. He fell into step beside her. "I'm a lawyer, too," she said. "But I did practice for several years. Hung out my shingle in the small town just down the road from my folk's ranch. Mostly helped people deal with the legal morass of life, divorce and death in this country. But that was before I had the accident."

Alex sensed silence was his best tactic. If he blurted out the wrong thing now, Tinsley might just stop talking.

"That accident changed a lot of things for me," she said, almost as if she were speaking to herself. "I had to face some hard truths about a relationship I was in. And I had to look at the practice I had. See if I was really doing any good for the people I took on as clients. Had to take stock generally of the direction my life was going." She took a deep breath. "I guess I'm lost right now. Don't know who I am or where I ought to head. So I came out here to stay with Delores for a while."

"She's your aunt?" That was safe enough, he figured. Tinsley was coming close to revealing her deep emotions, and he wasn't ready to deal with that in a stranger. So, the safe, conventional question. He already knew the answer, though. What he was after were the details.

"Mmm-hmm. Mom's her little sister. Mom went out West when she was eighteen to work for a summer at Yellowstone Park, and she fell in love with a local boy who wrangled horses for one of the dude ranches. That was my dad. After falling for him, she fell for the country. She's lived in Wyoming ever since."

"But you came back here."

"I needed a change of scene," she said.

And that was it. She said nothing more. They continued to walk, passing under a long stand of live oaks, dripping with Spanish moss. The air was much cooler in the shade. Cool and quiet. Like the woman walking beside him, Alex thought.

He felt her silence like a barrier between them. He was not used to women who didn't talk. Particularly women who wouldn't talk once you got them on the subject of themselves. Well, he thought. If she wouldn't talk, he would. Open up a bit on a personal topic.

"The reason I don't read to the literary group is because my material isn't really appropriate," he said. "I deal with historical analyses—what we've done to the local environment in the past and how we need to act responsibly in the future. It's controversial to some folks.

Dull as dishwater to others." He paused. "I love this place, this land and the people who live here, and it shows in what I write."

"Are you afraid?"

"What?" He stopped, dead.

She stared at him with that disconcertingly direct gaze. "Are you afraid, Alex?" she asked. "Is that why you don't read aloud?"

He shook his head, slowly. "I don't think so." He thought about it for a moment. "I feel...uneasy, though. I admit—"

"You were more than just uneasy when I was engaging your group in hot debate," she said, folding her arms over her chest. "In fact, you got up and left just as soon as you could. Did the conflict bother you?"

He rubbed the back of his neck. "Tinsley, I—"

"No! I want an answer. Delores nearly took my head off because I stirred up such a hornet's nest. You got up and ran out with your literary tail between your legs. What's the problem?"

Alex felt his face get hot. "The problem, Miss Cole, is that you have the manners of a . . ."

"A what?" She faced him and wiggled her fingers, egging him on. "Come on, spit it out!"

"Never mind!" He started to walk away, knowing even as he took the first step he was making the wrong move. She cut off his escape by stepping right in front of him, forcing him to look her in the eye.

"Oh, no, you don't! Don't weasel out on me, Alex Berringer! Is that what you think of me? Want to trade insults? Well, you have the backbone of a jellyfish."

Alex started to retort, when he saw the joy and excitement in her eyes. "You're loving this, aren't you?" he said, accusingly. "Getting a real big kick out of it. I saw that the other day. You had a great time dueling with Sanford Taylor and the rest of them. It was a party as far as you were concerned."

She sobered a bit. "I don't mind a good debate. I kind of like a fight, I have to admit. And, I don't run from conflict."

"And you think I do?"

She regarded him without speaking for a long time. Alex watched, seeing her thoughts right on her face and in the depths of her eyes, seeing the tension in her muscles ease and her body contour soften. It was a performance she was unaware of giving. He was the only audience and he decided it was a rare privilege.

"You're right," she said, finally. "I apologize. I have no basis for criticism. And I am a conflict junkie, just like you said. I love a good verbal battle. I'm a conversational scrapper. My manners are, by local standards, less than civilized, I guess."

"Tinsley," he said, reaching out to touch her cheek. "You are unique. That's all. You call things and people as you see them, no holds barred. And that's unusual for this part of the country. But there's nothing intrinsically wrong with your honesty."

"But a lot wrong, socially."

He shrugged again, a gesture she was beginning to recognize as one he used to avoid a direct answer to an awkward question. Then, the fingers that had rested on her cheek slid around to the back of her neck, pushed aside her hair and touched her skin. Gently, carefully, he drew her closer.

Tinsley let him. When they were almost close enough

for a kiss, he stopped. She felt her heart rate speed up, wondering if he would kiss her. Frightened that he would. Worried he wouldn't . . .

CHAPTER FOUR

BUT ALEX STEPPED BACK. "You're making this far too easy for me, Tinsley Cole," he said, a strange expression on his face.

"I didn't realize this was some sort of contest, where easy and hard mattered." Anger and confusion coursed through her, and she spoke with some heat. "If you wanted to kiss me, why didn't you?"

He surprised her. Instead of growling back an answer, he smiled. "Because, I *really* want to kiss you. If I'd only wanted a moment's touching, I'd have done it."

"Oh." Tinsley felt the wind fall from her sails. "I see. I guess." She turned, embarrassed again, and started walking rapidly. He moved into step beside her.

"Probably," he said, conversationally, "neither of us sees right now. We are very different, you know. In our approach, that is. Socially, I mean."

"You said it."

"Which does make this all the more interesting, you have to admit."

She glanced over to see if he was kidding. "I don't have to admit anything. We speak different languages, that's all."

"Hey, it all sounds like English to me."

"That isn't what I mean, and you know it."

His laughter was rich and deep. Too genuine to resist. She smiled, then joined in wholeheartedly. She hooked her arm in his elbow and pulled him along while they laughed. Several cars drove by and slowed, the drivers and passengers staring at them, but Tinsley didn't care. She felt happy and free, all her anger gone. Let 'em all think whatever they wanted, she decided. She raised her hand and let out a whoop of joy and energy. She felt good and didn't care who knew it!

Alex wasn't as unselfconscious. He enjoyed the closeness of the shared humor and the touch of her body next to his, but not the freedom of it all to the extent she was obviously relishing. In spite of his various rebellions over the years, he still cared what others thought. Old habits, too deep to die, kept him alert to the presence of outsiders.

And it wasn't too long before one particular outsider intruded.

Tinsley was calming down and seriously considering setting up another opportunity for a kiss when she noticed a car driving so close the tires were scraping against the curb. Alex pulled away from her abruptly, just as the driver leaned out and called to him.

"Hello, Cousin," the man said, drawling the words. "Nice day for a stroll."

"Hello, Clay," Alex replied. His tone indicated he was not at all happy to see this particular relative. Tinsley's interest was aroused. She looked carefully at the newcomer.

The man addressing them was younger than Alex, but his youthful appearance faded when his eyes focused on Tinsley. The irises were green, just like Alex's, but there the similarity ended. This man's eyes were cold and hungry. Old. *Predatory,* she thought. Instinctively, she moved closer to Alex. She felt him begin to put his arm around her, but he didn't complete the move.

"Who's your friend, Cousin?" The man turned off the engine of his car—a low-slung sports model she didn't recognize—and got out, disregarding the traffic that honked and drove around him. His hair was auburn instead of black, but the resemblance to Alex was striking. "Aren't you going to introduce me?"

Alex seemed to growl, his tone low and forced, as he went through the motions. "Tinsley, this is my cousin, Clayton Berringer. Clay, Miss Tinsley Cole. She's Delores Bishop's niece."

"Ah." Clayton's eyebrows rose. "I've heard about you, Miss Cole. From your poetry recital yesterday. Word's around you were quite, ah, entertaining." He took her hand, and for an awful moment, Tinsley was afraid he'd kiss it. But he merely squeezed and released. "You're from out West somewhere, aren't you?" he asked.

"Wyoming," she replied. "You'd better move your car before someone decides to rear end it."

"Don't worry, my dear." He turned and waved at the traffic. "If that happens, I know my cousin here will arrange for any blame to be removed from my record. Isn't that right, Alex?"

"No, it's not. Move the car, Clay."

"Oh, you seemed to be in such a good mood just moments ago." Clayton grinned at Alex, leered at Tinsley. "Come on, Al. You have the family money and with it comes the obligation to buy the rest of us out of trouble. Especially me."

Alex stood tense and still for a moment, the muscles at the hinge of his jaw working. Then, he sighed, clearly burying his anger. "Clay," he said. "I'm under no obligation to anyone, and certainly not to you. Now, please get out of here."

As Tinsley watched, the younger man's face turned ugly, then resettled into a bland expression. "Sure, Cousin. Whatever you say." He addressed Tinsley. "What do you think about this, Miss Cole?"

"I think you're being pretty stupid, since you ask. That's an expensive car."

Clayton's features shifted to ugly again. "Well, I see you've found a real rose in the garden of love, Cousin," he said, returning to his vehicle. "Be careful her thorns don't stick you too deeply."

"I'll keep your advice in mind. Be sure of that."

Clayton slammed the door and drove off, cutting ahead of a station wagon full of kids in baseball uniforms. The woman driving honked her horn. Alex winced. "Sorry for that," he said, speaking gingerly. He looked at Tinsley. "I swear I didn't choose to be related to that man."

She laughed. "He's quite a creep. But then, you know what they say about relatives."

"You're stuck with them." Alex smiled again. "But you can choose your friends. I'm glad you weren't offended."

"Why should I be? The guy's just a jerk. Are there more like him in your family woodwork?"

Alex hesitated before answering. Then he said, "Thankfully, no. Clayton is unique. Though, except for my mother, he's my closest living relative." He started walking back toward the Bishop home. His shoulders seemed bowed slightly, as though by a burden.

Tinsley ran a few steps to catch up. "What did he mean about you having an obligation to buy him out of trouble? That was a strange remark."

Alex just shrugged.

"Oh, I see. I'm being nosy. Sorry."

He straightened up. "It's not a particularly nice story. Let's talk about something else. Tell me how you started writing your poetry," he said. "I guarantee you that's a far more interesting subject."

She thought for a moment, wanting to pursue the cousin story. But it wouldn't be polite, she told herself. Not when he'd dismissed it so firmly. "No one's ever asked me that. I suppose if I had to sum it up, I'd have to say that solitude was why I started. I had lots of time alone, and I wrote."

"Solitude?" He stopped and looked at her. "You?"

"Sure. I'm my parent's only kid. That automatically made me fair game for a variety of lonely chores that other ranch kids shared with their siblings. I've spent long hours of my time alone, pitching hay in the barn, hunting lost calves on horseback, riding the fences looking for breaks and—"

"You're an only child, too?"

"Yep."

He touched her face with his fingertips. "We only kids are supposed to be spoiled, as I understood common wisdom. What happened to you?"

"What makes you think I'm not an absolute stinker? Spoiled rotten?"

"I...I don't know. You seem too transparent to be selfish. Too...outgoing..." His fingers were lingering on her skin. His expression was a bit dazed, as if he were entranced.

"How 'bout you, Alex?" She had some trouble getting the words to come out in a light tone. "Selfish?"

"Very." He moved a little closer. "I'm afraid I'm rich and spoiled, Tinsley. Selfish to the bone. Hardly the kind of man you'd approve of, given your hard-working background."

"Really?" She reached over and hooked her arm around his neck and pulled him in. But she didn't kiss him. She just held him a quarter inch from her face and waited to see what he would do.

Alex smiled and said, "Oh, my Lord," and kissed her.

CLAYTON BERRINGER drove around the block again, watching his cousin and the woman. It was the first time in years he'd seen Alex getting obviously social with a female during what his snotty relative called his "working hours," and that bothered him considerably. Not that what Alex did was actually work in the accepted sense, but his pet projects had taken all his energies and devotion since he'd moved to his hermit's retreat out on the island, effectively cutting himself off from normal social intercourse. Clayton smiled at the unintended pun. Then his smile vanished as he saw how close the two walkers were getting.

It was, after all, in Clayton's best interest to keep Alex from any serious relationship. His cousin must never be allowed to marry. No little Berringers to come between Clayton and the family fortune. No, no. He frowned as he watched the pair, scowled when they stopped and talked, cursed when she dragged him in for a kiss. A kiss old Al seemed quite enthusiastic about.

Clayton swore again and gunned the engine, shooting the Jaguar around the corner while cutting off a lumbering old sedan. The driver of the sedan honked balefully, but Clayton scarcely noticed. Time to talk about dear Cousin Alex to Aunt Soosie. She'd surely be interested to know what her little boy was up to these days. And Clayton would spare no details. Yes, indeed. Let her know her son was practically screwing that cowgirl in public. Let her know one more social disgrace waited just around the corner!

He shoved out of his mind the feelings of extreme envy that gripped him. Alex always made him feel so damnably inadequate. It wasn't fair.

So, he'd work on making things a bit more even.

ALEX HELD ON to emotional control with difficulty. The temptation to gather Tinsley in and really test the waters was almost irresistible, but he managed to limit his caress to her lips alone. That was enough. Her wide, sensual mouth was made for kissing, and he felt as if he could spend hours exploring the possibilities it offered.

He was turned on to a degree that hadn't happened to him in years. He *wanted* her. Right now, right here. A primitive surge of desire made him feel strong and dizzy at the same time. Her tongue touched his lower lip, and he shivered from the top of his head to his feet. His hands moved of their own accord to grasp her generous hips and pull her against him.

But she dodged, stepping back and out of his reach. "Wow," she said, gazing at him with the light of delight and laughter in her eyes. "You don't fool around, do you?"

"You surprised me," Alex replied, hearing the gruffness of passion in his voice. "I didn't mean to..."

"Oh, it's okay." She turned and started walking again. "I guess I shouldn't have set you up, but I couldn't resist." She glanced back over her shoulder. "Come on. I'll buy you a glass of lemonade. Silvie makes the best, believe me. We might even be able to talk her out of some cookies."

"All right." He caught up with her, feeling a little foolish. Clearly she hadn't felt a thing. She'd been teasing him. And he was an idiot for letting it bother him.

He'd be an even bigger idiot if he let her know.

Tinsley felt the tension in him as they returned to Delores's home, but she put it down mostly to the encounter with his cousin. She was sure that kissing her hadn't set him off. On the other hand, what did she know about this man? She counseled herself to take it easy until she learned more about Alex Berringer. He was not all he seemed at first sight. *That* she was sure of.

They walked to the gates without either of them making any further attempt at conversation. The afternoon had deepened, and the air was heavier with humidity, almost gray in color. Tinsley waved her hand slowly. "I used to come to visit Aunt Delores when I was a kid," she said. "But I don't remember being so aware of the differences in climate." She touched her hair. "I feel at times like I'm carrying around several extra pounds just from the moisture caught in this stuff. Air is so different, depending on where you are."

"I've traveled," Alex said, glad for a neutral subject. "But I've never lived anywhere else. I probably wouldn't notice any differences anyway. Air is a medium for poets to describe, not essayists."

"I'd like to read some of your writing, if I may. Sometime."

He shrugged. "It's pretty dull going by most standards."

"You don't *like* your own stuff?" She put a hand out and stopped him. "Why bother, then?"

"I didn't say I didn't like it. I'm just not sure you would."

She looked at him. "You're shy! I don't believe it."

Alex felt a hot sensation in his face and realized to his horror that he was blushing. "I'm not shy, I just think..."

"Oh, I'm sorry." She seemed genuinely contrite. "I've gone and embarrassed you. I just never know when to keep my big mouth shut, I guess. I'm forever putting my foot into it. Forget it, okay?"

"I'll be happy to let you read some material I'm working on, Tinsley. If you're sincerely interested."

She regarded him. "I'm sincerely curious, Alex."

"Fair enough."

She smiled. "Let's raid the kitchen. Apologies always make me thirsty." She grabbed his hand and half led, half pulled him along in a jog around to the back of the mansion.

The kitchen door was open, with only the screen door closed. The good smells of cooking wafted out. Tinsley paused, closing her eyes and breathing deeply. "This is another thing," she said, not letting go of his hand. "I can't remember aromas and smells being this clear and strong before. I make games for myself, identifying them."

Alex was enchanted. And disturbed. "Is that what you do? Indulge your senses? Just sit around amusing yourself all day?" As soon as the words were out of his mouth, he regretted them. He'd all but called her lazy, and that wasn't what he'd meant.

But she didn't seem to mind the question. "Right now, yes," she said. "Tomorrow, well, I don't know. I suppose you could say I'm searching."

"It doesn't take too much searching to find out where to take the South Carolina bar exam and hang out your shingle. Or are you planning on going home soon?"

She released his hand, now. "Really, Alex, I don't know." She pushed her hair back from her face. "Let's eat. I think better when I'm feeding."

Alex followed as she bounced up the stairs and through the screen door. He caught it as she let it start to slam behind her like a child would. Was she too childish? He wondered. What kind of solid, stable, adult woman would behave as she had so far?

None he'd ever met, that was for certain.

But once in the kitchen, settled at the table with a pitcher of lemonade and a plate of cookies in front of them, she showed him a different side of herself.

"I almost hesitate to come in here without permission," she said. "It's like barging into a church when the priest is gone. This is Silvie's domain, nobody else's, and she is queen, here."

Alex smiled, relaxing. "I like that. You have a gift for describing things by comparisons, you know."

A touch of color hit her cheeks. "Thanks. I think my problem, Alex, is I'm still not sure just who I really am. I mean, I'm over thirty. So far in my adult years, I've practiced some law, written some poetry, helped at the ranch, got involved with a man, but who am I and why am I here, really?"

"What man?" He was slightly startled by her frank admission of her age, but he was more interested in this man.

"Oh, he was one of my major mistakes in character judgment. I thought we had a relationship that meant something. We even had a wedding date set. But that all came to a screeching halt when I found out he was seeing a so-called friend of mine on the sly. Some friend, huh? I broke off the engagement." She smiled, and to his surprise, he saw no rancor or sadness in her expression. "I'm willing to bet he'd have married me and kept on seeing her. Isn't that something?"

"Weren't you angry? Jealous?"

"Oh, furious! Insane! But what good did it do? Raised my blood pressure, sure. Didn't change old Brad. Not for a minute. No, I learned a good lesson, then." She leaned forward and rubbed her back.

"Hurting again?"

"Reminding myself. I had the accident because I wasn't thinking about my driving, but about telling my folks the wedding was off." She frowned and sat back. "One thing I have decided, I won't get married until I find a man I can trust with my life. And not unless the guy and I feel something deeper than sexual attraction for each other. Something even more important."

"What might that be?"

She looked directly at him. Vision.

"Vision?"

"Yeah." She reached for another cookie. "My folks have one. The ranch. No matter how things were going between them, they always had the ranch to focus on, to keep the relationship in perspective. A reason to stay together, when things were bad, I guess."

"What's wrong with love for that? For a reason to stay together? It seems fine to me."

She just looked at him.

"My, you are deeply cynical, Tinsley. I'd never have suspected."

"Not cynical. Just experienced and wiser for it." She took a drink of lemonade. Ate another cookie.

Alex noted that she did not sip or nibble. She gulped and chewed enthusiastically. Watching her eat made him wonder what making love to her would be like. If she took to sex with the same energy, it would be an outstanding experience.

"How about you?" she asked. "Ever married?"

"Lord! No." The question caught him by surprise, and his response was viscerally honest.

"Oh." She regarded him. "Sore subject. Sorry."

"No, no." He poured more lemonade. The air conditioner was not on in the house, and the kitchen was warm. "Not a sore subject. I have no broken heart of anything like that. I just think I'm cut out to be a bachelor, that's all."

"Why?"

He shrugged. "I like being alone."

"So do I."

"But, I suppose I have given it thought. Marriage, that is." He poked a finger at the rings of moisture left by their glasses on the wooden table. "If I ever did find the right woman, I'd want a big family. I love kids. So, I guess I'm inconsistent." He drew a circle. Frowned. "You know, I don't think I've ever talked about this with anyone before."

"First time for everything." Her smile was mischievous. Then a dark, sad look came into her eyes. "Well, almost everything."

The expression on her face surprised him. He had no idea what her words meant, but he was unable to pursue the topic. Silvie chose that moment to enter her domain. Any gloom that might have been building in Tinsley fled, chased away by her obvious pleasure at seeing the older woman.

They fussed at each other cheerfully for a while before Tinsley got around to introducing Alex. When she did, Silvie didn't respond immediately. She sat where she was and glared at Tinsley.

"Come into my kitchen," Silvie muttered. "Like when you was little, sneaking cookies and stuff. Tinsley, if you wasn't such a big girl, I'd switch you, I swear I would." She grinned at Alex. "Now, I expect Alex here could handle you, but I know I can't anymore. Hey, Alex. How you doing?"

"Just fine, Silvie. Just fine. You?"

"No complaints."

"You two know each other?" Tinsley was surprised. With Delores's negative attitude toward Alex, she had hardly expected anyone else in the household to react positively to him, much less be on such friendly terms as Silvie seemed to be.

"For a long time," Silvie said. Warmth shone in her brown eyes. "But it ain't been 'til recently I came to find out what a good sort of man he..."

"Silvie means I used to steal apples from some of the trees in the back of your aunt's lot," Alex interrupted. "In the fall, of course. When you weren't here. I didn't even know Mrs. Bishop had a niece near my age. I wouldn't have gone off summers, if I'd known you visited then."

"Good thing you didn't know each other," Silvie said. "'Cause thinking of the two of you as children getting into trouble together gives the fair shivers to me."

"I didn't come out in the summer," Tinsley said. "Just at Christmas. I suppose you were too busy with your family to know anyone new was in the neighborhood."

"Not exactly." Alex didn't meet her gaze.

"In the summer, I was too busy at the ranch. So was everyone. Besides, the hot weather here would probably have kept me inside. What can you do in the summer when the heat's enough to fry eggs on rocks and the air's full enough of water to boil?"

Silvie chuckled. "The girl does have her opinions," she said. "One time, we all went out to her place, Mr. Alex. In winter for Christmas. And I like to froze to death! I never seen a place so cold. I swear."

Tinsley set her chin on her hand. "It's invigorating, Silvie. You just have to put on enough clothes to keep warm. In this climate, no matter how hot it gets, you can only take off so much. But when it's cold, you just keep piling it on until you're comfortable."

"Not enough clothes in the world make me comfortable out where your momma lives."

"When it gets too hot here, you just go in the water," Alex said. "Swim, sail, fish. Lie on the beach. There's always a breeze by the water."

Tinsley sat back. "No, thanks." She had a tight, hidden expression in place of the open, humorous one she had just worn. "I don't like water. I'll take the snow any day."

"What's the matter with water?"

"Tinsley doesn't swim, Alex," Silvie said, getting up from her chair. "She's afraid of the deep water." Any trace of dialect was gone, as it always was when she spoke of serious things. She picked up the empty cookie plate and took it over to the sink.

"You're kidding." He looked at Tinsley. "No, you're not, are you."

"I, uh…" She played with a crumb on the table. "I just never learned to swim. It's not uncommon back home. About the only deep water most of us see is a rushing creek in the spring. Snow runoff. I almost got caught in one when I was little. A cowboy happened by just as the shore collapsed and he dragged me out. So, I have bad memories and no reason to deal with them. The idea of all that water around and under me gives me the creeps."

"Anyone ever try teaching you to swim?"

"Not that lived to tell about it." She looked at him, anger in her eyes. "I don't need to know how. After the one time, I have sense enough to stay away from the edges of running water. I've gotten along fine so far. I can do a lot of other things. Do them well."

"I'm sure of that." Alex glanced over at Silvie's back. The woman was busying herself at the sink, seemingly out of the conversation. He wondered how deliberate that pose was. Silvie knew things about him he wasn't ready for Tinsley to know. Undoubtedly there were things about Tinsley he wasn't ready to hear yet. Fair was fair. "But there are teachers, then there are teachers."

"I don't need either kind."

He studied her eyes. It wasn't anger he saw. It was fear and defiance. "Okay." He put his hand palm down on the table. "It's just that I was going to invite you out to my place tomorrow. I don't suppose you'll want to go, now, though. What with having to cross that deep, dangerous water, and all."

"Very clever." She tapped her finger on the table. "Is the invitation real, or just to make fun of me?"

"Hey." He spread out his hands. "Why should I do that? I'm sincere, Tinsley. I'll even cook you dinner myself."

"Better go, girl," Silvie commented. "I hear he's a mean one with a skillet."

Tinsley turned around. "Is this a conspiracy?"

"Nope."

"No, it isn't. Look," he said. "I have life jackets aplenty. You'd have to wear one, anyway. And I've been swimming in the ocean since before I walked. You'll be quite safe with me."

Now she grinned. "Right. Like spiders and flies."

"Go with him," Silvie said, again. "He's a decent man. You'll be all right."

"I wasn't worried about..."

"I was talking about the water, girl! Get your mind up out of the gutter, please."

"Oh." Tinsley sank back down in her chair. Her face was red.

Alex sank back in laughter. In a second, the two women joined him. As he laughed, he embraced the warmth and friendliness of the situation. How long had it been since he sat with a woman like Tinsley at a kitchen table and just had fun?

A long, long time.

He couldn't remember, in fact, ever—

"What in the world is going on in here?" Delores Bishop's entrance had gone unnoticed. Her censorious voice did not. In spite of himself, Alex was now the one with the red face. For a second, Delores had seemed to be his own mother. That second was enough for all the old hurts to start aching. Enough for the good feelings to leave him. Entirely.

Ten unbearably uncomfortable minutes later, Alex Berringer beat a hasty retreat—his second where Tinsley Cole was concerned. On the drive to the dock and the boat ride home to his island, he swore he wouldn't set himself up like that again. Let himself relax like that and let his guard slip. He had too much to do right now to get involved with a woman.

Too much to do to let his libido control his mind.

CHAPTER FIVE

HE HEARD THE PHONE ringing as soon as he tied the motor boat to his dock. Too late in the day to be business, so he decided to let the answering machine catch it. That's what the thing was for, after all. To answer when he didn't feel like talking to anyone.

Alex stuck his hands in his pockets and stared down at the dock. The wood was worn and weathered, but tough and solid. It had stood up to its share of hard weather and hard use. It was good, reliable and...

It belonged to him.

He took a deep breath and looked up at the sky, out at the endless horizon. Endless. Like the possibilities he had for his life. Possibilities and responsibilities. He pulled back his lips, trying to grin. Unlike Miss Tinsley Cole, who could warble cheerfully about not knowing who she was or what she wanted to do, *he* knew who he was and what he was put here on earth to do. No problem there.

So, big fella, what is your problem?

Alex blew out the air he'd drawn in. He did have a problem, otherwise he wouldn't be feeling like ants were clawing at his nerves. *Antsy.* That's what he was. A beloved voice from the past echoed in his mind. "What's the matter, Al? You got ants in your pants, son?" He smiled. *No, Dad. That's not the problem.* Not all of it, anyway.

Now Alex scowled and turned away from the water. This was ridiculous. He was too experienced, too old and too busy to waste his time thinking about a woman just because she made him laugh and he wanted her in bed. Too old, too busy and too wise.

Sure, he was.

He entered the cool, dark house and felt the usual sense of relief flow over him. No matter what went on in the world outside, he could count on this place relaxing and refreshing his body and spirit. That's what a home was for.

But, it also held his office. Held his work. He glanced at the phone system. The message light was blinking. One message. He walked over, put his finger on the play button, then lifted it off. Whoever called would call back, if it was vital. Whatever was on the tape would wait. In fact... He set a program to place the whole system on hold. Now, if anyone called, he wouldn't even be bothered by the ringing. It would record, but he wouldn't hear. Nothing in his professional or personal life was so vital he needed to know about it right away. All would wait. It always had before, hadn't it?

He had work to do. Kicking off his shoes, he stripped off his socks and polo shirt. He tossed the clothes onto a chair and picked up a clean, T-shirt. He pulled it on and headed to his office.

TINSLEY GLARED at her aunt. "It's been over three hours, Delores," she said. "Plenty of time for him to get home and return my call. He's really hurt. And I am still in shock! I've never, in all the years I've know you, and that's all my life, ever heard you be so deliberately rude to anyone before."

Delores looked away. "I apologized."

"To me. To Silvie. Not to Alex."

Delores sighed. She was in the wrong this time. She had acted like a spoiled, jealous child. No excuse for the way she had barged into the kitchen and snapped at young Berringer. Not at all. "I was just so surprised to see you and him, sitting there, laughing like old friends, Tinsley. I . . . I suppose I just lost my perspective for a moment."

"Which is?"

"Pardon?"

"Why would the sight of me laughing and talking with a guy make you freak? I don't understand. As far as I can tell, the only negative thing about Alex is his creepy cousin, Clayton. So, I—"

"You met Clayton?"

"In a way. He pulled up beside us while we were walking and kind of harassed Alex. It was tense. I didn't get the point of some of the conversation, but I gather there's little love lost."

"Indeed." Delores relaxed a bit. She could afford it for the moment. The focus of her niece's attention was now elsewhere. "That is true."

"Why?"

"Well, I don't quite know. I mean, I do have an idea or two, but . . ."

Tinsley rested her chin on her palm. "Give me an educated guess. You owe me that."

Delores cleared her throat. Tinsley waited. They had finished dinner and were still seated in the dining room, enjoying coffee and mints. A little daylight still showed outside, silvering the window panes, but the room was lit by the large chandelier over the long, mahogany table. Delores sat at the head of the table, Tinsley to her right. Her aunt wore a dress, but Tinsley had kept on her jeans and shirt. She was too angry to comply with the house rules of decent dinner costume tonight. Uncharacteristically, Delores had allowed her to get away with the minor rebellion. Out of guilt, Tinsley was sure. She continued to wait, silently.

"Very well," Delores said, finally. "But let's go into the den." She glanced at the door to the kitchen where both of them knew Silvie lingered, waiting for the mealtime to end. Thinking Delores simply wanted to be thoughtful and let Silvie finish her work for the evening, Tinsley agreed to move. But soon, she realized that her aunt's motives were less noble.

They sat in the two wing chairs flanking the fireplace. "Alex Berringer's family is strange," Delores said, her voice lower than usual, almost conspiratorial. Another shock. Delores had moved because she hadn't wanted Silvie to overhear. This was not typical of her aunt. Tinsley settled back in her wing chair and waited. She was not looking forward to the knowledge she was about to gain.

ALEX THREW DOWN HIS PEN and shoved the legal pad across his littered desk. Papers and books fell to the floor, joining the pile already down there. He didn't notice.

He was too distracted to work. This was ridiculous. It had never happened before and should not be happening now. Not because of a woman he'd just met, a person with whom he had no relationship. If she was his lover, he could understand being distracted by thoughts of her. But they had only kissed.

Five minutes later, he stood up and swore loudly. He'd drifted off again, just thinking about the way her lips had felt, the erotic tickle of her tongue, her warm, full-bodied figure so near him...

Alex slammed out of his house and headed inland, toward the barn and stable area. It was still light enough for a short ride on the beach, and maybe a session with Jack

Tar would clear his mind. It usually did. Unless the big horse took it into his head to dump Alex into the sand again. Alex grinned. Most of the time, it was a real battle between horse and rider.

Alex reached the paddock and leaned on the fence. Jack, a huge black beast, came over, whickered and rubbed his soft nose on Alex's arm. "Want to blow out some carbon, boy?" Alex asked, scratching behind the animal's ears. "I sure need it. How 'bout you?"

Jack pulled back his big lips in a wicked, almost-human, grin. He stretched his neck over the fence and shook his mane.

"I see." Alex slapped his hand hard on Jack's withers, a gesture which didn't seem to bother the horse at all. "Well, let's get to it." He walked around the fence to the gate. Jack followed him slowly, pacing as if he were stalking prey. Alex began to feel better. The horse needed a good workout. A hard run would do them both good.

He entered the small stable and took a bridle from the tack room. He hesitated over the saddle, then decided against it. It would take too much time, and the light was failing. Riding Jack in total darkness would be inviting disaster. Grabbing a handful of oat treats, Alex threw the bridle over his shoulder and sauntered back to the paddock. Jack sidled into a corner and set his ears back.

Alex whistled softly and rattled the oats. Jack blew air out of his mouth, making his lips flap.

"Y'all going to ride Jack, now, Mr. Alex?"

The unexpected voice made Alex startle. He turned and saw ten-year-old Samuel Turner standing on the lower rail of the fence, his arms hooked over the upper. The child was grinning broadly.

"I was planning on it," Alex admitted. "But Jack doesn't seem too keen."

The boy climbed off the fence and into the enclosure. "He don't like to run at night, I think." Samuel walked over to Jack and stared up at the horse's face. "Think he's lazy when it gets close on to sundown." The animal pawed the earth.

"Samuel," Alex said, warningly. "He's not in a good mood, son. Why don't you . . ."

The boy reached up and grabbed the horse's halter. Alex felt himself redden as he walked over and slid the bridle on the now docile Jack. "Guess that's why I pay you to take care of this stinker," he said to Samuel. "You know his moods a lot better than I ever will."

"You just too busy, Mr. Alex." Samuel walked back to the fence and sat on the top rail. "Ain't you going to use a saddle?"

"No."

Samuel cocked his head to one side. "You got a problem, Mr. Alex? Something on your mind?"

Alex turned and looked at the boy. He was Silvie Turner's grandnephew, and he could see some trace of family resemblance in the firmly carved features that even on the boy's young face showed a determined character. "Yeah, Sam. I do," he admitted.

"Then you be careful. 'Cause Jack there'll know it, and he'll take you for a real ride, you ain't watchful."

"I'll keep that in mind." Alex grabbed a handful of mane and swung himself up onto the horse's back. He felt the powerful muscles quiver beneath him. Jack ducked his head, once, but didn't buck.

For now.

Samuel opened the gate, and Alex let Jack amble out. Once outside the fence, the horse stopped. Alex kicked his heels into the barrellike sides. "Giddap, Jack," he said, twisting his fingers in the mane and reins.

Alex yelled with exuberance as they flew across the marshy ground, over the dunes and onto the beach. A flock of sea gulls screeched and took off at the horse's wild approach. The tide was out and the sand was hard, and Jack's hooves pounded a primitive, basic rhythm on the surface. Knowing the beach stretched unbroken for miles, Alex let the horse run, making no attempt to control the ride. He needed this. Needed the warm wind in his face, the sound of the surf and the hoofbeats in his ears.

They raced on, past solitary old men fishing the evening surf. Some raised a hand as he tore by. Others scarcely looked up, accepting him as part of the natural landscape. Alex rode on, slipping out of himself and into the experience.

He was the island. He was the wind, the sand, the water. He was...

He was suddenly airborne—on his way past Jack's nose—and heading for a not-so-soft landing on the sand. Alex yelled again, as he hit the ground with his shoulder, and rolled for several feet before coming to a stop, sand in his face. Jack whinnied.

Alex sat up, brushing his eyes. Jack was dancing around, watching him. The horse's head was high, and his mouth was open. It looked as if he were laughing.

"You got me, boy." Alex sat still. If Jack took off, Alex would have a long, lonely walk home ahead of him. "I wasn't paying attention to business. I admit it. Now, let's just talk about this, shall we?" He rose slowly to his knees.

Jack put his head down and blew through his lips. He backed up.

"No, no. Don't do this, Jack." Alex spread out his arms, prayerfully. "I swear, I'll fill your feed trough with pure oats tonight. I'll talk to that man on the mainland with all those pretty little fillies, and we'll see about letting you stud.... Jack!''

Jack turned and took off, kicking a cloud of sand into the air. Heading homeward.

"Son of a..." Alex stood up, dusting himself off. So much for the Zen of bareback riding, he thought. At least with a schemer like Jack. Maybe he should rethink his absolute ban on motorized vehicles on the island and invest in a safe, reliable, nonsentient dune buggy.

Maybe, he just ought to sell the horse. Jack was too difficult to handle.

Naw. That would be too easy. He took a step and winced at the pain of a strained muscle. Maybe he ought to threaten to turn Jack into a gelding. Maybe that would scare the creature into some decent manners.

But the immediate problem was to get home. Alex hitched up his pants, dusted off sand and started slogging. He had the small satisfaction of realizing that he hadn't thought about Tinsley Cole for almost a full hour. She returned to his imagination with a vengeance. He sighed. The good news was that, at least, he now had something to occupy his mind on the long trek home.

FROM THE DECK of the small boat, the man watched, his binoculars picking up the shadow of Alex Berringer's form as the latter moved slowly back up the beach. Most days, the man figured he was just wasting time, observing the bastard. But then, it was his employer's money that paid for the time. So it didn't really matter.

Today, however, he'd finally seen something worth reporting. Something that might lead to a big bonus.

Something that might put Mr. High-and-Mighty Alex Berringer *under* the sand, instead of on it. Grinning with satisfaction—that part of the job would be a pleasure—he set the binoculars down and started the engine, aiming the boat for the mainland.

LATE THAT NIGHT, Tinsley sat up in bed, the light still on. Sleep was impossible.

Will the real Alex Berringer please stand up. She finally put aside the book she'd been trying to read. She hadn't seen a word in an hour, at least. Her mind was on the strange, attractive, mysterious, contradictory man who was making his way into her fantasy world so firmly, she could think of nothing else.

Was it worth letting him make his way into her real world?

She stretched, reaching up and noting with pleasure that her back didn't hurt. The healing was slow, but the muscles, seemed to be on the mend. No point in dwelling on the rest of it. She settled back, absently petting one of Delores's cats sleeping at her side and thought about her conversation with her aunt.

Delores had told her everything the older woman knew about Alex. His family had a long and distinguished history, but his father had cast a shadow on their reputation by his mysterious death at sea, possibly a suicide. It had happened over a decade ago, when Alex was in his teens, and the boy had been devastated. His behavior had deteriorated seriously for several months after the tragedy. Tinsley had listened in silent amazement as Delores recounted a sad tale of youthful grief expressed in wild partying and general hell-raising. There was even speculation about Alex trying to imitate his father's death by deliberately putting his own life in peril with his reckless actions. Then, suddenly, young Alex Berringer had gotten a grip on himself.

He'd returned to school, finished his senior year at high school with grades high enough to enable him to enter college at the state university. From there, he'd gone on to a law degree. Tinsley was impressed.

But Delores was not. "He turned his back on his family," she said. "Renounced any claim to the Berringer mansion and moved out to that...hovel on his island. He did nothing with his schooling. You would not *believe* the offers he turned down. He wasted his time and his money, if you ask me. Supposedly he is working on some philanthropic mission only he understands. I believe it involves children, but I don't know any details. And he spends the rest of his time running up and down the coastline, looking for stories to write about."

"But, he is published, isn't he?" Tinsley still didn't understand Delores's hostility, but she had begun to wonder if it wasn't based on fear. Fear that Alex Berringer had actually succeeded in his odd life. Succeeded by throwing over many of the rules her aunt had based her own existence on.

It made a strange kind of sense. Tinsley stroked the cat, who rolled over to present his furry belly for attention. Tinsley obliged and the cat purred in ecstasy.

Delores had admitted that Alex was published and his work did enjoy some limited popularity. But that, in her aunt's mind, meant little, compared to his giving up the sort of life everyone expected of a man with his *pedigree*.

Not Delores's word, of course. Tinsley had mentally supplied it.

In summary, according to Delores Bishop, Alex was a wastrel and a traitor to the expectations others had for him. Not once, Tinsley noted, did Delores mention Alex's mother. She wondered how Mrs. Berringer bore up under the double burden of a husband who'd died mysteriously and a son who had turned his back on his heritage.

Maybe she approved of her son's choices. Maybe that was why Delores neglected to mention her. She knew that Delores had neglected to mention a lot of things.

Tinsley got out of bed and went into the bathroom. While she washed her hands, she stared at herself in the mirror. Why had Delores omitted those things?

And why had Silvie supplied them?

From Silvie, later that evening, she learned Alex had turned some of his personal wealth, inherited after the death of his father, into a trust. That trust was used, in Silvie's words, to help folks, particularly kids. Though any child with the gumption and ability, Silvie said, could apply, Alex really tried to help the island kids, giving them the best opportunities available to use their skills and follow their dreams.

In a way, Tinsley realized as she listened to Silvie heaping praise on the man, he was encouraging a generation to look beyond the limited lives of their parents. To reach out and upward in society. She had commented on this and wondered aloud if he wasn't actually encouraging the end of a way of life.

Silvie hadn't agreed. "No, girl! Sure, some folks leave and don't come back. By my Jason's baby brother, David, he got some special training in some kind of sea stuff with Mr. Alex's help. He came back and started a business raising shrimp. He and his family all still live right out there on the island. They haven't turned from the old ways, just made things better for themselves."

So, Alex's character, Tinsley concluded, depended on whose opinion one listened to. She returned to bed and shut off the light, hoping for sleep. It had been difficult to see Alex as a no-good, as Delores had drawn him. It was equally difficult to see him as a Mr. Bountiful, the way Silvie painted him. She scratched the snoring cat under his chin, wishing she could relieve her curiosity but she couldn't. Not without confronting Alex. Tomorrow she would call him again. First thing. She was going to have to find out for herself which picture was true.

Or if both of them were false.

BRIGHT AND EARLY the next day, she began her mission of discovery. Alex's phone rang and rang, but he never answered. Tinsley fidgeted around until midday, when Delores left for a church meeting. Then, she made a decision.

"Silvie," she said, going into the kitchen. "I'm off on a quest. Don't know if I'll be back for dinner. Tell Delores not to worry, will you, please?"

"Where you going, girl?"

Tinsley didn't reply. She took an apple from a straw bowl on the kitchen table and bit into it.

"Going to the island, aren't you."

Tinsley took another healthy bite.

"Watch yourself, is all I have to say." Silvie turned her back and attacked a pile of cooking pans in the sink. She sounded more amused than worried.

"I can do that," Tinsley replied. She tossed the apple core into the trash. "Thanks, Silvie."

However, those were bold words, she discovered, when she confronted the problem of actually getting to Alex's place.

She drove to the dock with no difficulty. Alex's island was easy enough to locate, since it was called Berringer's Island. So far so good.

Now came the hard part. Skill with words and considerably more courage than she believed she possessed were necessary for the trip out. The only available transportation was owned and operated by a tall man with a suspicious attitude toward her and an apparent faith in his own good luck. First, he wanted no part of taking Tinsley out to Alex's place without a guarantee she'd been invited, and second, his boat looked like it had seen better days during the last century. A drop of water would send it straight to the bottom, Tinsley was certain. She could scarcely look at it, much less consider setting foot in it. But, if she wanted to see Alex . . .

"You all say Mr. Alex knows you, but he don't know you are coming out to see him?" The boatman glared down at her from a height of well over six feet.

"That's right." Tinsley glared back as best she could without seeming to be angry. If she annoyed this man too much, she would never get what she wanted. "I've tried calling all morning. Last night, I even left a message on his answering machine. But he never called back."

"Maybe he don't want company."

"Maybe not. But I won't know until I ask, will I?" She managed a smile. "Look. If he's home and he's busy, or doesn't want my company, I'll just ride back with you, all right?" She glanced at the battered boat, thinking she'd almost rather try flying without a plane than take two trips in it.

The man considered. "He's home, all right. I'da known if he came to shore, 'cause his boat'd be right here. And since I been out here all morning, I know he ain't taken the Sea Lady out. I'da seen her."

"Maybe he's unable to answer the phone." Tinsley stopped worrying about herself for a moment. She looked out over the water and felt a chill even though the day was warm. "Maybe something happened."

"Not on the island." The man stared out at the blob of land. "Naw. Not there. He got too many folks watching out for him there." He sounded confident, but a worried expression twisted his features.

"Even so..." Tinsley shivered. "What could it hurt to check?"

The man stared a moment longer, then looked skyward, as if remembering something important. Finally he looked at her. "My name's Timothy Blane, and I'll take you out because I'm going out myself. But I still got to charge you the regular rate. That'd be two dollars in advance, Miss. Get in the boat."

She did. The ride was worse than any nightmare she'd ever had.

CHAPTER SIX

ALEX HEARD Timothy's boat as it pulled up to his dock. No mistaking the chugging, stuttering sound of that antique motor. Should have been given last rites decades ago, but Blane swore by it, saying he was sure he could count on his old machine when everyone else's was at the bottom of the ocean. Alex pushed his chair back from the computer desk and rubbed his eyes.

He had made it home last night furious—madder than a wet hen—at himself and at Jack. He was tired and in pain. Jack had already been divested of his bridle and been put in the paddock by Samuel. The boy was waiting by the house, and when he saw Alex was all right, he just grinned and ran off in the direction of his own home. Alex made a point of glaring at Jack, but the horse paid him no attention.

So, Alex had gone to bed, too tired even to dream. He had slept in and now was trying to make up for lost time. Alex frowned as he headed out the door and down to the dock, resenting the intrusion even though he knew Timothy wouldn't interrupt him unless it was an important matter.

But when he got to the end of the dock and saw Blane's real reason for coming to the island, all traces of resentment fled.

"Tinsley Cole!" Her name burst from his lips as he saw who the passenger was. A highly reluctant passenger, apparently. Assisting her from the ancient boat was a little like prying a large limpet from a rock. She had a death grip on the gunnels and had jammed her lower body under the middle seat, but with help from both men, she managed to extricate herself and get out onto the dock.

"What's the matter? What happened to you?" Alex asked.

"She don't like water," Timothy said, his face expressionless. "But she had to see you, she said."

"I...I...I...I'm okay," Tinsley said, pushing both men away and promptly crumpling into a heap on the dock. She clutched at the solid wood. "*Now* I'm okay," she repeated. She looked up at Alex and smiled. "Hi. Why didn't you answer your phone? I called last night and all this morning."

Alex was speechless for a moment. She was as white as a ghost, no color at all in her face, yet her eyes shone bluer than the sky. Her smile was sunnier than the day. She looked absurd, sitting there, holding on to the dock. She also looked gorgeous, helpless and embraceable, and it was all he could do to keep from lifting her in his arms right then and kissing her silly. Kissing her until *he* was silly. Right in front of Timothy and anyone else who cared to watch.

"She say you ain't answered since yesterday afternoon," Timothy drawled. "And I saw the boat that's been sneaking around your island again last evening. Just before deep dark. Made me wonder if something had gone on. So, when she asked, I thought about it and out we came."

"I see." Alex watched as Tinsley got carefully to her feet. "Well, Timothy, thanks. I think I can take over from here," he said. "Don't move too fast, Tins. You may faint again." She nodded. He put his hand on her arm, astonished at the clamminess of her skin. She had truly been terrified. It was no act.

"'Bout that boat . . ." Timothy moved back to his own vessel. "We ought to see what's up."

"Yeah." Alex nodded, answering absently, more aware of the fact that Tinsley's skin was warming rapidly beneath his touch. "I'll talk to you about that later, okay?"

Timothy glanced at Tinsley. "Later's fine," he said. He dug in his jeans pocket and took out a crumpled dollar. "Here you go, Miss," he said, handing it to her. "Only one dollar, one way."

Tinsley took the bill, pleased to see her fingers weren't shaking. "Thanks for the ride, Mr. Blane," she said. "Sorry I was such a sissy."

"It's okay, Miss." He smiled at her, then turned to Alex. "She don't like water, for certain. You remember that, now." He nodded, then, as if agreeing with his own thoughts. He grinned, got back into his boat and gunned the engine. It spit and sputtered, but caught and roared obediently. By the time he turned his vessel from the dock, Timothy was chuckling audibly.

As he plowed away through the water, Tinsley heard his deep laughter quite clearly. Alex's arm by now had slipped across her shoulders. His closeness felt good. Comforting. "I'm flying home, when I leave here," she said, settling back against him. "I swear, if I have to sprout feathers, I'll do it!"

"We'll get to that," Alex said. He squeezed her shoulder gently, then stepped away. "Don't worry about it. Are you all right, now?"

"Fine. It was just Timothy's boat, I guess. I could *feel* the ocean under me. I suppose I overreacted a teensy bit."

Alex bit back the urge to smile. "You were frightened," he said. "Come on into the house. I'll fix you a cup of tea."

"Tea?" She waved a hand in front of her face, fanning herself. "It's too hot. I sure could use a cold drink, though. Why didn't you answer your phone?"

He slapped his hand on his forehead. "I forgot to reset the phone system." He took a few steps toward the house. "I had sort of an accident last night, and—"

"You're limping! What happened, Alex?"

He looked at her. "I think we need to talk," he said. "At a certain level, I'm not honestly sure what happened. I fell off a horse, but I'm not sure why. And, what about you? You rode in a boat and nearly scared yourself to death. Are you sure why you're out here?"

"Well, no. I guess not. I . . . I just . . . I had some questions. I . . . You fell off a horse? What horse?"

"Come into my house, Tinsley." He gestured for her to lead the way down the wooden walkway. "Let's both sit down, take some deep breaths, and talk."

"But . . ."

"Move!" He smiled as he barked the order. His open palm waved in the vicinity of her rear, but he didn't touch her.

Tinsley moved, laughing at his gesture. Her residual fear from the harrowing ride across the channel faded as she reached Alex's home. A Southern mansion, it definitely was not.

His house was a simple cottage. But an unusual one. Small and unpretentious to a fault. A grove of pine trees sheltered it, scattering their needles on the sandy yard to make a lawn of brown, aromatic material. It was only a short distance from the beach, but it was lifted up on tall pilings, so that high sea surges would pass under it. The walkway from the dock led over the beach and yard right up to the front porch. The exterior was covered in weathered wood, unpainted and gray in color. The roof was shingled, also in a weathered wood material. To her unpracticed eye, it all looked hand-done.

Inside was hand-done, as well, but only in the sense that the owner had made no effort to organize or decorate. It was a mess. She stopped at the open front door, amazed at the confusion. "This is certainly a lived-in place," she said, trying to be diplomatic.

"My cleaning woman doesn't come but once a week," Alex said, sarcasm in his tone. "Sorry."

She hardly noticed the defensive bite in his words. She was fascinated by the litter, her eye trying to make sense of it. "Oh, it's all right. Don't apologize. I didn't give you any warning I was coming, after all. It's your place, and you have a right to keep it any way you want." Tinsley moved farther into the big room, stepping over piles of books, newspapers, magazines and boxes.

Alex unsuccessfully wrestled with resentment at her obvious disapproval of his home. Granted, she was only speaking the truth, but it rankled, nevertheless. "Why, thank you. I feel so complimented," he said. He moved around her and went over to the cooking alcove. Taking two glasses from the drain board, he loaded them with ice from the fridge and poured tea from a pitcher. He felt heat on his face as he pushed aside a week's worth of dishes in order to perform the task. The dishes were clean, but stacked up and waiting to be put away.

As he cut lemons, Tinsley came out of her fog. "Oh, you meant *iced* tea," she said, brushing her hair back from her face with both hands. "And I stood there and demanded a cold drink. Then, I come in and insult your house. The way you live." She went over to him. "Alex, I apologize."

He handed the tall glass to her. "Why bother? It's the truth. I live in a constant state of confusion around here. I like it. I know where everything is. It suits me." That wasn't true. The place was a shambles simply because he could never find the time or the inclination to tidy it, but he felt obligated to defend himself.

"Okay." She drank some tea. "This tastes great. Thanks." She took a breath and chugged down the rest of the liquid, the long muscles in her lovely throat working as she drank.

Alex watched, fascinated. "You don't do anything halfway, do you?" he asked.

Tinsley exhaled, noisily, and set the glass down on the few inches of unoccupied countertop. "I guess not," she said. "But I was thirsty."

"More?"

"No, thanks." She looked around. "Really, do you prefer this? Or is it just that you actually can't get it together?"

Alex looked at the ceiling in exasperation. And embarrassment. She'd called his game without knowing she'd done so.

Tinsley ignored his expression. She moved over to one of the big windows facing the channel and stared out. "I was worried about you," she said. "You left in such a hurry yesterday. I wanted to know why. I couldn't get you on the phone. So I asked about you. Insisted on information, really. Delores told me some things. Silvie, other stuff. And when you didn't answer the phone at all, I thought I should come out and confront you. Talk, I mean."

Alex set down his glass. "So, you know I'm a disgrace in my mother's sight. And that the rest of my family thinks I'm crazy?"

She turned, shocked at the bitterness in his tone. "No. Delores didn't say anything about..."

"Oh, come on, Tinsley. I don't suppose it's all that big a deal where you come from to challenge the expectations held for you since birth. Perhaps no one has such expectations out there." He looked away. "Perhaps that's an improvement over our system here."

"Alex, you are babbling nonsense. I don't understand what you mean."

"Then, let's talk about you."

"Me?"

"Why'd you brave your fear of deep water and come out here? Why didn't you just wait. Eventually, I would have remembered to reset my phone system."

Tinsley tapped her fingertips on the window pane. She didn't look at him. "I have one big weakness, Alex. It isn't my fear of water."

"Let me guess."

"Don't bother. I am the original Curious Cat. My Dad's always said one day it'd either kill me, get me thrown in jail or make me rich and famous. So, honestly, that's why I came out. My curiosity concerning you was driving me nuts. I had to ask you about what I learned last night. About you. Are you annoyed or angry? I guess I wouldn't blame you, either way."

Alex didn't reply immediately. She listened and heard him make a strange sound. When she turned to look, she saw his expression was twisted and strained. "What is it, Alex?" she asked, her heart sinking. She'd made a terrible mistake, she thought, invading his privacy and then being so direct about her motives. She had it on the tip of her tongue to apologize again and say goodbye. Then, he spoke.

"This is all a little scary, Tinsley. That's exactly what my father used to say to me, when I was small."

"Oh?" She moved closer to him, drawn by the sorrow in his eyes and the odd, warm, sympathetic feelings inside herself.

"Yes." Alex put his hands behind him and leaned against the counter, knowing he would reach for her, if he could. And that an embrace now would lead to some really inappropriate behavior, at least on his part. "I was always into something, checking it out, looking it up, running it down. My father, at least, approved my need to question everything."

"And now, you approve of it in others, don't you?"

Alex blinked, momentarily unable to follow her. "I...I recognize and appreciate initiative, if that's what you mean."

"Silvie told me. About your encouragement to kids." She turned back to the window. The view had changed. Instead of a blank land-and-seascape, the scene was populated by a boy and a horse. The black horse was huge, the child's features vaguely familiar. He had the animal by a halter lead, and as she watched, he broke into a jog, giving the horse a chance to trot along the beach. "She said you helped people who would put your assistance to good use. Who's that? Is that the horse that threw you?"

Alex came over to stand by her. "The boy is Samuel Turner, Silvie's grandnephew. The horse is mine. Jack Tar is his real name, but I frequently call him other things. He didn't throw me. I fell off. Sort of." He rubbed his sore leg.

Tinsley looked at him. One light blond eyebrow rose, slowly.

"All right. He threw me. But it was only because I wasn't paying attention. It was my fault, I suppose. Jack's a tricky beast." Alex frowned. Then he started to laugh. "I went out to ride him because I couldn't get my mind off you, if you want to know the truth."

"Are you kidding?"

"No. Not now." He pressed his forehead with a knuckle. "Frankly, Tinsley, your bluntness seems to be catching. If you want to know more of the truth, I haven't been able to stop thinking about you since I saw you the other day, reading your cowboy poetry."

"Whew!" Tinsley blew out her breath. "I'm not really sure how to respond to that."

"Don't, then. It's not necessary. Not now, anyway." Suddenly he sensed the beginning of a good idea. "I think I see a way we can do some mutual advantage negotiation, here."

"What do you mean?"

"I just had a thought." He stared out into space, then at her, then focused on the room. "I need to chew on it for a while before I share it. Let's get out of here for a bit. Mind taking another walk with me?"

"No. Of course not. I'd like it, in fact. I want to see your island." This would be a chance to get him to relax, she thought. On his own turf, he might open up some more. She wasn't sure what was going on, but she knew it was something other than what she had bargained for.

Maybe it was something she should run from. Maybe not. Either way, she needed to find out. "How long have you lived out here?" she asked. "This place looks old."

"Only about five years. But the structure's been here for almost fifty. It was originally a fisherman's shack. I fixed it up with the help of some friends. The last hurricane damaged it pretty extensively, but I rebuilt, just like a lot of other folks did."

Alex led her out the front door and down onto the beach. The sand was deep, white and soft and sifted into her tennis shoes immediately. "This side of the island gets very little surf," he said. "It's peaceful and quiet. Waves are bigger over on the ocean side. Unless it's storming, then it's anyone's bet how high the water will get."

"Isn't it dangerous, living here year-round?" Tinsley walked as far from the water as she could without being too obvious. She didn't actually mind the stuff as long as she wasn't riding on it, but she still was nervous from the harrowing voyage in Timothy's floating death trap. "I mean, if it stormed hard enough, you could drown." The idea made her shudder.

"And if it stormed hard enough where you live, you could freeze. There're risks, no matter where you set your roots, aren't there?"

"Can't argue with that." She gave up kicking sand out of her shoes and slipped them off. The hot sand felt good on her bare feet. "Life isn't much fun without risks, anyway, in my opinion." She hooked the shoes with her fingers and carried them. "I admire your courage, though. Living way out here." He didn't reply immediately, and when he did, he had changed the subject from himself to her.

"Let me teach you to swim."

"Oh, no. We already covered that, Alex."

"We talked about it. We didn't close the book. Why not give me a chance?"

She shot a glance at him. He wasn't looking at her. He was just gazing straight ahead at the long stretch of beach, and he was squinting against the glare of the sun. He wore old jeans and a new white T-shirt. No shoes. He hadn't

shaved, the dark stubble giving him a rugged appearance. "What about that mutual advantage stuff you
mentioned back at the house?" she asked. "What did you
mean by that?" Overhead, a flock of gulls flew by,
screeching.

Alex stopped. "You must be one hell of a courtroom
lawyer, lady," he said. "I've never met anyone so able to
turn a conversation around. You're evading the issue."

"I'm not. I just don't want to deal with it. That's different."

"Not in my book."

"I guess that's because we aren't reading the same
novel, then." She aimed a kick at a piece of driftwood,
but remembered in time she wore no shoes. Sand flew,
instead. "I also guess I made a mistake coming out here.
I just thought ... Oh, I don't know what I thought."

"You wanted to be with me."

Tinsley stopped. "I, what?"

"Look, Tinsley." He put his hands on her shoulders. "I
find you really intriguing. Pardon my directness, but I just
have to say this. You're on my mind, constantly. You
might as well actually be around. I can't speak for you, of
course, but for myself, I want to understand what's going on with these feelings I have. And, as far as I can see,
you really don't have anywhere else in particular to be, do
you?"

"Well, since you put it that way, no. I guess not."

"All right, then. You need something to do. I need help
here. Would you go to work for me?"

"As a cleaning lady?"

"No, no. As an assistant. You're too qualified to be an
office manager or secretary. You're too unfamiliar with
my work to be a partner. So, assistant."

Tinsley shook her head. "I don't want a job. I just came out here to ask you . . ."

"What?"

"Well, like why Delores was able to bug you enough to make you leave yesterday. I thought we were having a good time."

"We were. Delores pushed a few of my personal buttons, and I overreacted. And the only way you're going to find out enough about me to understand that, is by working with me." He smiled, then grinned, showing his teeth.

Tinsley stared. "By golly, I've been conned! Did you have all this planned?"

"Not a bit of it. I swear."

"I shouldn't, but I do believe you." She brushed her hair away from her face. The breeze blew it back. "This is really crazy, Alex."

"I know. Shall we begin?"

"Begin? Where?"

For a few moments, Alex had felt he was in control of the situation. He had guided, and she had followed. Now, he wasn't at all sure where to go. "Ah, I suppose . . . Ah, I don't know." His thoughts ran down like an unwound clock. He couldn't think. So, he did what he found most natural and appealing. He looked at Tinsley Cole. He let himself really look at her for the first time since he'd helped her out of Timothy's boat.

She had apparently paid even less attention to her clothing and appearance today than she had yesterday. Her mane of hair was drawn back by two barrettes, placed haphazardly and accomplishing little in the way of control. She had a slight sunburn on her nose and wore no makeup at all. Her jeans were faded and baggy at seat and knees, and the tank top was old and frayed along one seam.

But it was clean and pale pink and made her skin glow. The very fact that her jeans didn't fit made her look all the more sleek and athletic. Desire for her hit him again, and he wondered at the frailty of his own character.

He wanted her to say she'd work with him so he could get her into bed. That was his motivation, and it stank to high Heaven! He was a louse, and he couldn't help it.

"Could you start work tomorrow?" he asked, not meeting her gaze, need overcoming conscience. "I . . . I'll have to use at least the rest of this afternoon and evening to sort things out."

She could tell he was lying as plainly as if his nose started to grow. "Alex, give me the whole truth, please. I wasn't born yesterday or even last week. You don't want an assistant, do you? You don't need one."

"You saw my place."

"Sure. But you've managed fine so far. Why the sudden desire for order?"

Alex stared out at the water. Sunlight glinted on the waves. "Okay. Maybe because desire is the operative word, here."

"English, please!"

He turned. Looked right at her. "It's not easy for me to be so blunt, but here goes. You turn me on, Tinsley. I want you. I have ever since I first saw you."

"I know." She smiled, pleased at his honesty. "Maybe that's another reason I came out here. Besides my curiosity, of course."

"I'm not hearing this. You don't mind my saying I want you?"

"Why not? If it's true, I appreciate hearing it. Look, Alex, just because we're interested in one another doesn't mean we're going to do anything, does it? I'm long past needing to scratch an itch the first time I feel it. Aren't you?"

"I really don't know." He stuck his hands in his pockets. "I thought I'd outgrown this sort of thing. I guess I haven't. Where you're concerned, I'm making no promises."

"I'm flattered." She spoke softly, her tone sincere. "Really. I like you, Alex."

Alex's conscience buckled under the sweet pressure of her words. He reached for her and put his fingertips on her bare upper arms. Her skin certainly wasn't clammy now. It was hot and smooth to his touch. She gazed at him, and the sound of the surf started pounding in his ears. She put her hands on his chest, her palms flat against him. But she didn't push him away. A tiny frown appeared between her eyebrows, then faded. Her lips seemed to soften as her mouth opened slightly and she moved toward him. Alex felt his breath catch in his throat. Felt desire become a solid weight in his body.

And then, the pounding became rhythmical. Hoofbeats echoing his heartbeat. He heard Samuel yell, the boy's warning call sounding over the roar in his head. Alex turned his head. Jack Tar was racing along the beach directly toward them. His ears were flat against his big head and his eyes were wild.

"Get back!" he yelled at Tinsley, shoving her to safety while he faced the horse. He had no idea what he was going to do, but he knew he had to stop the animal before it hurt someone.

Jack Tar lowered his long head as he thudded closer and closer. Alex could see his strong, yellow teeth as the horse's lips pulled back. He braced himself, ready to grab at the halter and the rope that trailed behind. Ready for pain and disaster...

Suddenly his feet went out from under him, and Tinsley was standing in his place. Jack thundered up to them and by them and swerved toward the water, driven by a banshee yell from Tinsley. Alex picked himself up and watched as she waved her arms and screeched, the sight and sound of her making Jack plunge deeper into the surf. The horse whinnied and slowed, his progress impeded by the water.

And she followed! Right into the ocean. Showing no fear at all!

Alex continued to watch as she waded after the horse, moved to his side and started to stroke his back. By now, Jack was motionless, except for his ears and withers. The ears moved back and forth, the withers quivered. Alex dusted off the seat of his pants and walked down to the water's edge. Tinsley was speaking softly, droning words to the animal as she petted him. She was also standing hip-deep in the ocean.

"Thanks," Alex said. "I didn't know what to do."

"I did." She moved around to Jack's face and ran her hand along his long nose. "I've had many a time like this on the ranch, but never had such a convenient runaway ramp." The water lapped at her tank top, turning it a deep rose color.

"Runaway ramp?"

"Like for trucks." She scratched behind Jack's ears. The stallion put his head down and made a noise suspiciously like a contented sigh. "You know. On long, high grades in the mountains, they put runaway ramps, roads off to the side, for trucks that lose their brakes. So they can stop with relative safety." She put her hand in the heavy mane just above Jack's withers. "The water sure worked for big boy, here."

She placed her other hand on Jack's broad back. Alex saw her lips move as she murmured reassuringly to the animal. Then, he understood what she was up to. The words of warning came from him without his being conscious of speaking them until they were already shouted.

"Hey, don't! Tinsley, what're you . . . ?"

She mounted the horse, her long legs grasping his middle tightly. Even in his fear for her, Alex could see by her expression she was not taking this step lightly. She was worried. Watchful.

But not as frightened for herself as he was for her. He started to speak again, to warn her, to yell for her to get off. But some instinct told him to keep silent. Samuel came running up, his breathing so labored that he couldn't talk. Alex heard him gasp in alarm at the sight of Tinsley on Jack. He put his hand on Samuel's shoulder. The boy said nothing.

Jack raised his head. The big horse blew air from his wide nostrils and walked sedately onto shore. From her high perch on his back, Tinsley Cole smiled down at the two worried faces, staring at her. She felt great, and the exertion hadn't hurt her back one little bit!

CHAPTER SEVEN

"LOOK." TINSLEY RUBBED Jack Tar's big flank, ruffling the black hair carefully so that skin was visible. "See this?" She pointed to a small raised welt beaded with tiny spots of blood. It looked to Alex like an ordinary bruise until he studied it closely. Too perfectly round for a normal bump.

Tinsley went on. "Something hit him. That's why he bolted." She caressed Jack's hide. "Good boy," she murmured. "Gooood boy."

Alex observed the scene with amusement and concern. Big bad Jack looked ready to lie down and roll over for her to scratch his tummy. She had the beast totally under her spell, he realized. Alex knew how Jack felt. Tinsley was darned good at casting spells. But what she was suggesting did raise some surprising questions.

"What could have hit him?" Alex scratched his head. "I can't imagine anyone on the island throwing rocks or harming Jack in any way. He's kind of a local pet. When he behaves, that is."

"Even when he ain't," Samuel stated. "All the folks think Jack's fine." The three of them were in the paddock, examining Jack. Samuel, still extremely upset by what he saw as a personal failure, sat on the fence, watching the proceedings closely. So far, no amount of reassurance had wiped the look of defeat from his young face. Now, with Tinsley's revelation of the strange welt, he looked hopeful, at last.

"There was this boat out in the channel," he said. "Maybe they was shooting off something. Hit old Jack by accident."

Tinsley shook her head. "Unlikely. The accidental part, anyway. Jack was tagged on the butt. Right where it would have the greatest shock impact on him without causing obvious damage. If he was shot at, it was deliberate. Count on it."

"How in the world can you tell that just by looking at him?" Alex asked. "I admit you know horses better than I do, but . . ."

"I did a little work in security on the local rodeo show when I was younger," she said. "I learned about some nasty techniques for getting horses to buck up to expectation. Usually, something sharp or irritating was stuck under the saddle, but the really clever jobs involved nailing the poor animal from a safe distance with some kind of missile that wouldn't draw blood. Just startled or scared the hell out of the bronco."

"But, why Jack? Why my horse?"

"I don't know." She turned and looked at him, giving him the full impact of her blue gaze. Sensual and serious at the same time. "But, you do."

Alex had no response. Her statement was just too ridiculous.

"She's right, Mr. Alex," Samuel piped in. He jumped off the fence and came over to the horse. "I heard my pa talking about how you made some rich folks real mad 'cause you wouldn't sell the island to them. He says you're saving it. Maybe one of them rich men shot at Jack. Hurt him to hurt you." The boy's eyes filled with tears, and he patted the horse's neck, gently. "A bad thing, Jack," he muttered. "Real bad."

Tinsley was mildly startled at the child's words. She'd already come up with a culprit: Alex's unpleasant cousin, Clayton. Now, here was Samuel, suggesting in strong terms that some others might have a stake in causing trouble for Alex. The man had no shortage of enemies, it seemed. For such a quiet, mild person, it was an astounding revelation. And more. It was...

Interesting. She had to find out more, she told herself. So, volunteer. Get involved in his life. "Were you serious about that job?" she asked. "Not just putting me on, I mean?"

Alex hesitated, taken aback by the sudden change of topic. "Of course, I was serious," he said. "I wouldn't have even mentioned it, otherwise."

Tinsley held out her hand. "I'm employed, then. When do I start?"

He didn't take her hand. "Why have you changed your mind? Because of what just happened? Are you just intrigued and want to hang around because of that? Or because you really are interested in helping me with my work?"

"Does it matter?" Her expression was open and ingenuous, neither confirming nor denying his suspicions.

"I really don't know. At a certain level, I suppose it doesn't."

"And at another?"

"I've never been much of a gambler, Tinsley. I don't know if I really trust your motives. But it looks like this time I'm going to have to take a chance. I'll have to wait and see. If you want the job, it's yours."

This time they did shake hands.

Samuel had been following the conversational volley by looking first at one of the adults, then the other. Finally, clearly frustrated, he declared, "I don't know what you all're talking about, but don't you think we oughta tell the sheriff about Jack, here?" He stood in front of the horse and put his arms around the thick neck as best he could. "I mean, somebody *hurt* Jack."

"Samuel, we can't prove that. We'd just be wasting time." Alex hunched his shoulders and buried his hands in his pockets. "I'm sorry."

"He's right," Tinsley added. "Just because Jack's got a sore spot on his hind end and acted insane for a few moments doesn't constitute evidence of criminal activity. Now, if he'd been shot with a dart or something, and we could find it, that might be a different story."

"I'll go hunt in the sand," Samuel volunteered. "I'll find that evidence!"

"You can look, if you want." Tinsley rubbed the welt. Jack snorted, but didn't shy. "But I'm willing to bet you won't find a thing. Ever heard of an ice bullet?" She looked at Alex.

"No."

She patted the horse again. "Made of dry ice, fired from a relatively short distance with a low level of explosive, it'd just ding the target and disappear. Could be a sling-shot sort of thing was used. Dollars to doughnuts, that's what we're dealing with, here."

"Whew." Alex regarded her. "You're way beyond me on this. I've never even imagined such a thing. You do have a mind for the devious. I salute you."

"Well." She grinned. "Maybe I can think like a criminal, but I can't swim, so we're even, I guess." She looked at Samuel. "How about some lemonade, guy? I think I remember seeing a big old pitcher of it in Alex's refrigerator.''

"But, Jack...."

"Don't you worry about Jack," Alex said. He moved to the horse's injured side. With a tenderness that surprised even himself, he moved the hair aside and studied the welt. "I'll get some cream on it that'll help it heal and keep the flies off. You go with Tinsley, okay, Sam?"

"Okay." Samuel sounded delighted. Then, he sobered. "But you be careful, Mr. Alex. Jack's in a mood."

Alex sighed. "When isn't he?"

"That's another thing I can work on," Tinsley said, putting her hands on Samuel's shoulders and steering him toward the house. "He shouldn't have bolted quite so wildly. Jack needs some serious training, I think." She looked back at Alex. "You don't know much about horses, do you?" she asked. Then, before he could answer. "That was pretty brave of you trying to stop him like you did. Even if you went about it wrong, it took courage."

Alex confined his response to a modest nod, knowing his bravery was really nothing more than a stupid macho knee-jerk reaction. He would have been trampled right into the sand, if she hadn't intervened. Not much call for pride, there.

"Are you a cowgirl, Miss Tinsley?" Samuel had a tone of awe and respect in his voice.

"Kind of." She started telling the boy about her childhood on the Wyoming ranch. Samuel was obviously all ears.

Alex watched them as they moved out of clear earshot and disappeared around the side of the screened porch into his house. She'd made a conquest of Samuel, today, that much was sure! He slapped Jack on the neck and went to the tack room to find the medicine kit. But, he reflected in a moment of self-awareness, Samuel was the second guy to fall around here.

Because, she'd already made a conquest of him.

"WHADDAYA MEAN it was a dumb idea?" The younger man slapped his palm down on the polished surface of the big oak desk. "It went perfect. Like clockwork. The horse went crazy. Nuts! If she hadn't been there, it woulda run him or anybody else down, believe me! Now, all I got to do is make sure he's on board, and no one else's around to stop the horse. He ain't much of a rider."

The older man cleared his throat. "You should have waited until that specific opportunity presented itself. As it is, Berringer is alerted. He won't be so careless with the stallion from now on. You spoiled a marvelous plan with your damned trial run."

"You don't know that." The man turned his back and scowled at the wall. The wood paneling was festooned with framed papers declaring honors and degrees conferred on the man behind the desk. The occasional photo of that person with politicians and celebrities spoke of power beyond the mere academic and honorary. The young man was suitably impressed. It meant the guy had enough money to hire him and pay when the job was done.

But when it came to this kind of thing, none of that power and honor or money meant squat. Just know-how and experience. He had both. Plus, the guts to do the job, when it came down to it. "I mean, you ain't run nothing like this before. So, you ought to trust me."

"Indeed." The tone was dry. "I suppose I have little choice."

"Okay." The man nodded, satisfied. "Then you want me to go ahead with it? Soon as I see a chance?"

"Not just yet. Young Master Alex is involving himself with that cowboy woman, I understand. Let's wait and see how that goes, first."

"Why in hell should we do that?"

"Because." A sigh. Patient tones. "A man in lust or love is a careless man. He'll be confused and not thinking clearly. Then is when you should strike. Do you understand?"

The man laughed. It was a dark and ugly, grating sound. "Yeah. I get you. I sure do! Okay. I'll hold off a while. Until he looks like he's really out of his skull over the broad. Then, it'll be all that much easier to crack it. See, what I figure is, if the horse don't kill him, I will. Brain him with some driftwood like he hit it on the way down. He falls, it still looks like an accident." There was excitement in his tone. Relish at the prospect. Something the old guy wouldn't understand, he thought.

"Ahh." The man at the desk smiled. "Excellent. I was concerned you were leaving far too much to chance. I can see now that you have thought this out. You actually have a strategy. I find that encouraging. Nevertheless, wait a while." He paused. "But not for too long."

"Got you." The young man grinned and held his thumb up. Then he slowly and deliberately turned it downward.

THAT EVENING, as they sat on the back porch enjoying the soft warmth of the air, Tinsley told Delores about her new job. Predictably, her aunt was not pleased.

"You have a law degree," Delores said. "You've practiced long enough in Wyoming to have respectable professional credentials. And you're willing to stoop to being a mere secretary? An office cleanup person for a man who—"

"A man who needs my help. Who asked for it. Who's remarkably patient with my fear of deep water. Darn it, Delores. A man I like! Is that clear enough?"

Delores didn't answer. She just sighed. Aggrieved. In the background, crickets chirped their night romances and a few birds continued to sing.

"Look, I don't mean to be snappish." Tinsley held out her hand in a gesture of peace. "I understand you don't like what you know of Alex, but all I'm asking is that you give him a chance. Or at least let me make my own way without all this...this..."

"This interference?" Delores stood up and went over to the porch railing. "Dear, I know I've tended to do that where you're concerned. It seems I just can't help myself." She stared off into the distance for a moment. "I feel responsible for you, just as if you were still a child. Not right of me, perhaps, but I can't help it." She sounded miserable and self-accusatory.

Tinsley longed to get up and put her arms around her aunt. But she knew the rules. If she did, she would be acknowledging that Delores was right and she was wrong. No. She had to stand, or in this case sit, her ground. Funny, but if this had been her mother and if this scene had taken place in Wyoming, just the opposite kind of behavior would have been appropriate. As she sat still, Tinsley pondered that. She was in the same nation as Wyoming, certainly. But it was a different world.

Delores finally broke, as Tinsley was sure she would. "All right," she said, giving another deep, troubled sigh. "You must do what you think is right for yourself, I suppose. You are a grown woman. But, darling, I just don't want to see you hurt again. That's all." She came back to her chair, a wicker frame rocker, and sat down. The wicker squeaked softly as she started rocking. The invisible crickets sang along.

"Thanks, Delores. I appreciate that." Tinsley reached over and patted her aunt's hand. Now, touching was okay. The skirmish had been won. Was the battle still to come?

THE NEXT DAY she woke up with poetry running through her brain. The vision of big, powerful Jack Tar thundering across the sand, and the equally big and powerful man attempting to stop the headlong, insane rush was a strong picture. Her creative instincts just couldn't ignore it, even though the fantasy she found herself constructing had nothing to do with the reality of her bumping Alex out of the way and chasing the horse into the surf. Well, wasn't that what poetry was all about, anyway? Making reality more structured and beautiful than it really was?

Yeah, right. It could also get you into trouble, if you took it too seriously and distorted real life. She knew that well enough!

Tinsley got out of bed and headed for the bathroom. She was supposed to meet Alex at the dock in forty minutes. That would be a good dose of reality for her.

As she showered, however, she thought about how kind and patient he had been with her the afternoon before when he had brought her back across the terrifying water in his motorboat. He had her put on a thin life jacket that didn't make her feel like she was in a straightjacket and had suggested that instead of cowering in the center of the boat, she take up a position right at the bow. Right at the front, where she would be able to keep her gaze and attention on the shore rather than on the water directly beneath them. Knowing land was just within shouting distance, he had said, would reassure her until they actually reached it.

Strangely enough, it had worked. She had experienced none of the sweating anxiety that usually gripped her in such a situation. Even more strangely, she reflected as she toweled off and took the dryer to her mane of hair, she was almost looking forward to the trip over this morning.

Or, maybe, she was just looking forward to seeing Alex again. Looking forward to being around his intriguing combination of strength and gentleness. Of power and peace. Who knew? She didn't, that was for sure.

But when she stood on the dock at eight o'clock and watched him roar up in his little powerboat and place it precisely where Timothy indicated, she was fairly sure it was the man she was anticipating, not the mission. Timothy moved swiftly, efficiently, tying up the boat, and Alex got out. He greeted Timothy warmly, then turned his attention to her.

"You look bright-eyed and bushy-tailed this morning," he said, smiling at her. "In fact, you look wonderful."

Tinsley felt heat on her face, and it wasn't from the morning sunshine. "Oh, I took a little more trouble today, seeing as I was starting a new job. I guess I wanted to impress my boss."

"Well, you succeeded." Alex regarded her. For the first time since he had seen her at the literary society meeting, she was dressed up. Not in skirt and stockings or high heels, but more appropriately in a smart-looking pair of tailored khaki slacks with a crisply ironed linen blouse. She had a beige sweater thrown across her shoulders. The blouse was almost the same rose pink color as the old tank top she'd worn yesterday, but today the flattering shade had some help from a touch of makeup on her face. Her pale hair stirred like a living thing in the slight breeze. She was totally gorgeous and desirable. He wanted to wrap himself around her and hold her forever!

"Let's get on back," he said, calmly. It took an effort. "Think you can manage the trip without a problem this time?"

"I can only try." Tinsley swallowed her fear and climbed into the boat. Looking at Alex helped. He had on his usual polo shirt and jeans, and he still hadn't shaved, making him dashingly appealing in her eyes. This time, she watched him instead of the approaching shore.

And she wondered why he hadn't shaved. Was he somehow aware how much his go-to-hell appearance turned her on? Or did he just not care enough to groom for her? That was an unpleasing thought.

But the view of him was pleasing enough. The wind of their motion made his dark hair ruffle and plastered the shirt to his body. She could even see the dark pattern of hair on his chest under the material. She started to imagine what he would look like with the shirt off and was doing so well with her fantasy that she almost forgot she was on a boat over deep water.

Until a sailboat cut carelessly across their bow and Alex swore and turned sharply to avoid the larger craft. The turn threw her to the right, and Tinsley nearly went over the side. She lost her balance, slipped to the bottom of the boat and slid down toward the stern, arms flailing for something to grab. She didn't scream or yell. She simply hooked on to the nearest safe support.

Which happened to be Alex's leg. She wrapped her arms around his thigh, pressed her cheek to his knee and closed her eyes. She knew her whole body was shaking, but couldn't control the reaction. Her worst nightmare had almost come true! Just when she had felt so at ease. So safe. She panted, trying to get enough air to keep up with her racing heart.

Then the boat settled, her center of balance returned to normal and Alex's hand rested on her head. "It's okay, Tinsley," he said. "Nothing's going to happen to you. I'm right here. I'm in control. We're almost home." His tone was soft and reassuring, but deep and resonant enough for her to hear over the sound of her blood rushing in her ears and the horrible *slush-swoosh* of the water under the boat. Tears squeezed out past her shut eyelids.

She didn't move. Finally he stopped the boat. She felt it bump up against the dock. Then and only then did she open her eyes and release her grip on his leg. "I'm sorry," she murmured. "This is really darned embarrassing."

Alex kept his hand on her head for a moment, his touch caressing her hair. "I can see how it might be for you," he said. "But for me it's one hell of an ego trip. I can't remember when a woman made me feel like I was actually rescuing her from something terrible."

"Well, you did. And it wasn't just a feeling. I nearly fell overboard." She moved forward, anxious to get onto dry land. "Why did that idiot sailboat cut in front of us like that, anyway? They ought to get a ticket for reckless...sailing or something."

Alex laughed. He followed her onto the dock and tied the lines firmly. "A sailboat has total right-of-way, Tins," he explained. "They're dependent on the wind, so all power-driven craft are obligated by law and by common decency to yield to them. If I'd ignored the sail and gone right on, I'd be the one getting ticketed."

"But I nearly fell in!"

"That's right." he straightened and regarded her. "And that's why you're going to start to learn to swim today. If you're planning on working with me, I can't be worrying that if you do ever end up in the drink, you'll drown out of sheer panic.''

Tinsley fought a rising tide of negative emotions: anger, fear, frustration... terror. ''You're right,'' she said, hugging herself to keep from starting to shake again. ''Of course, if I'm riding the water taxi at least twice a day, sooner or later, I'm liable to get... wet. I have to learn to cope, even if I won't ever enjoy it.''

''That's the way.'' He spoke so softly, she wasn't sure she heard him correctly. It was the kind of undertone, encouraging sound she used on children and animals.

Well, he was using it on her, now. And with good reason. ''When can we start?'' she asked, unclasping her arms and raising her chin. This fear would not defeat her!

''Later.'' He smiled.

''Oh, but I didn't bring a suit.''

''Don't worry. I've taken care of that, too. Got it covered, so to speak.''

Tinsley looked at him carefully; something she saw deep in his sea green eyes suggested that it was entirely possible he had arranged for that sailboat to cross their path. She saw nothing malicious, but a lot that boded good-natured mischief. Another facet of his personality?

But once inside his house, he was all business. ''This will be your office,'' he said, leading her through the big main room to a card table set up with a view of the beach. On the table were stacks of notebooks, files and loose papers. ''Sorry I couldn't provide better furniture,'' he added. ''But this was the best I could do under such short notice.''

''I've worked on worse.'' She poked at the debris on the table. ''But rarely with this impressive a workload already in place.''

Alex chuckled. "It's not as bad as it looks. All I want you to do today is sort out this stuff by topics." He fished among the papers until he located a sheet from a yellow legal pad. "See? All you need to do is stack the material per topic in one place. I've listed—"

"Alex, this is Stone Age! Primitive beyond reason. Don't tell me how to do the job. Just tell me what you want done."

"I just said..."

"You just said you wanted another mess made. If I stack this stuff up, even in order, all it's going to do is make more confusion. Suppose I work today, die of a heart attack or something overnight? You'll never find this material again without me."

He looked at her solemnly. "You're planning heart failure tonight."

"No. Of course not. I just wanted to make a point. Now, before we go any further, we have to take care of one thing."

He frowned. "What's that?"

"A contract, of course. Defining our mutual obligations and my pay. You're a lawyer. You didn't think of that? I'm very surprised."

"In point of fact," he said, grinning now, "I did." He moved over to his own desk and produced a piece of paper from a mountain of notebooks and manila folders. He handed it to Tinsley. She read it quickly.

Then reread it carefully. "I can't sign this," she said, finally. "It's crazy."

"Why?"

"You're paying more an hour for scut work than I earned as a practicing lawyer in Wyoming. That's why. I won't take advantage of you like this!"

"Why not?" His expression was bland, unrevealing. "You didn't write the terms. I did."

"You are out of your mind."

"Maybe so." He took the paper from her and picked up a pen. "But it is my mind, my job offer and my bank account. So, if I choose to pay you even a million dollars an hour, and I can prove I can afford it, it's my business, not yours."

Tinsley thought for a moment. "I guess I can't argue with that." She took the paper back. "But I want to add a few clauses."

"Feel free."

"Okay." She looked around. "Typewriter?"

Alex looked embarrassed.

"Okay. No typewriter. Mind if I work off your word processor and use the printer?"

"Well, it's kind of quirky." He looked even more uncomfortable, now.

"The printer?"

"No. The word processor. You see, I built the computer and designed the software myself. And—"

"You did!" Tinsley hurried over to his desk and stared at the machine. It was totally unlike any she had ever seen before. "My gosh, Alex! I'm really impressed. Is there anything you can't do?"

"Organize myself." His smile was definitely sheepish. "That's what I want you to help me do." He dug through the mess on his desk and came up with a clean sheet of typing paper. "Just write out whatever you want to add. I'll run it into the appropriate file myself and print out the revised copy. That'll be simpler than spending the rest of the week teaching you how to run this system."

She took the pen and paper. "But I'm going to have to learn it." She waved at her card table desk. "And I'll need a terminal of my own, eventually. I'm not just going to sort through your stuff and stick it all in various boxes according to your alleged topics. I'm going to take the material from the primary sources and set it up for you in reference files in your data bank. That job alone will cut thousands of hours from your time.''

"But..."

"Don't argue, Alex. If you're going to pay me this much, I'm going to earn it." She slapped the page with the pen. "If you don't agree to that, we might as well stop right now."

He ran his hand over his head. "I like to see the primary material firsthand myself. I don't know if I want to work off your digest of it."

"So, go back and check me out. But at least you won't have to spend hours transferring the material. No one's going to stop you from adding or subtracting from what I do."

"I guess not." A strange look came over his features. "Go ahead, Tinsley. It seems to me your mind is working far better than mine right now. We'll do as you suggest."

"You won't regret it." She went back to the card table and sat down. "I promise you that!" She seemed to radiate energy as she applied herself to the task. Her enthusiasm was an almost palpable thing as her fingers made the pen fly across the page. It made him feel tired, just watching her go! What was it going to be like, having that lovely dynamo around day after day?

"I certainly hope not," Alex said, turning away so that she couldn't actually hear him. "But," he added solely to himself, "I have a feeling I might."

One thing was for sure, as long as she was in his life, it was not going to be the same.

CHAPTER EIGHT

BY THREE THAT AFTERNOON, Tinsley was exhausted. Once she had made the changes she thought ought to be in the contract, she turned the paper over to Alex and went right to work, sorting through his material. Her plan was to arrange it all according to topics, as he had requested, then to learn the computer's software and deal with it as she had suggested to him. Sorting, she figured, would be the easy part.

It wasn't.

His interests were eclectic to the extreme. Difficult to track and separate. She quickly lost the thread of any discernable pattern. For instance, the material on fishing showed no common denominator except locale—he was deeply involved in work that had to do with the industry around the South Carolina coast. He had notes for an essay on responsible harvesting of the seas surrounding the island. He had the draft of a legal document detailing the rights of indigenous fishermen as opposed to big commercial operations. She found a surprising amount of material in favor of economic commercial fishing. He was biased, it seemed, but not closed-minded.

He had researched material on historical naval topics. Sea battles in the area. Possible locations of wrecks. Even treasure maps from the old pirate times and the earlier Spanish treasure vessel traffic. Exciting, romantic stuff, she thought. Enough to intrigue a scholar and writer for a lifetime. But there was more.

Duller material on economics—crops that had been tried and failed. Ones that were successful. A fascinating piece on the return of some rice culture, a crop that had all but disappeared until recently. Social customs. Politics. His list took up both sides of the legal pad page, and she was sure he was into more subjects. He just hadn't wanted to overwhelm her.

His intellectual capacity, she decided, must be truly amazing.

On the other hand, he didn't have the sense to keep enough toilet paper on hand, she discovered. She rummaged in her pockets and found some Kleenex tissues. *Thanks, Alex,* she thought. *You do have flaws.* A classic absentminded professor, if she ever met one. He needed a keeper, that was for sure!

And not just any helper. One that really cared about his work and would support him in the smaller details of life, the nitty-gritty of living. Tinsley pushed back her chair and rubbed her eyes. Yes, she was totally exhausted.

"Ready for a break?" Alex sounded cheerful.

She glared at him. "I'm ready for a vacation. This is a *job!*"

"I never said it would be easy." He stood and stretched, making the fabric of his shirt pull tight across his chest. "But I knew you'd turn down a cakewalk. You need a challenge to stay happy, I think." He rolled his shoulders and reached down to the keyboard. He punched in a code and the printer started clacking away. "The contract'll be ready by the time we get back."

"From where?" An uneasy feeling settled in the pit of her stomach.

"Swimming."

"Oh."

"You agreed. While in full possession of your faculties, you agreed it was a good idea. So don't sit there, shrinking. It doesn't wash. You're too tough for that." He spoke forcefully, but his tone was kind. "Come on. I'll get your suit."

Tinsley stood up. Her legs felt weak and shaky. "Alex, I don't think..."

"What?" He narrowed his eyes and glared. Challenged her. Taunted. Without saying a combative word, he invited her to fight.

"All right, damn it! If it'll make you happy, I'll get in the water. But don't expect me to like it. Now or ever. Where's the damn suit?"

Alex bent over and rummaged in a desk drawer, then held up a scrap of silvery material. "Right here," he said. There was no mistaking the glint of mischief in his eyes now. No mistaking it at all.

But, when, in the privacy of the bathroom, she did try getting into the suit, it proved to be quite modest and a little bit too big. Tinsley regarded herself critically in the mirror.

She filled it all right, but the extra material indicated he'd misjudged her size by about ten to fifteen pounds. She patted her fanny, speculatively, checking the jiggle factor. Was she getting heavy? Looking fat? She had led a relatively sedentary life since the accident. No, her behind wasn't sagging yet. Firm enough, encased as it was in the silvery spandex. And, best of all, the maillot style covered her scars. She looked all right.

Now, if she could just control her fear....

Alex had a towel ready for her when she emerged from the bathroom, but when he tried casually to toss it to her, it fell short. He was too busy staring to aim accurately.

She was a goddess! He'd imagined how her figure would look in a swimsuit, but no amount of erotic daydreaming could have prepared him for the reality. A true Venus, she was sculpted in abundance above and below a narrow, trim waist. Because of her size, he had assumed she was soft, but when she moved, he could see that hard muscle lay right under the surface of that satiny skin. "Suit fits all right," he managed to say. His throat was suddenly dry and the words sounded a little croaky.

"Yeah. Thanks. It's slightly big, but I like it. It's not too tight and doesn't bind me anywhere." She made an adjustment on one of the straps, unaware she was demonstrating that not all of her was rock solid. Some parts did move.

Enticingly.

Alex wrapped his own towel around his hips just in case his body responded too obviously. This was not going to be easy, he warned himself.

Silently repeating Alex's promise that her introduction to swimming under his tutelage would not be scary, Tinsley followed his lead down the beach. The afternoon was hot and muggy with humidity, but the breeze from the water kept her feeling comfortable. Alex set a brisk pace, making her move quickly. Probably, she thought, so she wouldn't have time to worry. She slowed a little to show him she was all right, but he kept right on, striding across the sandy ground until he was ahead of her.

That gave her a chance to observe him from behind. She didn't need to be thinking about poetry to be aware she was watching it! Instead of bathing trunks, he wore an old pair of cut-off pants. Hard to tell what the original color had been. Now they were sort of muddy sand.

But they fit like a second skin and were stretched and bleached white over the small, tight roundness of his rear.

Poetry! His long, lean torso with his broad, muscular shoulders was a sonnet; his strong backbone line, a quatrain. The legs she had admired when they were encased in jeans looked even better bare. Again, long and lean, but with tight, defined muscles. Perfect, matching stanzas! Tinsley lowered her head so that if he turned around, he couldn't see her staring and grinning. What a lecherous female she was getting to be!

"We're almost there," Alex said, not turning around. "How're you doing?"

"Fine." Hadn't thought about the water at all! She smothered a snicker. "I'm fine, thanks."

Alex still didn't turn to look at her, fearing if he did, he might forget about swimming and try teaching her some more intimate lessons, but he listened carefully. He heard the catch in her voice clearly and knew she was terrified. Poor woman! But he had to do this for her own good. If she had gone over the side this morning, she would have been in a great deal of danger, even with the life preserver on. She needed to learn enough about the water to control any panic response, at least.

So, they would start where the island's children—who frequently swam before they walked—began their lessons. In the tidal pools. Alex turned and reached for her hand. "The island has a strange geography," he said, looking only as far as her eyes. "Up here it kind of bends and folds, letting the tide come inland when it's high." He started to lead her into the trees.

"Inland?" Tinsley stepped gingerly over the pine needle carpet on the ground. "I don't get it. I thought we were going in the ocean."

"Not just yet." He pushed aside some low-growing pine tree limbs and directed her onward.

He didn't say anything more, so she followed, curiosity growing. He still held her hand, and the contact felt good. Warm.

Warm and a little sweaty. The breeze from the water was now blocked off by the thick growth of trees. The air was hot, wet and still. It smelled lemony, of the pines. Her skin began to prickle from the heat and the sweat. She was about to make a comment on her discomfort, when she heard the high, happy sound of children's laughter and squeals of excitement. "Alex, what is going on here?" she started to ask.

He held aside some boughs, showing her. "Ye olde swimming hole," he said. "Island style. Look."

Tinsley did. Then, she laughed. About a dozen small children frolicked in the shallow pools in the clearing before her. Some were so tiny, they had to be supported by older siblings. But most were on their own and obviously at home in the water. They splashed and paddled and swam and leaped in the stuff. There was plenty of horseplay, but no one was acting as lifeguard or referee. "You've brought me to kindergarten, haven't you." she said. "Where's the teacher?"

"The kids mostly teach themselves," he replied. "Generations of island folks have learned how to handle the water right here. Once they get past the infant stage, they're left to play pretty much on their own."

"Isn't that a bit negligent? I mean, the potential for accidents..."

"You mean drownings?"

She nodded. The word was not one of her favorites.

"As far as I know, it's never happened. Not here, anyway." He frowned. "From time to time the sea does get one of the people who make a living off it or one, like my father, who loved it too much to stay away from it, but..." He broke off.

She put her hand on his arm. "Alex, I'm sorry. I wasn't thinking about your father. Just the kids."

"It's okay." He turned toward her, his expression open and vulnerable, in spite of the casual tone of his words. She smelled the tang of pine and the subtle aroma of his skin and sweat. His eyes were deeper green than any ocean. The heat she felt from him hotter than any sultry, Southern afternoon air and sun. She swayed toward him, ready for an embrace and kiss. She felt her body heating up and swelling in anticipation of his touch, maybe even his promise of lusty passion...

"Hey, Mr. Alex!" Yells. Shouts. The kids had spotted him. The erotic moment was gone. She stepped back as he was surrounded by small, brown bodies. They laughed and danced and all tried to hold his hands at once. Clearly, the man was a special favorite of these little water sprites. Alex greeted each and every one by name, squatting down to speak directly to them. Tinsley was amazed.

And yet, she reflected, she shouldn't be. This was his home, after all. These kids were the children of people he saw every day. He had declared a particular fondness for children. Her emotions shifted sharply, and she lost the sexy feelings entirely. The sight of him, surrounded and having fun with the little ones, brought a mistiness to her eyes. It looked so... right. She swallowed away a lump in her throat.

"Mr. Alex, who's that lady?" One of the boys was pointing at her. "She a movie star?"

"No, Caleb, she isn't." Alex put his hand on Tinsley's shoulder, presenting her to the group of children. "This is Miss Tinsley Cole. She's my associate...uh, my new helper. She's working with me at my house, you see. Uh . . . in my office.''

"She ain't cleaning it up, is she?" a sharp-eyed little girl asked. "That's my momma's job!"

"Tinsley," Alex said. "This is Emma, Clara's little girl." In a lower voice, he added, "Clara cleans for me."

"Emma," Tinsley replied. "I'm not cleaning. Your momma's job is safe, believe me. I'm just helping Mr. Alex with his books and that sort of thing."

"She came here to play with you all," Alex announced, giving her a gentle push into the clearing. "She's from out West where there isn't much water, so she's going to get used to it a little bit at a time."

"Yea!" The kids liked the idea.

Tinsley wasn't so sure she did. They grinned and ran back into the pools, splashing and shouting and calling for her to follow. She couldn't just stand there like an idiot. "Thanks a lot," she said to Alex.

"Good luck." Another slight nudge. This time, his hand rested for a moment on her bottom. Almost a caress. Then he slapped her, gently. Tinsley yelped and stepped forward into the fray.

Actually, it was quite pleasant. None of the pools were much deeper than her knees, and the water was cool and refreshing on her warm skin. She bent down and splashed it onto her face and arms, enjoying the sensation.

The children didn't stay interested in her for long. Once they discovered she was only going to plod around, she was quickly abandoned for riskier sport. Alex was out in the deepest pool, tossing kids into the air. They landed, shrieking with glee, until they went under water. Tinsley shuddered with each disappearance, but the little heads always bobbed back up, grins intact.

They were having a terrific time! Alex was having a terrific time. She decided she should, too.

She waded around until she found a relatively quiet place. The pool was shallow, but long enough to allow her to stretch out, much like she would in a bathtub. She sighed and settled, enjoying the sun, the water and the cacophony of voices from Alex's direction. She paddled her arms, making small waves in the pool. Kind of fun. Kind of relaxing. She felt comfortable enough to close her eyes. If this was his idea of swimming lessons, it was sure all right with her.

"Hey, Miss Tinny. Wanna play ducks?"

Tinsley opened one eye. A little girl, about four or five years of age, was sitting in the pool near her. Like the other children, her bathing costume was constructed of old bits of clothing. In this child's case, it was a strange combination of a tiny pair of boys' jockey shorts and a red bandanna halter. Her chubby, brown form looked right at home in the water.

"What's 'ducks?'" Tinsley asked, sitting up and smiling. "And what's your name?"

"Janna." Giggle. "This's ducks." Janna disappeared underwater. When she came back up, she blew out her cheeks and said, "Quack, quack." Water streamed down from her short, black hair into her face.

Tinsley looked around. Alex was surrounded by yelling, rambunctious kids. Water was flying all over the place, and his entire attention seemed on the children. Not on watching her at all. She looked back at Janna. "I guess I'll try," she said, her chest tightening. She felt some fear, but pushed it away. What could happen? This water was so shallow. Why not? She bent her head down. When she lifted it, her water-soaked hair fell over her face. Sputtering, she pushed it aside. "Quack, quack," she cried. Janna collapsed in laughter.

So did Tinsley.

From his pool, Alex registered her every move. Janna was his agent. He'd sent the little girl over to Tinsley with the suggestion she invite her to play. Janna was the most adventurous of the small ones, and he knew she'd give Tinsley a challenge without threatening her. As the woman lifted her face out of the water and laughed, he knew triumph. He'd been right! Right as rain.

The children were the key to unlocking her fears and ridding her of them. He felt a surge of joy. Then, when he saw Tinsley pick up Janna and hug her, other feelings moved into his mind and heart. He tried not to think too much about them.

Yet.

The rest of the afternoon Tinsley played in the tidal pools with her new friend, Janna and several other younger girls. Finally the sun began to drop behind the trees and the tide to go out. Tinsley found herself disappointed when Alex announced it was time to get back.

"Can we do this tomorrow?" she asked, toweling off. "I had a great time."

"Sure." Alex was drying off, too. He had his back to her. "But the tides are supposed to be higher tomorrow, so these pools will be somewhat deeper. Think you can handle that?"

"Yes, no problem." Tinsley gave Janna another hug and waved goodbye to her other new friends and followed Alex through the trees back to the beach. After a few minutes of walking in silence, she asked, "How much deeper?"

Alex shrugged. "Depends."

From the way he said it, she knew it was going to be much, much deeper. She was just going to have to trust him. Was she ready to do that? She wasn't sure.

When they returned to the house, he said little until they went over the terms of the contract. Then, he was again all business. Stern without being harsh, but also without much warmth. It was almost, Tinsley decided, as if he were holding himself back deliberately.

But why would he do that?

"I've set your pay as a salary rather than an hourly wage," he said.

"But I know I'll be here a certain number of hours each day. Won't it make things easier for you to pay by the hour?"

"Not if you think about the future. My research carries me all over the state. Not just here. I might find myself taking you to the university, for instance. For days of digging in the archives." A small smile. "Suppose I paid an hourly rate then?"

"I see your point." She hadn't imagined the possibility of such a long, involved commitment to this job. But, she reminded herself, one never knew what the future held.

She decided to agree to the rest of his points, also, since he accepted her changes without argument. At least they were in accord on legalities, she thought. And they both seemed committed to treating one another fairly. That, in itself, said a great deal for the possibility of trust. She looked forward to long, interesting discussions with him. Maybe she'd learn what made him tick.

Later, however, Alex made no attempt at conversation as he took her back to the mainland. She, for her part, was too jittery to bring up anything. He let her fight her fears alone in the bow of his boat, giving her the luxury of privacy to deal with her demons. But he drove slowly, carefully, avoiding even the slightest wake of other boats, and she was able to maintain her dignity. Her faith in him went up several more degrees. When they reached the dock, Timothy Blane was waiting. He greeted them both, cheerfully, then gave the weather report.

"Gonna blow tonight," he said, setting the lines and gesturing to the darkening sky. "Should be rough in the morning."

"How rough?" The question burst from her. "I mean, will the channel be too bad to travel on?"

"No." Alex answered. "I expect you here on time tomorrow."

She looked at him and saw no particular expression on his face. But in his eyes, she was sure she saw a challenge, a dare. Maybe more. "Okay," she said. She held out her hand. "Tomorrow morning, then."

He shook her hand. All business. Only that certain something in his eyes... She said goodbye and headed for her car. But she heard him talking to Timothy the moment her back was turned.

"I'll be crossing back later on tonight," he said, quietly. "Don't wait around for me. Go on home."

"It ain't no problem."

"I know." He put his hand on Timothy's shoulder. "But don't trouble yourself, anyway. Hear me? It's gonna rain like sixty."

"I hear you. I'll head on home come dark. You seeing The Lady?"

"Yes." Alex's reply was low, soft and full of emotion.

Tinsley resisted the urge to slow her pace and overhear some more. She reached the car, one of Delores's old ones, a Buick that had seen better days, but still ran perfectly well. Opening the door, she felt the hot burn of jealousy. Whoever The Lady was, Tinsley hated her. And that was silly! The only claims she had on Alex Berringer were business, combined with a growing friendship, spiced by a healthy dose of lust. She had no right to feel jealousy over anything he did with anyone else.

That night, she picked at her dinner, giving Delores an opening for inquiry. "Things didn't go so well out at Mr. Berringer's island today?" Delores asked. "You look somewhat unhappy."

"Oh, things went fine. But I... Oh, I just don't know."

"Out with it. What happened? Did he behave like a gentleman or not?"

"Oh, he was perfectly mannerly. Say, do you know if he's got a girlfriend? Someone called The Lady, maybe?"

Delores's fork hit the plate with a clang. "Hardly, my dear! Where in the world did you hear that?"

Tinsley sat up from her slouching position. "Alex himself. I overheard him tell Timothy he wasn't going home until late. Then Timothy asked if he was seeing her tonight, and he said..."

Delores started to laugh. Delicately and with restraint, but she obviously found what Tinsley had said to be vastly amusing. "Darling," she said, wiping the corners of her eyes. "The Lady is what many local people call Alex's mother. She is eccentric, I admit. Especially since the tragedy. But she does have a regal air about her that has earned her the nickname." She picked her fork back up. "Now," she said. "Do you feel better?"

His mother! Tinsley resisted admitting it, but she did feel much better. Dinner suddenly became very appetizing and she dug in with enthusiasm. Yes, she felt just great.

ALEX FELT HORRIBLE. He sat at the opposite end of the long dining room table from his mother, attempting to eat while his digestive system warned him he would pay for every acid bite. The visit had been required, but had been a mistake, given his present emotional state. Tinsley Cole had unsettled him seriously, and he wasn't up to dealing with his mother right now.

"And so, I can scarcely raise my head in polite society," his mother continued. She was on a roll. Right over him. Her small, thin body sat bolt upright in her chair, her spine a stiff yardstick, her dark eyes fixed on him, accusingly. Her gray hair was pulled tightly back in the customary severe style. Her classic features were becoming more harsh and hawk-like as the years passed, he noted. Not much left of the soft beauty of her youth.

"Why, it isn't bad enough you've become a hermit," she snapped. "It isn't humiliating enough you've chosen to squander your money on unworthy, frivolous causes. No! You have to flaunt your affair with that...that cheap woman from out West. I tell you, Alex. You actually seem to delight in humiliating me."

"Any humiliation is totally unintended, Mother. I wasn't even aware I was having an affair." He sipped at the soup. It burned his tongue. He responded more sharply than he had intended. "I'm enlightened this evening. An affair. Me? Just imagine. Even if it is a cheap and tawdry one, it's nice to know about it."

"Don't be sarcastic with me, Alex. Clayton told me all about her."

"Ah. And Cousin Clayton knows my alleged paramour intimately? Good to know it's all in the family."

"You are impossible. I won't discuss this unpleasant subject further." Susan Berringer turned her attention to her dinner, ignoring her son for a while.

The silence didn't help Alex's digestion. By dessert, he was extremely uncomfortable and deeply saddened. He'd come to dinner, at his mother's invitation—an unusual occurrence in itself—hoping to make some progress toward bridging the gulf between them. Clearly, his time had been wasted.

But, she was his mother. And the hostility between them upset him beyond measure. He left as soon after dinner as was decently possible. His emotions were too fragile for him to risk staying. If he broke down in front of her, he felt he would lose any progress he had ever made toward earning her respect. Her disdain for a man who lost control of himself would be monumental. And Alex wanted that respect. He had long since abandoned hope that she would offer him her love.

He drove toward the dock and his boat. And his lonely house on his island. For the first time since he could remember, he did not want to go home alone. Rain beat down on the windshield, and sorrow beat in his heart. He wished he could cry. Like he had when he was small. When he'd learned of his father's death. He yearned for someone he could trust enough to share those tears with. Right now, there was no one on the planet he felt that way about. Not one single human being.

ALEX WAS NOT the only Berringer suffering deeply that night. After her son left, Susan Berringer sat alone in her huge living room. Her tiny figure seemed doll-like in the vast space. The night was rainy and gloomy and one of her staff had set a fire in the fireplace. She sat in the dark with only the fire for light. Rain beat at the windows, and the wind sighed in the trees outside.

And pain, confusion and loneliness sighed in her aging heart.

CLEAR OVER on the other side of town, lying on his single bed in his small bedroom, Clayton Berringer burned painfully inside. Grief was not the acid eating at him, however.

Stark envy was.

That night, none of the three Berringers slept well. One didn't sleep at all.

Tinsley Cole, on the other hand, slept like a baby.

CHAPTER NINE

THE NEXT MORNING, Tinsley waited on the dock a full twenty minutes before Alex showed up. Rain fell steadily, making the early hour darker than it normally would have been. Timothy wasn't on duty yet, either, so she waited alone.

Because of the weather, she pulled the Buick close to the end of the pier and sat inside, watching the water. Wondering at herself, that she would actually be looking forward to crossing that water with him. Wondering about what the future was going to bring. Wondering why he was so tardy.

When she finally saw the shape of his motorboat arrowing through the gloom, she buttoned her rain jacket and got out. The level of excitement she felt was far greater than the situation warranted, but she didn't try to control her emotions. She reached his docking place just as he pulled up. "You're late," she said, loudly, in order to be heard over the roar of the motor. "Why?"

Alex cut the motor. He was covered by a yellow rain slicker and hat. "Sorry," he said. "I didn't sleep well last night. I had some trouble getting up."

She bent down and peered at him. "You look like hell. Are you sick?"

"No." His tone was as harsh as a slap in the face.

She stepped back. "And if you were, it's none of my business?"

"Just get in the boat, please." He handed her the life jacket. "The channel's a bit choppy today. It's not likely to get much smoother, either. The sooner we cross, the better."

She put on the jacket under her raincoat, but hesitated before entering the boat. "Are you sure you're all right? I don't want you conking out on me about halfway across. Like an airplane pilot having a heart attack and leaving the terrified passenger to fly alone." She spoke in a light tone, trying to make a joke.

Now, he smiled. "I swear. No heart attack." He made the sign of a cross over his chest. But he had a closed look in his eyes. She wasn't going to learn anything right now, she realized.

The ride across was tolerable. The rain lashed her face, but it felt quite invigorating. For the first time in months she felt cool and comfortable. The temperature was still in the seventies, she knew, but the rain tempered the heat. Alex again steered the craft for maximum safety and comfort, and she almost relaxed. They arrived at the island without incident.

His house was warm and welcoming, even though he was distant and distracted in his behavior and conversation. "I'm really not working on all cylinders this morning," he said. "I'll be, uh, in and out. You go ahead and finish what you started yesterday."

"Alex, I . . ."

"Coffee's over on the counter." He pointed. "Help yourself. I'm going to check on Jack. He hates rain." Then, adjusting his rain slicker, he went out through the front door.

Tinsley stood unmoving for a moment, thinking. She took off her coat, poured some coffee and went to her desk. She sensed that checking on Jack was just an excuse to get out and be alone. But that was his business. He did, after all, have a perfect right to his privacy and moods. It was no concern of hers. She stared at the pile of paper on the desk.

Alex walked through the downpour, his shoulders hunched against the chilly rain. Jack had been fine, though edgy as he always was when a storm was brewing. Alex had felt a definite empathy with the animal. He was edgy himself. He wanted to work out his mood before he rejoined Tinsley. She didn't need to be subjected to his depression. It was his problem, not hers.

Though, he thought as he splashed through some puddles, just seeing her, waiting for him this morning, had made him feel a little better.

He walked on, considering this.

Tinsley was deep in books and paper when Alex came back. A cold wind blew in with him, and she bent over her work, protectively. "Shut the door," she yelled. "Is Jack okay? What's going on out there?"

"Yes, he is. Dry as a bone in his stall. Bit more of a blow than I expected, though," he said. He took off his slicker, shook it and hung it, still dripping, on a hook by the door. "I'm going to listen in to the weather report. Mind?"

"No. Of course not. Just don't open that door again without warning me, please." She looked at him and noted that he seemed more relaxed, now.

"I won't." He sat down at his desk, ran a hand over his hair and turned on a small radio. A weather announcer's voice droned, unemotionally reporting conditions. They were not good.

Tinsley tuned the voice out. She returned to her work, eagerly. She managed also to tune out her concern about

Alex, since he seemed all right, and she concentrated on the job at hand.

Alex listened to the weather commentator while he worked. The information registered at one level in his mind, while he concentrated on the computer screen. His job today was to restructure his personal program so that he could teach it to Tinsley. At the rate she seemed to be going, she would be ready for it soon. He glanced over his shoulder, taking in the sight of her blond hair as she hunched over a pile of books on the card table.

She was a worker! He had no idea she would set herself to the tasks he had given her with such energy. Of course, given what he already knew about her, he told himself he ought not to be surprised. She was both greyhound and bulldog in temperament. Maybe even part bloodhound. From time to time, as she worked looking through books and magazines, he heard her make little noises of triumph and discovery. Alex turned back to his screen. Then, a strange thought hit him: it would be wonderful irony if she proved to be an ideal assistant. Ironic, since that had been the last factor on his mind when he'd offered her the job.

By lunchtime, the storm outside had worsened. Tinsley was so involved in reading and taking notes, however, that Alex had to shake her shoulder to get her attention. "Hey," he said. "I think I ought to take you home. It's getting real nasty out."

"Home?" She blinked, then rubbed her eyes. "Oh, no. Not yet. I'm just getting a handle on this material about—"

"It's not important. At least not as important as you are. The water's already very rough. They've put out small craft warnings for the whole coastline. I don't want to put you through..."

Now, she looked up and focused on him. "Alex, do you want me to go? Do you need to be alone?"

Her question threw him off balance. "No! Of course not. I was just—"

"Then, quit worrying. If it's too dangerous, I'll just sleep over. You've got a couch." She pushed away from the card table. "Let's eat lunch," she said. "I'm starved." She went over to the kitchen area and opened the refrigerator door.

Alex could think of nothing else to say. He helped her assemble the sandwiches, silently. Any casual words he uttered right now would stick in his throat, he knew. If she slept over, he doubted their relationship would be the same in the morning.

They both ate heartily, as if they hadn't been given a decent meal in days. But they did not speak of either the weather or of night ahead.

The rest of the afternoon passed quickly for both of them. It was hours later when Tinsley yawned, stretched and got up from her chair. She walked over to the window and stood beside Alex. He didn't look up.

The storm had settled in for some serious work. Wind blew the rain at a slant, sometimes even sending it directly horizontal to the water. And the water in the channel boiled and sizzled as if it were in a gigantic pot on a monstrous stove. No way was she riding across that tonight! "I hope you have an extra toothbrush," she said.

"Umm." His fingers worked the keyboard. Click, click, click.

Tinsley folded her arms across her chest. "Is this a hurricane?" she asked.

"Umm, no." Click, click. "Hurricanes come in the fall. This is just a hard spring thunderstorm."

"Oh."

Click. Buzz. Beep. "Say, I just remembered. I asked you to come over for dinner, didn't I?"

"What?"

He turned, smiling at her. "The other day. In your kitchen. Delores's kitchen. Remember? Silvie encouraged you to accept."

She did remember. "That seems like a hundred years ago."

"It does," he agreed. "But will you accept the invitation if I extend it again?"

She pointed to the window. "Do I have a choice?"

"No." Mischief in his eyes, now. They were clear of any shadow of pain or strain. "Isn't that great?"

She had to agree. She tried calling Delores to tell her what the situation was, but the phone refused to function properly, giving her only static and an occasional beep, so she figured Delores would be able to work the details out for herself.

Dinner was everything she expected and more. With her help, Alex prepared salad, halibut steaks, boiled new potatoes and fresh asparagus. For dessert, he produced a pecan pie so rich she could feel it going directly to her thighs. "Do you eat like this all the time?" she asked, groaning. "If so, how in the world do you stay under four hundred pounds?"

"Mind over matter." Alex poured coffee. "Actually, this is special. Cooking is fun for me, but I don't often have the chance to share the product of my labor. That pie's been in the freezer for quite a while, for instance."

"Tasted terrific." She took a sip of coffee.

"Thanks." He looked away from her. "Funny, but I think you're the first woman I've served dinner to who didn't spend the whole meal telling me she ought not to eat it." He took a swallow of coffee. "Particularly when I presented that pie."

Tinsley laughed.

"I'm serious," he said. "I appreciate your attitude."

"I'm glad," she replied, softly.

They sat silently for a few minutes. Rain beat rhythmically on the roof, and the roar of the surf sounded steadily, just as rhythmically. Tinsley listened, growing even more silent inside. She heard her breathing, then Alex's. Also rhythms. She looked at Alex. "Maybe I will understand the ocean, someday," she said, again speaking so softly she was almost whispering.

Alex sat very still. Magic hung in the air between them. "Will you let me teach you to sail, Tinsley? Could you trust me enough to let me take you out into deep water?" he asked. Desire, anticipation, made his voice husky.

"I don't know."

Silence again for a while. Then she got up and put her cup in the sink. "Alex," she said. "We both want to sleep together. But I don't know if we're really ready for that yet. This night wasn't exactly planned, and maybe we need to know more about one another before we share something as important as sex. What do you think?" She turned around and fixed him with a level, steady gaze.

He didn't move. "I want to make love to you more than I can ever remember wanting to make love to a woman before," he said. He looked away from her. Shook his head. "I can't believe I'm telling you this, straight out in such plain words."

She smiled. "It's okay, Alex." She turned back to the sink and started washing her cup. "The air needed clearing," she added. "We might have been heading for a heavy-duty romantic scene that wouldn't have meant a damn thing." She bent to task of drying the cup.

"How can you be so sure?" He stood up and put his hands on hers, effectively stopping her busywork. She looked up at him. "Are you so determined to avoid romance that you have to throw ice water on any magic moment?" he asked, his eyes dark with emotion.

"Don't get mad."

"I'm not!" He stepped back, angry at himself. "No. Yes, I am! I was feeling..." He shoved his hands into his pockets and turned his back to her. "I thought you felt it, too."

"I did."

He guided her around until she faced him. "Just answer me one question, Tinsley. Are you playing, or are you in any way being serious with me?"

She had to think.

Alex watched her. Saw her brow furrow. Observed the shifting emotions in her eyes. "You just don't know, do you?" he said, touching her face with his fingertips. "Well, fair enough. Neither do I." He drew a line along her cheek down to her chin. Lifted her face for a kiss. Touched her lightly with his lips. Breathed in the scent of her warm skin....closed his eyes, savoring the small taste of her he could allow himself....

Hot desire flared through her. Tinsley gasped at the strength of it. If he had grabbed her and plastered her with a deep kiss, she wouldn't have reacted like this! No. This was her honest response to his restraint, pure and simple. She put her hands behind his neck and looked at him. "I'm serious," she said, firmly. "But I wasn't sure until just now."

He frowned.

"Just trust me," she said. "I don't think I'd want to explain it, even if I could, but you can rely on me. I'm not taking anything about you lightly." She traced a finger around the curve of his ear, smiling when he closed his eyes and shuddered with pleasure. "Not my work for you. Not our friendship. Nor this . . ." Her mouth covered his.

They began to make love.

Tinsley felt right about it. She let the notion that she had known him only a few days nudge her conscience for a moment, then dismissed it. Alex was a good man; she liked him, and she wanted him. So, why not?

She stood very still while he touched her, heating slowly, steadily with the fire he was causing to build in her body. New feelings for her. Nothing quite like this had ever happened to her before. Not even when she had thought she loved the man. Did she love Alex? She didn't think so. But his touch! Oh! What it was doing to her!

His fingertips moved across her skin so softly they felt like feathers. His gaze locked on hers while he caressed her face, her neck, her throat. Tenderness and desire flowed from him to her, and she began to shiver. He ran his fingers under the neckline of her skirt. Shivering changed to trembling.

"Tinsley." He whispered her name, pressing his face into her hair. "If you don't want me to do this, you'd better tell me now."

"Don't stop," she answered, embracing his waist. "I'm already going crazy." They moved into the bedroom. Flinging the covers to the floor, Alex guided her down onto the bed. She reached up for him.

Alex settled over her. His need for her was so overpowering, he was afraid he'd lose control and go wild with passion. Take her solely for his own purpose, and forget about her pleasure. He would not do that, no matter what it cost him! With exquisite, painstaking care, he undressed her, leaving his own clothes on as a way of keeping some rein on his body.

Her nakedness filled him with awe. She was smooth ivory, sculpted with such full-bodied perfection, he could scarcely believe his senses. Then, the lust began to change to something even hotter. More enduring . . .

Tinsley lay as still as possible while he kissed and caressed her. In his eyes, she had seen his struggle to go slowly. No matter how much she wanted to race right on to the finish line, she wanted him to set the pace.

And she was enjoying the pace he set! No other lover had taken his time with her like this. She sighed with pleasure and smiled as he lavished attention on her most sensitive places.

But she could be patient for only so long. Shudders of pleasure began to run through her, and she lost some of her sense of self-consciousness in the tendrils of sweet sensation starting deep within. "Alex," she said, murmuring his name with some urgency. "Take off your clothes."

"Soon," he replied. His voice was much deeper than normal and broke a little when he spoke. "We have all night," he said. "I promise." He shifted his position on the bed, so that while he still held her, touching her intimately, he could look into her eyes. "This will be a night you won't ever forget."

She believed him.

His hand moved, his long fingers dancing an erotic pattern over her, in her, and Tinsley responded. The first orgasm thrilled her, but left her tingling, needing more. She was hungrier for him than ever.

"Alex, take off your clothes, please," she pleaded, tugging at his shirt. "I need you. Need to see you."

"Stand up." He pulled her off the bed and to her feet. Outside, it started to thunder. He positioned her so that the light from the lamp on the bedside table fell on her body. Then, he stepped away and started to strip.

Tinsley watched, sensing he wanted it this way. Her legs were weak, so she leaned against the bed for some support. But as she watched, she felt herself growing strong again.

He was gorgeous. Perfect, in her eyes. She had seen him yesterday wearing cutoffs, but total nudity gave him a beauty and dignity she hadn't expected. Lean, tanned, muscular, but not overly so, he also had a pattern of dark body hair that emphasized his form. And his arousal. Tinsley's eyes widened in appreciation. She smiled. Then she moved closer. To touch him.

Alex felt fire go through him, and his body quivered with the soft stroking of her hand. He started to warn her to take it easy, if she really did want him to last all night, but then she moved her hands up to his neck, his chest, his face. One long, slim leg rubbed and twined around his. She loved him with her touch, with her hands and mouth. With her eyes and the way she looked at him. Suddenly, in the midst of his growing passion, he saw her. Really saw her.

Without saying a word, she revealed a side of herself he was sure she wasn't even aware of. He put his hands on her waist. "Tinsley, I..." He wanted to tell her, but something stopped him. "I l..."

She looked at him, puzzled.

And the lights all went out.

Thunder boomed and his computer's backup system screamed with tinny, electronic protest as it hauled itself into action. The bedroom turned white-bright for a moment as lightning flashed. Tinsley was in his arms.

"Don't be afraid," he said, embracing her tightly, talking against the soft silk of her hair. "Just blew out the power connection to the mainland, that's all. Don't worry, though. I've got my own generator."

"You sure do!" Her body moved against his. "And it's already on." Tinsley laughed and fell back onto the bed.

Alex fell on top of her. Her legs went around him, her arms held him a happy prisoner against her heat and strong-soft roundness. And he forgot anything that he was trying to say to her. It didn't matter, anyway. Now, all that mattered was what he could do. All that mattered was what they were doing together. He covered her mouth with his and slid into her.

It was like coming home. Home to a wild, insanely erotic, sexual celebration of life. Alex lost himself in it all. Lost himself in his love for Tinsley Cole.

Overhead, the storm boomed and flashed, working out its elemental frustration on the water and land. But it didn't disturb the lovers.

Later, Alex woke, a chill gripping him. He blanketed Tinsley with most of his body, and where they touched he was warm. But his back was cold. He reached over, trying to snag the covers from the floor, and his movements woke her, as well. She murmured his name and touched his face tenderly.

"I'm so glad you told me how you felt tonight," she said. "It showed me that you were vulnerable."

"Oh, my God!" Alex sat up. "Tinsley, I'm so sorry! Please, don't think I meant to..."

"What's the matter?" She sat up, too. Frightened.

"I didn't use any protection." He slapped his forehead. "My God, how could I be so thoughtless! When you said the word, *vulnerable*, I remembered. Too late...."

"Not a problem, Alex." Her voice sounded dry, emotionless. "If we'd talked about this before we did it, I would have told you."

"Told me what?" He put his hand on her shoulder. She shifted until he removed it. "Tinsley? What's wrong?"

"My back." She turned sideways. "The scars. You've seen and felt them, of course."

"Sure. But..."

"From an accident. I can't get pregnant. So, unless you're worried about catching a disease, which from me you shouldn't be, since I haven't had sex in..."

"You can't have children?" He touched her again, gently tracing the scars. "For sure?"

She shrugged, all of the good feelings gone from her now. But she said nothing.

"Tinsley, I..."

"Forget it." She moved away again. "It's just something I've learned to accept. Actually, I was lucky. The spear of metal went in, and it could have cost me a kidney or something else. Instead, it messed up my insides enough that I probably will never have any children."

Alex listened to the flat, unemotional words, hearing the pain and sorrow beneath them. She was hurt and using her toughness to mask the grief. He embraced her tightly, so she couldn't pull away.

"No one's totally whole and perfect, Tinsley," he said. "This is not a very safe world."

She closed her eyes, squeezing the lids against tears. "You can say that again," she said. Then she cried. And he held her. Held her until the tears stopped flowing. They made love again. This time with a slow, sultry abandon that brought them to such powerful simultaneous orgasms neither could speak. Release and satisfaction was total for them both. Sleep, when it did come, was deeper than either had known for a long, long time.

Sleep that lasted late into the morning when the sun shone and the waves lapped gently at the beach. And three people came looking for them and ended up knocking on Alex's front door, together.

CHAPTER TEN

ALEX ANSWERED THE DOOR. He squinted in the sunlight, holding a hand over his eyes to shade them from the glare. The three people on his doorstep were indistinct shapes for a moment. Then, he recognized the only woman. Or rather, she identified herself in no uncertain terms.

"Where's Tinsley?" Delores Bishop demanded. She stepped past him into the house. "Where's my niece?"

"She's in..." Alex gestured toward the rear of the house. "But, I don't think you..." Delores wasn't listening to him. She was already at the bedroom door.

Alex turned back to the other two. One of them was his cousin, Clayton.

"She thinks rather less of you this morning, dear Cousin, than she did yesterday. If that's possible." Clayton drawled the information. He didn't try to come in. His smile was a sneer. "Hitched a ride out with me just to rescue her darling niece from your clutches. Terribly upset to think the poor girl spent the night with you."

"Clay, you really are an ass, you know." The third person spoke now and moved into Alex's line of sight. His presence made Alex forget the awkwardness of Delores's invasion and Clayton's sarcastic comment and thinly veiled accusation.

"Joe!" he cried out, grabbing the older man by the hand and pulling him into the house. "What're you doing here? Good to see you!"

"Easy, there." Joseph Meadows grinned, the expression wrinkling his tanned face. "We had a fishing date, you and I, remember? My freezer's empty, and I need to restock."

"No." Alex frowned. "I didn't. I..." The sound of feminine voices raised in argument cut him off. Tinsley and Delores emerged from the bedroom.

"Alex," Tinsley said. "I'm sorry about this." She gestured at her aunt. "I had no idea she'd make such a fuss. I'd have called you this morning," she said, turning back to Delores, angrily, "if I'd even dreamed you'd behave as if I were still twelve years old!"

"You should have called anyway." Delores was clearly furious, but keeping her dignity. She was dressed in a skirt and sweater, high heels and stockings. Not a hair was out of place. "It would have only been common courtesy to me to let me know you were in no danger," she added.

Yes, Alex thought. Common courtesy was Delores's watchword. She looked as if she just stepped out of a page of *Southern Living* magazine. Aristocratic, as only a vintage Southerner could be.

Tinsley, on the other hand, looked as if she'd just been over Niagara Falls in a barrel. No sense of aristocracy there. Earthy and sexy, though. She'd pulled on her clothes, but it was obvious she hadn't been in them for long. Alex was sure it was also very obvious she had been making love to him half the night. Tousled and unkempt as she was right now, the sight of her still excited him. Lovemaking, however, was clearly not on her mind.

"I couldn't call you last night," she snapped at Delores. "I tried. First the phone acted like there were ghosts on the line. Then the power went out. His phones depend on electricity."

"I was told Mr. Berringer has a generator," Delores said, glaring at Alex. "Surely, he could have turned it on and enabled you to contact someone to let me know you were all right."

"Ah. It is my fault, I'm afraid." Alex ran a hand over his hair. He was extremely conscious of the fact that he wore only an old pair of jeans. That he hadn't shaved or bathed, either. If Tinsley looked scruffy, he could only imagine the impression he was giving. Delores made him feel like true pond scum.

"I never got around to cranking it up," he said, meaning the generator. He moved over to the sofa and picked up a T-shirt, which he pulled on quickly. He still felt naked and grubby.

"Oh, I shouldn't say that," Clayton said from his stand at the front door. "Looks to me rather as if you did quite a bit of cranking last night."

Alex turned, his fists already balled, fury rising like a red cloud in his brain.

"Hey." Joseph stepped in front of him. "Too early in the day for that sort of exercise, isn't it, Alex? Not worth the bother, anyway, don't you agree? Clay, why don't you take yourself on back to your place. I'll give this lady here a ride home when she needs it."

Delores agreed readily. She hated scenes. Righteous anger, such as she felt was one thing. Violence was quite another.

"Yes, that would be fine with me," she said. "Clayton, I do appreciate your help, but perhaps it would be best if you left now." She gave Joseph a look of deep gratitude for his timely and diplomatic intervention.

"As you wish. So glad I could have been of some help." Clayton smiled, nodded, sneered and departed.

Delores breathed a sigh of relief. "Thank you," she said to the older man. "I don't believe we've met."

"No, we haven't," he said. "Alex?"

Alex, who was still struggling to clear his head of anger at his cousin, mumbled "Delores Bishop, Joseph Meadows." Then he turned to Tinsley. "Are you all right? I apologize for Clayton's idiocy." He moved toward her. "I . . . I should have . . ."

"You didn't do anything wrong," she said, her stern expression showing her indignation, but also keeping him at arms' length. She did not want to be hugged or touched, that was plain enough. "It's not your fault if people can't keep their noses out of other people's business." She glared at her aunt. "What in the world possessed you to bring that man out here?" she asked.

"Clayton was kind enough to offer me a lift in his boat," Delores said. "I came down to the dock to see about hiring a ride out, and he was already there. I was worried sick about you, and I wasn't ready to risk my life by venturing forth in the dockman's vessel." She glanced at Joseph Meadows. "Clayton's was the only other boat around. He saw my dilemma and helped me."

"How convenient." Tinsley frowned, thinking. "I wonder why he was out so early in the morning."

"Maybe he wanted to see if I'd been drowned overnight. It would certainly have made his day." Alex put his hand on her shoulder. "But, don't let him upset you. He's not worth it." He turned to Joseph. "I really did forget our fishing date, Joe. Slipped my mind entirely, I have to admit."

Joseph grinned. "Introduce me to your young lady, Alex," he said. "I'd like to meet the woman who can make you forget fishing." He laughed, warmly. "Never thought to see the day, actually."

Tinsley held out her hand. "I'm Tinsley Cole, Mr. Meadows. Delores's niece, in case you haven't put that together. And as of yesterday, Alex's office assistant. I don't like traveling on the water under the best of circumstances, so when the channel got too rough last night, I decided to stay over here." She looked at Delores. "It was a sensible decision, given the situation. You shouldn't have worried."

"Perhaps not." Delores lost some of her emotional momentum. "But, it looks...wrong, Tinsley."

"To who?" Tinsley ran her hand through her hair. The tangles were impenetrable. "Anyone around here really care? It's sure as heck not anyone's business, if you ask me."

"Delores is right," Alex said, surprising her. "I should have taken you home before the storm hit. It would have been the proper thing to do. But, that's hindsight."

Tinsley got mad. It was as if he were dismissing their night together as a tawdry, cheap event. "Well," she said. "Sorry if I've tarnished your reputation. I guess now you're branded as a fallen man."

"Tinsley!" Delores looked shocked.

But Joseph Meadows laughed again, bringing some warmth and sanity into the situation. "Yes, my dear young lady," he said. "You've ruined Alex, socially. Now, you'll just have to marry the lad. Redeem him. It's the decent thing to do, you know."

His joke brought some perspective to the situation. Tinsley started to laugh, joining Joseph. Both of them seemed to think the idea hysterically funny. Alex and Delores looked at each other. They weren't laughing.

"How about some coffee, Mrs. Bishop," he said, ignoring his friend, Joseph, and his lover, Tinsley, who were by now, wiping tears of mirth from their eyes. "I have a special blend I think you'll find quite good."

"Thank you," Delores said, grateful that someone had maintained proper decorum. Even if it was, to her mind, the real villain of the piece. "That would be lovely," she added. "May I help you make it?"

Two cups of coffee apiece later, the quartet seemed ready to call a truce on hysteria and hostilities. Tinsley, who had taken time to shower and tend her hair while the brew was perking, noted that Delores's attitude had changed considerably. Softened, in fact, to the point of being downright friendly. Credit, she was sure, belonged to Alex's friend, Joseph.

Well, she thought. No wonder. If Alex looked like her fantasy of a sexy young adventurer, Joe Meadows could pass nicely as an older version. His steel gray hair, neat beard, tanned and weathered skin and blue eyes, as well as a physique that was still in shape and tough, made him an attractive enough man to turn any woman's head.

And, Delores's head could use some turning. She needed something else to think about besides Tinsley's reputation and well-being, Tinsley decided. Loving someone and caring about them was one thing; haunting them and interfering with their privacy was quite another.

Alex was aware a number of undercurrents were flowing around his table. Much was still left unresolved between himself and Tinsley, since they'd had no chance to discuss the events of last night. They needed to try to work out what had actually happened to them. It had been more than just a night of passionate sex for him. But he had no idea how she felt. He needed to know.

Meanwhile there seemed to be some unexpected electricity, low-voltage, but nevertheless evident, moving between Joe and Delores Bishop. At first Alex chided himself, thinking that his own heightened feelings were drawing conclusions where there was no reality. But as the two older people began to talk to one another and leave him and Tinsley out, he knew he was on target. He listened for a few minutes, then spoke, taking a chance that his intuition was correct.

"I wonder," he said, interrupting carefully. "Mrs. Bishop, you've come all the way out here. And I do apologize for my part in inconveniencing you. But, since you are here, how about joining us for some recreation?"

Delores frowned, her expression growing censorious again.

"Let me rephrase that," Alex felt his face get hot. Why couldn't he just talk to the woman without getting all these residual negative emotions?

Joseph stepped in, saving the moment. "What Alex means, Delores," Joseph said, "is to ask you two delightful ladies to join us for some fishing. Today should be especially enjoyable, since the storm's cleared out the air. There's nothing like the sea air after a good squall."

"Joseph is a retired navy man," Alex said, his tone warm again. "He's so in love with the sea, he believes it's the only part of the planet worth two cents. But he's right. Today should be perfect. Would you like to go fishing with us?"

Both Tinsley and Delores hesitated, each for her own reasons.

"I'm hardly dressed for such an outing," Delores said, reluctantly. "Though I must admit the notion sounds appealing to me. I can't remember when I went out ocean fishing." Her expression became sad. "Certainly not since my husband passed away."

Alex saw Joseph's eyebrows raise.

Tinsley swallowed hard. "I don't think I'm ready, Alex. Sorry. I just can't."

"Oh, take your time getting ready, my dear," Joseph said, his gaze still on Delores, though he addressed Tinsley. "We've already missed the morning, so it really doesn't matter when we set out."

"That's not what she means, Joe." Alex tried to cover Tinsley's hand with his own, but she pulled back, refusing the contact.

"My niece doesn't care for the water," Delores said. She stood up, her posture stiff again. "And I think we should get home in any case. I do thank you for your kind invitation. However, it was an outing the two of you planned for yourselves in the first place. We would only be in the way."

"Nonsense." Joseph stood up, too. "As far as your clothing is concerned, I can run you back to the mainland while Alex is getting his boat ready. It'll take him a while, since he forgot the date. You can change. We can be back in a jiffy, and..."

The front door flew open, and Samuel burst in. "Alex, Alex," he cried. "Something's wrong with Jack. You gotta come! I think he's dying or something!"

Tinsley was out of the door before Alex could move. She raced across the muddy field behind the house to the paddock. Samuel was right behind her. Jack wasn't inside the fence.

"He's in the stall," Samuel said. Tears were glistening on his face. "He musta gone in there last night. To get out of the storm, maybe."

Tinsley ran around to the stable door, thinking of the horses at home that lived outdoors in all sorts of wild weather. Would Jack willingly get into an enclosure just to keep dry? It didn't seem likely, but she didn't know the horse that well, yet. Maybe he had an aversion to getting too wet.

Apparently, he had. He was in one of the two stalls in the small building. The Dutch door leading out to the paddock was open, though the stall door was shut. He could have wandered in out of the rain. But had he closed the gate behind himself? She hesitated at the stall. Jack stood with his legs splayed, his head down, blowing hard through his nostrils. She heard Alex come in behind her. "Get a vet!" she yelled. Then she went into the stall, all her concern centered on the horse. She swung the door shut, so that no one else would follow.

Alex shouted at her, but his warning went unheeded. His heart nearly stopped when he saw Jack's head go up, the ears plastered back, the eyes wild. Tinsley started talking, her voice slow and soothing. Jack trumpeted in fury. His hooves flashed, hitting the door with a thunderous thump. Samuel screamed. Tinsley continued to speak softly. She was just a pale blur in the darkness of the stall. "Get Samuel out of here," she said. "And be quiet, for goodness' sake!"

Alex picked the boy up and carried him outside. "Stay there!" he commanded, turning back to the stable. He heard the dull, heavy thump of something hitting the wooden wall of the stable, and he ran inside.

Tinsley was still standing, but wasn't going to be for long. She was cornered in the back of the stall, one arm cradled to her body. Her right cheek was bruised and bleeding. Blood trickled down from her shoulder where her shirt was torn. Jack seemed to be stalking her.

But she was still talking to him. Her voice sounded to Alex like slow water rippling over smooth stones in a warm river. Her tone was hypnotic. Jack was moving, but in what seemed to be slow motion. Alex opened the stall door and reached for a pitchfork at the same time.

"Don't hurt him," Tinsley said, seeing him and the weapon, but not changing the timbre of her voice. "He's been poisoned, Alex. He's out of his head. He doesn't know what he's doing."

"I do." Alex took a step into the stall. Jack lifted his hind hoof. Cocked his back leg. "When I move, you move, understand?" Alex said to Tinsley. "Get yourself out of here."

"Alex, don't..."

"I won't hurt him, I swear." He lifted the pitchfork in both hands, holding it like a quarterstaff in front of him. "Get ready..."

Jack kicked, Alex lunged, and Tinsley moved. She ducked and ran out of the stall, whirling in time to see Alex pin the big horse to the wall. But not by the points of the pitchfork. He held him there with the wooden handle against his thick neck. Jack screamed and thrashed and struggled. Whatever was wrong with him was beginning to weaken him. Alex's muscles bulged and strained, and he groaned. It was clear he wouldn't be able to hold out for more than a few seconds. Tinsley looked around, frantically.

The blanket seemed to come into her hands by magic. Samuel thrust it at her. "Cover his eyes," he yelled. "If he can't see, he might get quiet." She ignored the sharp pain in her shoulder and went back into the stall. She stepped next to Alex and threw the blanket over Jack's head.

The stallion immediately ceased fighting.

Alex lessened the pressure on the animal's neck. Jack started quivering violently. Tinsley spoke to him again in that special, soothing way. The horse lowered his head almost to the floor. Then, his legs buckled, and he collapsed with a huge sigh. Tinsley began to cry. Sinking down beside him, she rubbed and patted and stroked the animal, willing him to be all right.

"Are you hurt?" Alex asked her, stepping back and setting the pitchfork down. He was shaking as much as the horse. "Tinsley, are you..."

"I'm all right. Just scratched and shaken up. I hit my head and had the wind knocked out of me, but I'm all right. It's Jack who needs you now. Get a doctor for him," she said, not looking at Alex. "He's dying, can't you see?" Tears ran down her face. "Get him a vet. Now!"

"One's on the way." Joseph's voice made them both look around. He stood at the stable door. He had a rifle in his hands, a grim expression on his face. "Both of you, get out of there."

Neither of them moved. "Did you call for the chopper, Joe?" Alex asked. "If he lives through this, we're taking him to the mainland." He hunkered down beside Tinsley and put his hands on Jack's body, willing the big animal to survive. Suddenly aware how much the stallion had come to mean to him.

"I did." Joseph relaxed a bit, seeing they were in no immediate danger. Delores came up behind him, her arm around Samuel's narrow shoulders. "I called for Bob Duncan and his crew. If anyone can save your horse, they can," he added, his tone kind.

Alex nodded. "He'll be all right," he muttered. "He has to be. Come on, boy, fight it! You can, if you want!"

Tinsley heard the love in his words. She felt a sudden, powerful wave of empathy—triggered by their mutual concern for this huge four-legged creature. This sense of emotional unity with another person was unlike anything she'd ever felt before. She looked at Alex.

Did she love him?

They didn't have to wait long for the vet. Soon, the late morning air was cut by the stuttering sound of a helicopter. Minutes later, a trio of veterinarian professionals surrounded Jack. Alex started talking rapidly with one of them, a tall man with fiery red hair. Tinsley moved away, rubbing her hurt arm, then putting one hand to the growing bump on the back of her head. Delores grabbed her and pulled her out of the stall.

"You could have been killed," her aunt stated, crying. "Oh, Tinsley, I was so frightened for you!" She plucked at the rip in Tinsley's shirt, her fingers trembling. "Let me see. Did that beast bite you?"

Tinsley gently pushed her away. She looked at the wound for the first time herself. "He plowed me into the wall," she said, her voice steady. "Didn't bite me or kick. He wanted to, but held himself back, I think. I just scraped the hell out of myself. Got a bad bump on the noggin, too." She grinned ruefully. "I suppose I'll have to have a tetanus shot or something."

"You were lucky," Joseph Meadows said. He had put his rifle away. "But you're right about your injury. Let me give you a ride to the mainland. You should see a doctor."

Tinsley shook her head. "Not yet. I need to talk to the vet."

"About what?" A new voice asked the question. Tinsley turned. Alex and the red-haired man came out of the stall. Beyond them, Tinsley could see Jack was now standing, albeit shakily. His head was still down, and he was being supported by men on both sides of his large body.

But he was up!

She looked at the vet. "I think Jack was poisoned," she said. "He acted like he'd eaten something like locoweed that's made him crazy. I've seen it before. And this isn't the first time he's been the object of a kind of violence."

"I think you're right about the poison. It's acting like an alkali product." The vet nodded. "But how did you guess? And what other kind of violence? Do you mean his being shot at on the beach the other day?"

Alex introduced them. "Bob, Tinsley Cole knows more about animals than you can believe," he said. "She's from Wyoming," he added, as if to explain her expertise. "Tinsley, Bob Duncan is the best big animal specialist on this part of the coast. I'm sending Jack over to his place for a while."

"He's going to be all right, isn't he?" She massaged her shoulder. "I mean, no lasting damage, is there?"

Bob Duncan shook his head. "I don't think he's in danger, now. But I want to observe him. Old Jack's had two bad experiences in a short time. Alex told me about the beach scene," he said. "And, frankly, I agree with your suspicions. That's twice you saved Jack's bacon, Miss Cole." He looked at Alex. "I don't think you're dealing with coincidence here, and I want you to promise me you'll call Tottie about it. If you don't, I will. Somebody may be trying to get at you and using Jack to do it. If you don't care about yourself, think of the damn horse, will you?"

Alex nodded. He looked grim.

"Tottie?" Tinsley asked. "Who's that?"

Alex came over to her. "The sheriff," he said. "Now, before anything else happens, you are going to the doctor, yourself."

"I'm all right," she protested. "I don't need . . ." Suddenly edges of her vision grew gray. She reached out, clutching for support at empty air.

Alex swore and caught her. "All right? All right! Like hell you are! Bob, what's the matter with her?"

His voice came to Tinsley from far away. She felt herself being lowered to the wet grass. The smell of it mingled with the scent of the soil and the acrid aroma of the stable. Bob Duncan bent over her and pulled down her lower eyelids. He ran his hand over her head, and Tinsley winced.

"Maybe a slight concussion," he said. "I'm just an animal doc, but I know some of the symptoms are the same as in my patients. I suggest you get her to a hospital, though. She ought to be X-rayed, at least. I think she took a good crack on her skull."

Tinsley heard Delores let out what sounded almost like a wail, although she knew her aunt was too dignified to actually howl. She struggled to sit up. The world whirled, but she hung on to the solid earth. "I don't need a doctor," she stated, firmly. "I am fine, I tell you." Then, she fainted.

SHE DIDN'T STAY OUT for long, but when she came to, she was already on her way to the hospital in Carleton Cay. Since Jack seemed to be in better shape than she was, she got priority use of the helicopter. Tinsley was frightened, recalling the only other occasion she'd landed in an emergency room. She remained unusually quiet and docile until the doctor pronounced her to be in no danger. She had a mild concussion, but nothing to worry about.

Over vociferous protests from Delores, she declared her intention of returning to Alex's island. "I have a job," she stated. "And I'm not calling in sick when I have no real reason."

"He won't be there, Tinsley," Delores said, trying logic. "He certainly won't expect you to go. He and his friend, Joseph Meadows, have taken that horse to Savannah for tests. He really wanted to come to the hospital with you but there was no room for him in the helicopter and he had to make a report to the police. You'll be out there all alone."

Tinsley thought about Samuel and the other children. "No," she said. "I won't be alone. I promise." Then, she relented a little. "Look, Delores. If I try staying in bed, I'll go nuts, and drive the rest of you that way, too. The doctor said I was all right. I feel all right. I will call you as soon as I arrive. Alex never locks his door so I'll have no problem getting in."

Delores shook her head, but Tinsley saw by the expression in her eyes that she had given up the fight. She even consented to drive Tinsley out to the dock after she had packed a small bag with some extra clothing. Just in case.

When they reached the dock, however, Tinsley suddenly understood why Delores had been so obliging. She had figured Tinsley would change her mind. And with good reason. The only transportation available was Timothy's miserable little barge.

Tinsley looked at her aunt, hesitated a moment, then said, "Well, I'll see you when I see you, Delores. Please, don't worry about me. Okay?" And before Delores could say anything or try to stop her, she got out of the car and into Timothy's boat.

"Take me to the island, please," she told him, when he came over and looked at her with a puzzled expression on his face. She settled her bag into the bottom of the boat and held on to the sides. But she did not cringe or cower. "I've got work to do for Alex," she added.

Timothy seemed to consider this. Then, without a word, he threw off the lines, got in the stern and fired the motor.

The ride over didn't really bother her. She had too much on her mind to be scared, she decided.

When they docked, Timothy tied up and stopped the engine. "Deputy came by a little bit ago," he said, taking her bag and carrying it for her. "Asked me if I seen anything out of the ordinary. Asked about Alex and you."

"Somebody fed Alex's horse a nasty dose. Did you see anything?"

"No, ma'am. Just Mr. Clayton's boat."

Tinsley frowned. "Clayton Berringer has no particular love for his cousin, does he?"

Timothy said nothing.

Tinsley felt a surge of annoyance, but stifled it, quickly. She was still a stranger, an outsider here. No reason for Timothy or anyone else to confide in her.

But the police had questioned Timothy. Probably, they would want to question her as well, since she had been with Alex both times his horse was attacked.

And she wanted to have more for them than just her eyewitness account. When they reached Alex's front door—unlocked as she had expected—she thanked Timothy, handed him his fee, took her bag and went into the house.

She set her bag down and went over to the kitchen area. The coffee was cold, but she poured herself a glassful and drank it like water. She found an orange and a fresh loaf of bread and brought the food over to his desk. She sat down in front of his computer. She reached for the switch to turn it on.

She hesitated. Did she have the right to look at his personal file?

Tinsley answered her own question. She worked for Alex. Had signed a contract to that effect, including a clause that swore her to keep personal information she learned about him to herself. She'd put that in when she redrafted the paper. So, she was, theoretically, trusted by him with anything she came across in the course of her daily tasks.

They were lovers. Now, she knew that entitled her to nothing at all, but she had made a kind of emotional and ethical commitment to him by going to bed with him. And, even more important, they were friends. She had confided some of her darkest secrets to him, had exposed far more than just her body.

So, she had some entitlement to his secrets.

And, most important of all, she knew he was in some sort of danger, even if he didn't seem to buy the idea. Instinctively, she knew. She also knew that, given enough information, she might discover who was causing his problems. She prided herself on her powers of deduction.

She thought about all of this a little longer.

Then she fired up the machine.

CHAPTER ELEVEN

THE PROGRAM was a nightmare, but she muddled her way through it. Muddled and messed and searched until she found some extremely interesting material.

It put a whole new light on the "Jack incidents."

Alex had been under attack before. Not through Jack, but by other means. Through his love for the sea. At least three times, from what she could find, something had happened with his boats that endangered his life and damaged the vessels. Insurance claims and reports told an alarming story.

Tinsley opened the yellow legal pad she had taken from her card table desk. Placing it to the right of the computer keyboard, she began to take notes. The longer she worked, the more concerned she became. How could he have missed all of this? Was he just deliberately being blind?

Or was he ignoring the evidence because it might bring to light some ugly truths he didn't want to face?

By late afternoon, she was too tired to focus on the screen. Alex hadn't returned, hadn't called, so she figured he was still involved with Jack and with the sheriff. Tinsley stood up and stretched, feeling tension and pain in her head, neck, shoulders and back. The pain was particularly bad in the area of her old injury.

She needed to get out and clear her mind for a while, she decided. Maybe take a walk or something to get the cobwebs out of her brain and the tension out of her body.

A soft knock sounded at the front door. Tinsley opened it. "Janna?" she asked, smiling at the small figure standing in the doorway. "What are you doing here, honey?"

ALEX WEARILY heaved himself out of his motorboat and tied it to the dock. The sun hadn't set yet, but the colors of evening were starting to stain the sky. At least it was clear. No rain or storm tonight.

Also, no Tinsley.

He would call her as soon as he got something to eat. Find out how and where she was. A quick phone call to her aunt's home hours ago had connected him with Silvie, and she had said Tinsley was still at the hospital but she was fine. There were no other details and Alex hadn't asked for any. Before he talked to Tinsley, he did need to eat. He hadn't had a bite since dinner last night, and his blood sugar was undoubtedly so low it wouldn't measure. He was tired and cranky, angry and sad. Tinsley Cole was out of his life.

No way was she to come back to the island. His conversation with Sheriff Tottie Reynolds had convinced him of that. The sheriff had taken one look at the evidence of the last few months and pointed out things he hadn't been willing to see himself. He was in trouble. A target. Tinsley would be, too, if she continued to hang around, working with him. Just as his enemy or enemies had used Jack, used his boats, they would surely strike out at her, if she was seen to be of importance to him.

If she was seen to be of importance! That was almost funny, now. She was so important to him, she was never out of his mind or his heart. If his first connections with her had been close to a sexual obsession, now that they had related on the levels of friendship, work *and* sex, the connection was something much stronger and much more significant.

The tragedy was, he would have to let her go. For her sake. And, in a way for his. He knew that he'd never forgive himself if something bad happened to her.

He walked home, slowly, hearing his footsteps thud with hollow sounds on the planks of the pier.

When he entered his house, however, his mood changed abruptly from one of melancholic meditation to outright anger. Someone had entered his sanctuary and had been rifling his computer. Alex bent over the legal pad lying on the side of his desk and read. He could not believe his eyes.

The handwriting was Tinsley's. But she was in the hospital. Wasn't she? Or recovering at her aunt's home. A victim of the violence aimed at him. . . .

"Hi." The front door banged open. "Welcome back."

Alex whirled around. Tinsley stood in the doorway, her lovely, lush body silhouetted against the darkening daylight. She was drying her white-gold hair with a towel. She wore the silver swimsuit and a smile.

"What the hell are you doing?" he shouted, masking his emotional turmoil with anger. "What. . .? Did you do this?" He held up the pad, shaking it until the pages rattled.

"Sure did." She seemed unmoved by his wrath. She continued to fluff her hair with one hand. "Mighty interesting stuff, I found, too."

"Tinsley, I didn't give you permission."

"So?" She put the towel down, dropping it to the floor. "I took the responsibility myself. You weren't here."

"But . . . My private files! How did you get to them?"

"Hey. I didn't read anything that wouldn't be available for anyone snooping the system. And I don't mean your personal stuff," she added, holding up her hand to keep him from interrupting. "I left your journal and private letters alone. Just took the kind of data any decent hacker could get hold of in an afternoon's work. I mean the files of your insurance claims, public tax records of your holdings and investments and expenditures. Your education fund for the kids..."

"Tinsley, why?" He sat down. "Why are you here? You shouldn't be, you know." He knew he sounded like an idiot, but he couldn't even think straight, much less converse intelligently.

"I know nothing of the sort." She picked up the towel. "Did you look over the notes I made this afternoon?"

"Yes. I couldn't miss them. Them and the fact that my computer was left on with no one in the house."

Now, she looked a little bit sheepish. "Janna came over to see if I could go swimming. I shouldn't have left it on, but I didn't think I'd be gone long."

"Janna?"

"Mmm-hmm. We had so much fun, the time just went by. I won't forget to turn it off next time. Promise." She headed for the bathroom. "I'm going to shower and change. What do you want for dinner. It's my turn to cook."

"I... I'll have to think about it."

"Okay. I won't be long."

Alex sat in his chair, feeling paralyzed. He listened to the rushing sound of the shower. Heard Tinsley singing, off key. Looked at the legal pad.

He picked the pad up. Then his mind caught up with what his eyes were seeing. She had found out. Had detailed the pattern he had been so reluctant to face. He swore and tossed the pad across the room.

The sound of the shower and the singing stopped.

Alex went over and yanked open the bathroom door. Steam rolled out. Tinsley, wearing nothing now, just glanced at him. She started drying off with another towel.

"You can't stay here," he said. "It's too dangerous."

"Hell I can't," she replied, calmly, cheerfully. "We have a business contract. I have a job to do. You offered it to me, remember?" She leaned over and cleared a spot on the medicine cabinet mirror with her hand.

"That was before I started seeing a pattern in things that—"

"That someone's out to get you?" She inspected her nose, which was rosy with sunburn. "I don't know why it took you so long to figure that. You must be a very trusting, unsuspicious soul at heart. Unlike myself."

"I . . ." His brain functions began to shift. From outraged employer to aroused lover. She had to know what she was doing to him, standing there, clean and naked and . . .

"I think I understand," she said, wrapping the towel around her body. "You're in heavy-duty denial because the other incidents with the boats looked like your own carelessness." Her eyes met his gaze directly, and her look was kind. "Alex, I've seen you in your boat. You're careful to the extreme. I don't think you goofed up."

"I—"

"Look," she said, moving so close he could see the tiny freckles across her cheekbones and shoulders. The sheen of moisture on her soft skin. "I have a thousand questions, things I want to know. Including, how Jack is. But first, I want to make love with you. Because I'm not going to be able to think straight, until I get that out of my system.''

Alex touched her face. "I feel the same, but I'd have put it better. That's not a very romantic overture."

"I didn't mean it to be. I'm simply telling you the truth."

"Now, it's my turn for truth. If we make love again, I don't know if I can stand to let you go. And you have to. You're right. I am in some sort of trouble. I talked to the sheriff, explained about everything that's happened to me in the last six months, and she agrees . . ."

"*She* agrees?"

"Tottie is . . ."

"Tottie is standing right here in your living room, Berringer," a female voice called out. "Been knocking on your door for the last five minutes. You and the lady want to come out, or would it be better if I helped myself to something to drink and waited 'til you all're done with whatever it is you're doing."

Tinsley watched as Alex turned bright red. "*That's* the sheriff?" she asked. He nodded, clearly embarrassed right down to his toenails. Still wrapped in her towel, Tinsley followed him out into the front room.

"Hello, Tottie," Alex said. "Make yourself at home, why don't you?" His discomfort at the intrusion was plain and so intense, he actually forgot his manners for once. He went over to the window and stared out at the water without formally introducing the newcomer.

A woman wearing a brown uniform sat in one of the easy chairs. Tinsley extended her right hand and held the towel with the left. "Hello, Sheriff," she said, shaking the woman's hand firmly. "I'm Tinsley Cole."

"Tottie Reynolds." The sheriff stood up, topping Tinsley by several inches. "Glad to meet you. Heard enough about you to feel we've met already, though." She didn't grin, but the corners of her eyes crinkled with humor. "You all, uh, want to get dressed before we sit to talk, Miss Cole?"

"Call me Tinsley, for goodness sake. It'll take just a second." She glanced at the sheriff. "You didn't interrupt anything. Close, though." She smiled, woman to woman.

Now, Sheriff Reynolds did grin. Alex's back seemed to stiffen in further embarrassment.

After she had dressed, Tinsley gave Tottie Reynolds her statement about the two incidents involving the horse. She was careful to explain how her ranch background and her work in rodeo security had helped her to understand what had happened to Jack. Tottie seemed satisfied with her report. "But," Tinsley added, "I don't think that's the only time someone's been out to cause Alex harm."

Alex had moved from his post by the window, but he sat quietly, not saying a word. He seemed to have drawn into himself.

"What do you mean?" The sheriff looked interested. "Or rather, I should ask, how do you know?"

Tinsley pointed at the computer. "It's all there in green and white for anyone who cares to look. In Alex's insurance records. The problem with the gas line in his little boat. The broken thing . . . ah, the rudder, I think, on the one he uses for fishing. One of the sail parts tearing at a critical time. Other stuff I really didn't understand. I don't know anything about boats." She studied the woman, seeing knowledge in her calm, brown eyes. "But you know about all this, don't you."

"Alex mentioned he'd had one or two accidents lately."

"And I have a suspect for you." Tinsley got up and went over to get the legal pad.

"Tinsley!" Alex spoke in a warning tone. "Don't!"

"Why not?" She turned and faced him. "Your cousin was here this morning. He had plenty of opportunity to slip Jack something. He has a boat, so he knows how to sabotage..."

"He had opportunity and knowledge, but what he doesn't have is guts, Tinsley." Alex stood now. He went over to the kitchen area and took a soft drink out of the refrigerator. "Clay might gossip and conspire in drawing rooms, but he would never, never have the courage or grit to do something that involved any risk to himself. Believe me. I grew up with him, and I know."

"Man can acquire lots of grit when the stakes are high enough," Tottie Reynolds commented. "Say, you got one of those cold drinks for me?"

"Sure. Sorry, I forgot my manners. Want a beer?"

"Pop'll do me fine." Tottie took the can of pop and snapped the top. She took a long sip. "Tinsley," she said, setting the can down. "You have any experience in law enforcement?"

"Not exactly."

"How exactly?"

"Well, I am a lawyer."

Tottie just looked at her.

"All right. So I don't know that much about investigation. But I do know how to research and draw logical conclusions. I have no proof Clayton is the one, but he sure has motive. Alex, are you aware if you die right now, Clayton gets everything?"

"It's the way my family has handled the bulk of the Berringer estate for many generations. I can allocate certain parts of my wealth for distribution as I choose. As I already have. But not the major portion. That goes directly to my nearest, eldest male relative, if I'm not married. To my wife as trustee for my oldest male child, if I am.''

"Medieval," Tinsley said. "Male primogeniture.''

"Nevertheless, that's the way it is. I'd change it, but it would take almost an act of congress. Up to now, I've seen no reason." He had a closed expression on his face, and when he sat down, Tinsley thought she could actually see the wheels turning in his head.

"So, you figure since Clayton would inherit Alex's money, he's the one doing this stuff?" Tottie asked.

"You have a better idea?''

"No. Maybe a notion or two, but no ideas. Some suspicion, just like you." Tottie Reynolds finished her drink and stood up. "But without proof, all the suspicion in the world don't mean a thing." She turned to Alex. "I suppose you still won't let me assign anybody to keep an eye on you?''

"No, indeed.''

She looked at Tinsley. "You seem like a woman who can take care of herself, so I won't bother warning you," she said. "But you be alert, you hear? This man, he's walking along the edge of a high cliff, these days. Some powerful folks don't like him, much.''

"What? What?'' Tinsley knew she was missing something important. "What do you mean?''

Tottie nodded her head at Alex. "Ask him. If you're staying here, you need to know. Good to meet you." She shook Tinsley's hand, said goodbye, and left. Tinsley was sure she had just had a first meeting with a potential good friend.

Alex got up and stood by the window, looking out at the water. "You aren't staying, Tinsley," he said. "I don't want you to.''

"Is that personal, or because of what's going on?''

"It doesn't matter. Get your things packed. I'll take you back to your aunt's home."

"Do you own this whole island?"

He turned around. "Most of it. Not all. Some of the people here have title to their own property. Others rent from me. I encourage them to buy the land, when they can. Why?"

"Because if you kick me out of your house, I'll just find someone else to stay with. I made some friends among the women today when I went swimming with Janna. It was Moms' Day at the swimming hole. Dixie, Starr, Lila. A bunch of neat ladies. We got along just fine. I bet one of them could put me on to a family willing to rent out a bedroom, if they couldn't make room for me themselves."

"I don't want you hurt."

"Me, neither. But what else is new? Alex, look. I'm no heroine, myself. I don't find a bit of fun in real danger. Not when it's serious. But I've committed to you, and I won't walk out just because the going gets a little rough."

He didn't look directly at her. "It is possible, you know, that the problems I had with my boats were things I did myself. Perhaps I have a kind of death wish, an unconscious desire to imitate my father."

"Horse manure!"

"Okay. But I just won't accept that Clayton's been the one doing these things. You don't know him like I do. All you see is the unpleasant surface personality he's managed to glue on. His mask, if you will."

"Deep down, he's a confused, lost boy?"

"In a way, that's true." Now, he did look at her.

And what she saw in his expression almost made her weep. She saw compassion. Real, deep compassion. He'd been ready to knock Clayton into next week for insulting her, but he still cared for his cousin. Then, the truth hit her.

Alex Berringer was a good man. So decent of heart he really couldn't see the evil in others. He needed her to help him see the clear intent of his enemies. She wasn't budging, no matter what he said or did to get her out of his life! If she had to, she would lie, steal, cheat and do whatever else it took to keep him safe.

So, time to lie. "I won't leave because I've fallen in love with you," she said, amazed that the lie felt like the truth. "I can't leave you, Alex."

Now, he smiled. But it was a sad expression. "Horse manure," he said, softly. "Don't lie to me, Tinsley. I can tell with you."

She felt her face get hot. "What do I have to do? Tear off my clothes again? I went to bed with you, didn't I?"

"Tinsley, you don't love me." He came to her and touched her face again, in that gentle, tender way he had. "You may be getting fond of me, surely. I'll give myself that. But love? No."

"Well…" She sputtered, looking for words. "Well, you can't know how I really feel, can you?"

He looked less sure. "No, I can't. That's true."

"When did you eat?"

"Huh?"

"When did you eat? Did you get any lunch? Or were you so wrapped up in what was going on with Jack and me and yourself that you forgot to eat?" Not waiting for an answer, she moved past him to the kitchen. "Sit down before you fall down," she said. "I'll fix dinner."

Alex sat. He looked at the computer screen. "How did you manage to find out all this stuff?" he asked, tapping the screen. "I thought you didn't know much about programming."

"I don't." She put a pot of water on the stove. "I just figured it out."

"How?"

"Because I made myself think how you would think." Potatoes plopped into the water. "Not so hard, really."

Alex considered that.

"What other suspects does Tottie have?" Tinsley rummaged in the freezer until she found a pound of hamburger. "What powerful people don't like you?" She put the meat in the microwave and set it to defrost.

Alex didn't answer right away. His fingers clicked at the keyboard. "They want me to sell the island," he said, finally. "Sell it out from under the people who live here, whose families have lived here for over a hundred years."

"They? Who they?"

"Developers. People with financial interests in the region. There's a resort on the island five miles south of here, and they want to use this one for a golf course. They're shortsighted enough to think that a golf course has more lasting economic and social value than honest laborers who make their livelihood just as their fathers, grandfathers and great-grandfathers did."

Tinsley found an onion and started chopping. "Well, maybe a golf course does seem more progressive to most people than subsistence fishing."

"The fishermen here are well beyond subsistence level." He sounded angry. "They are gradually working into modern systems of harvesting the fish."

"With your help?"

No reply.

"Alex, it doesn't take a genius to figure out that family tradition or not, you've been pouring tons of money into the local population's pockets. I see your work as good. Others might not. They might see it as wasting their future, or, at best throwing it away.''

''You mean, Clay? Sure, he's upset about it. So's my mother. But I doubt she's trying to harm me. Physically.''

She heard the emphasis on the last word and knew something more about him. His mood yesterday morning must have been caused by his visit with his mother. She was harming him all right! But psychologically, not physically.

Interesting.

They said nothing more to one another for a while. Alex continued to work at his computer, and Tinsley cooked. She cleared the table of the coffee cups from the morning and thought of Alex's friend, Joseph Meadows. There was another potential source of information about him. Would Meadows look kindly on her investigation, or would he be like Alex, convinced she should keep out of what didn't concern her?

She thought about that. Tottie Reynolds had only told her to take care. Not warned her off. Maybe that was a male thing around here—warning women off where there was potential danger. Maybe Tottie, as a woman who must have overcome great odds to rise to her position in her profession, understood. Warning off only meant there was something of value at stake.

In this case, Alex.

She rummaged around in the cabinets until she found a clean tablecloth and set it on the table. Napkins, plates, bowls, silverware. Food. ''Dinner's ready,'' she announced.

Alex looked up. ''Smells wonderful.'' He made a few more clicks and shut down the computer. ''What're we having?''

"Oh, it really doesn't have a name." Tinsley set out some rolls and butter. "It's what you make when you don't have the ingredients for regular food. Kind of a trail stew, actually."

"Trail stew?" He came over and sat down, eyeing the steaming mixture she ladled into his soup bowl.

"Yep. Meat, potatoes, onion, tomatoes, salt, pepper, and stuff."

"Stuff?" He took a spoonful. "Well, whatever it's called, it's good."

"Thanks."

More companionable, comfortable silence as they ate. She watched him devour several bowls and almost all of the rolls. He must have been half-starved. But he had allowed her time to fix a real dinner and had worked while he waited. Finally, she couldn't stand it any longer.

"What were you so busy doing just now?" she asked. "On the computer, I mean."

He didn't look up. "I was making it secure. Tinsley, are you absolutely determined to stay out here with me?"

The question caught her off guard. "I packed for overnight," she admitted. "That's all. But, I—"

"It's all right." He fixed his gaze on some distant point. "I won't fight you about it."

"Why not?"

"Let's just say, when I really consider it, I see no point." Now, he did look directly at her, and the intensity of his gaze was unsettling. "Anyone with half a brain can already see you're very important to me. An enemy, if I do have one, will know striking at you will be worse for me than if I'm hurt myself. So, even if I do send you off, you're in danger. Better you're with me. I can . . ."

"Protect me?" She said it gently. But she was worried by the idea. "Alex, if you start looking over your shoulder at me all the time, you're liable to just fall into a hole and break your neck. Or something.''

He laughed. ''My, you do hold a high opinion of me, don't you.''

''Yes, damn it! I do! But that's not the point. You're kind of... Well, absentminded, I suppose. And gentle. That sums it up.'' She took a deep breath. ''You concentrate on a thing that interests you, and everything else goes by the wayside.''

''So, you think I need a bodyguard?''

''I don't know about that. But, you do need...someone around.''

''To do what?''

''To... to keep you on track. Keep you from drowning in your own clutter. To help you get perspective, I suppose. Focus you. To—''

''To do what I hired you to do?''

''Exactly.''

He got up and took his dirty plates and silverware to the sink. ''Jack's going to be all right. Bob wants to observe him for a few days.''

''Good.''

He ran hot water over the dishes. ''Joseph wants to call on your aunt. He was very taken with her this morning. I suspect she'll be hearing from him, shortly. He's not a man who wastes time when he makes up his mind about something.''

''G-good.''

''I, however, am. I take a lot of time, Tinsley. I move at a slower pace than many people. I think. I work things out before I act.''

''Well, there's nothing wrong with that. I—''

"You think and act all at once." He turned around and looked at her. "I admire that, but I don't do it. Be patient with me, Tinsley. That's all I ask."

She looked at him, and her heart melted. "I will," she said, meaning it with every fiber of her being. "I'll be patient, Alex."

That promise lasted about five minutes.

He insisted on cleaning up, since she had cooked. So, curious as usual, Tinsley went over to his computer. It took only seconds to find she was blocked out. "What did you do?" she yelled. "This thing won't even let me see the time of day!"

"I'll get you your own terminal tomorrow," he said, calmly. "And I'll set up access to those portions of my data I want you to see."

Tinsley seethed.

"Odd though the concept must be to you," he said, busily scrubbing the iron skillet, "I do have a right to privacy. And to imagine your fertile imagination running rampant all over my material frankly gives me horrors."

She glared at the dead screen. He was right. But how was she going to curb her curiosity? And did she really want to?

CHAPTER TWELVE

THEY WENT TO BED together that night, but they didn't make love right away. The air was still and sultry, even when Alex opened all the windows to let in the ocean breeze. Unsure of what to expect from him or even what she wanted herself, Tinsley slipped into an old cotton nightshirt. *Sexy as all get-out,* she thought as she got into his bed.

Alex seemed to agree. He kept on his jockeys and lay on the far side of the bed, the sheet pulled up to his waist and his hands tucked under his head as he stared at the ceiling. Overhead, a big fan lazily stirred the humid air. The moon was full, and silver light flowed in through the windows, making a chiaroscuro scene out of the room. A study in black, gray and platinum.

"So," she said, feeling tense from lying so close to him, yet not touching. "What do you really think about all this?"

"Um. All what?"

"Why, your situation, of course. The apparent enemy who's out to do you harm."

Alex chuckled. "My God, Tinsley. Do you really intend to have a discussion right now?" He turned on his side toward her. "Here we are, alone in bed again. The whole night ahead of us. And you want to talk?"

"Well. We weren't doing anything else, as far as I could tell."

"Appearances are often deceiving."

"Alex! Are you teasing me?" She rolled over and glared at him across the empty inches of white sheet.

"Some." He smiled, and the corners of his eyes crinkled. "Actually, I was thinking about you just now."

"Why think? I'm right here."

"Of course. But I wanted to think for a while. Remember, I told you I tended to do that before I acted."

"Not last night, you didn't."

"True." He reached over and touched her cheek. "I was overcome with desire."

"And tonight?"

"I am overcome with desire."

Tinsley felt a shiver start deep inside at his words and the look on his face. He hadn't kissed her, hadn't made a grab for any of the standard erogenous areas, but just one sentence from him had aroused her more than she could ever remember.

"But, I'm still thinking," he added.

"What about, for crying out loud?"

"Why you're still here, for one thing. How did you get into my files, for another."

Tinsley swore and rolled onto her back. "I told you. I figured out how you thought and went from there. It wasn't so hard. I can't exactly explain it. I know enough about computers to run one if it's already set up for me, but not enough to work one from scratch according to the system. So, I make up my own way. It usually isn't so easy. You were a cinch to crack. Why in the world does it bother you? You said you'd fixed it so I couldn't again."

"Doesn't mean you won't try." His hands slipped behind her head, his fingers twining in her hair. "I wonder why?" he asked. Then, he moved over to her and kissed her. Deeply.

After that, Tinsley was sure neither of them did any more critical thinking. His hand moved down her body and slipped under the hem of her nightshirt. But he didn't rush things. He kissed her mouth fervently and caressed her body gently.

Then, she began to touch him. His skin was hot and silky, his muscles like solid oak beneath her fingertips. When she dug in, however, his flesh was supple and sensitive. She made him groan with pleasure, until his eagerness began to outpace hers. Soon, the few garments they had worn were stripped off and they were both engulfed by their need for each other. They made love with intensity and passion that left them weak, yet completely satisfied.

The next morning Tinsley woke up alone in bed. Sunlight poured like hot gold through the open windows. The room was like an oven. She smelled the coffee. Heard music from a radio.

But no sense of Alex's presence.

She got up, smiling and remembering. Whatever else was going on, the sex was great. Pulling on her nightshirt, she went into the main room, searching for the coffee.

The pot was on and full. She poured a cup. The front door was open, with just the screen shut to keep out any wandering insects or small birds. The breeze was slight and doing little to cool anything off. Tinsley set the cup down on the counter and went around the entire house, shutting windows, just as she had seen her aunt do during the hot mornings when she was a child. Open everything at night, shut it all during the day, was the rule when no air-conditioning was available.

That task done, she rummaged in the refrigerator and found an orange. Peeling it, she set the segments on a plate, took her coffee cup and went outside to enjoy her breakfast on the front porch.

The channel was smooth, only slight ripples of waves lapping at the beach. Boats of various sizes and styles cruised the water, but none came near the island. At first, she thought she was alone and wondered why Alex had left her alone. Last night he'd been so concerned for her safety. Then, she saw the fishermen down the beach.

And up the beach.

She wasn't alone at all. She was so well guarded she might as well be in prison! One of the men glanced over, saw she was watching and waved. Tinsley waved back, then settled down. Maybe it was annoying to be guarded, but it showed something good about the man who had ordered it done, didn't it?

"Morning. Miss Tinsley?"

Tinsley looked over to the side of the house. A woman carrying a straw basket full of cleaning supplies made her way down the sandy bank to the side steps leading up to the porch. "Yes, I'm Tinsley," Tinsley said, standing up. "Can I help you?"

The woman laughed, a full, rich sound. "I doubts it, honey. I'm Clara Sinclair. Here to clean up Alex's place."

"Oh, yes. Hi!" Tinsley wiped her orange-sticky hand on her shirt and held it out. The other's grasp was firm and friendly. "I think I met your daughter over at the kiddie swimming place. Come on inside. You are a welcome sight!"

Clara grinned as she went through the front door. "My girl told me how you're trying to learn to swim, just like a baby, she says."

"I'm making progress." Tinsley wasn't too thrilled with the comparison, but had to admit it was accurate.

"Never too late," Clara said, setting her basket down. "Shoot! That man makes a mess, don't he?"

"He does, indeed." She thought of the bedroom and the telltale sheets. Oh well, what did anybody think she was doing here at night, anyway? Still, she would try to change the sheets before Clara got to the bedroom. However, she hadn't seen a washer or dryer about the place, yet.

"I do the wash, too," Clara announced, as if reading her mind. "So, you got stuff, you just throw it on the pile. I'll get it back by tomorrow morning."

"Okay. Thanks." Tinsley accepted defeat. If she argued, she would upset the arrangement that obviously meant a great deal to Clara. She remembered the daughter's fierce defense of her mother's territory.

Clara started in the kitchen area. "You go on and shower or whatever," she said. "I'll tidy up here first."

Tinsley hesitated, feeling she ought to at least offer to help. Clara stopped clanking pans and dishes and regarded her. "My man drowned at sea just about the time my last baby, Emma, came," she said, no laughter in her dark eyes now. "She's the child you met. Mr. Alex, he saw to it my oldest boy, Nash, got in the University and stayed there. He's a businessman now. Lives out in California. Sends me lots of money, so I don't need to do this, honey."

"I didn't . . ."

"It don't matter. I'm gonna clean up for Alex until the day I drop dead. Cause I purely want to." Now, she did smile. "And you can go right on courting the man, cause he needs a wife, anyhow. He acts all strong and such, like he likes being alone all the time, but he's lonely, count on it. You understand?"

Tinsley blushed to her toes. With Clara's soft laughter ringing in her ears, she fled to the bathroom and a much-needed shower.

"YOU IDIOT!" The hand slammed down on the desktop with such force, the newspaper article lifted and moved several inches. "Why did you try such a stupid trick, poisoning the damn horse? Berringer wasn't even scratched. Just the girl, and she sustained no serious injuries."

"But, I didn't—"

"Don't bother lying. It had your nasty touch. And it's ruined any possibility of using the animal to get the real job done. No telling how long he'll leave the beast on the mainland, and I need action now. Find some other way to go after him."

"But..."

"Now! And if you take that bitch of a woman with him, I'll give you a bonus." Slam!

"TELEPHONE'S FOR YOU," Silvie told Delores, a smile in her voice. "I think you might want to take it out in the library where you can have some privacy."

Delores looked up from her needlework. She was sitting in her chair in the living room, brooding and stitching. "Is it Tinsley?"

"No." Silvie's grin widened. "It's a man."

Delores set down her embroidery. Touched a hand to her hair. "Really?" she asked.

Silvie nodded, pleased to see the look of excitement and anticipation replace the sorrow on her old friend and employer's face.

WHILE CLARA did her thing around the house, Tinsley, cleaned and dressed in jeans and a fresh shirt, hunched in front of Alex's computer, working. Several hours passed as she worked. Clara moved quietly, but every once in a while, she would walk by and make *tisk-tisking* noises. Finally, she got Tinsley's attention.

"What?" she asked, pushing her hair back with both hands and regarding the woman. "Why the disapproving clicks, Clara?"

"You ought not to be working so hard, Miss Tinsley. Ain't good for you. Get yourself out in the sun, girl. Go swimming again." She pointed at the kitchen. "Have some lunch."

Tinsley realized she was hungry. "I'll eat," she conceded. "But, then, it's back to the computer. I've got a job to do."

"You really working for Alex?"

The question made Tinsley stop dead. "Yes, I am. What did you think?"

Clara didn't meet her gaze. "We all...uh. That is, I thought you was his woman."

"I suppose I am. But I'm also his employee. Anything wrong with that?"

"No. Ain't nothing wrong with it." Clara looked sad. "But we all... We wondered if he was thinking of getting married at last." She raised an eyebrow. "He said anything to you about it?"

Tinsley sighed. It wasn't likely she would escape the scrutiny and gossip of such a small place, and she wondered why it hadn't occurred to her before that this would happen. "No," she answered. "Neither of us has mentioned it. And it isn't anything I'd consider right now, so tell everybody to quit speculating, will you?"

Clara looked disappointed. "Man needs a wife," she said again, turning back to her work. She *tisk-tisked* again, then was silent.

Oddly, Tinsley felt guilty when she took her sandwich from the kitchen and went back to sit in front of the computer while she ate. Marriage to Alex was out of the question, she knew. She was never going to be able to give him the children he yearned for. She was able, however, to put her brain to work for him. That was enough for now.

But, by the time Clara announced she was done and ready to take off with the laundry, Tinsley had made little headway. She pushed away from the desk and got up to help Clara carry out her load.

"Thanks for everything," she said to the woman.

"You're welcome." Clara smiled. She stepped off the porch and took her basket from Tinsley. The load of laundry was bundled into a sheet and balanced on her head. "I'll be back in the morning," she said. Then, she started to chuckle. "I guess you won't be working anymore today." She pointed out to the channel. "Here he comes, now."

Tinsley turned. Around the end of the island came Alex's motorboat. He sat at the tiller, and the bow and center of the vessel were crammed with boxes. Big boxes. He waved, and she could see his smile.

And her heart beat faster.

"THIS ISN'T EXACTLY state of the art," Alex said as he made the last connection, turning her new computer into a working operation on her new desk. It transformed the room. With Clara's work of the day still evident, and the stacks of stuff from the card table set into a corner, the place looked almost neat. "But it links easily with mine, and I think it'll give you no problems," he added.

"That's good news." Tinsley ran her hand over the top of the screen and sat down. New chair, too. It felt comfortable. "Now, what do I do?"

He showed her. Data eventually emerged onto the screen. "What's this?" she asked.

"My most important project. The kids."

She looked up at him, puzzled.

"I've set aside money for several years, as you know, for educational opportunities for island children and adults who are interested. But I've managed it piecemeal, on an individual basis, as it's come along. There's no continuity, no program." He moved back, putting his hands into his pockets. "If something happens to me, it'll all be lost. What I want from you is security."

"Alex, I don't understand?"

"Yes, you do. Better than I do. You see, Tinsley, I've never actually practiced law, and you have. You have a more analytical mind, as well. I want you to build me a trust fund so watertight no one can touch it, even if I'm not around. I want legal barriers against pirates. Against my family. Against any future owners of this island. Then, I want parameters governing who gets the money for education, who gets it for improving their businesses, who gets it in a personal emergency. I want—"

"I understand." She slapped the tabletop. "You want me to write your last will and testament! Well, you can just forget that!"

"Why?" He pulled over his chair and sat down, his elbows resting on his knees, his green eyes watching her intently.

"You hired me as a research assistant, near as I can tell. I won't play into your morbid scenario, Alex. No matter what."

"Scenario?" He clasped his hands together. "Morbid? I don't think so. Tinsley, none of us knows how long we have on this earth. You, yourself, had a close brush with death. You should be sympathetic."

"I . . ." Her eyes filled with tears. "I did. But that was different. It was an accident. No one was out to get me."

"And, in spite of all the talk that's gone on around here, we have no concrete evidence anyone's out to get me." He held up a hand, cutting off her protest. "No, we don't. If we did, believe me, Tottie would have been far more involved. She isn't one of these law people who sit around until after the crime has occurred. You should have sensed that just from meeting her. Tinsley, we don't know for sure. Not about Jack. Nor about the boats."

She couldn't answer. He was right.

And, he was wrong. She knew it with every fiber of her being.

"Tinsley, if I die, this island will be sold by Clayton to that cartel of developers I was telling you about. They aren't men who will care about Janna or Clara, or any of the other people who live here. Sanford Taylor's one of them. Remember him? Do you think he'd care if little Janna had no choices in her life?"

Tinsley settled back in her chair. "No."

"Then help me with this," Alex pleaded. "Be more than my research assistant. More than my lover." He spread out his hands. "Be my friend, Tinsley."

That did it. She couldn't refuse him. Tears filled her eyes and spilled down her face. "I'll need access to a law library," she said.

Alex smiled, the expression lighting up his whole being. "Done!" he said, joyfully. "Done."

"So, ELLEN," Delores told her sister over the telephone, two weeks later, "she's moved out there. Has applied and is studying to pass the South Carolina bar exam with the apparent intent of becoming his private lawyer, and no one in town can talk about anything else! It's disgraceful. I tell you, she's lost her mind. I am simply heartbroken!"

Ellen Cole considered. "You're certain they're... You know, living together?" Although the euphemism bothered her, she knew it would sit better with her sister's Southern sensibilities. And, years ago, with her own. "She's not just staying out there so she doesn't have to ride in a boat everyday?"

"Absolutely. They are... lovers. Making no secret of their affections. And my own household is ranged against me on this. I can't believe it, but Silvie and Jason are delighted. They keep talking about her *marrying* the boy! Evidently, so is everyone on the island. And some people here in town, as well. That's the only thing that keeps it from being a total scandal."

Tinsley's mother felt a jolt of true alarm for the first time. A romantic fling was one thing, but marriage was quite another! Tinsley was just too fragile, emotionally, after the horrible time she had over Brad. "I remember his father, Frank Berringer," she said. "He wasn't such a bad guy. But Susan is just plain witchy! Even as a little girl, as I recall. With a mother-in-law potential like that, I don't want my daughter anywhere near an altar! She's not thinking clearly. What should I do?"

"I don't know, Ellie. Maybe, if you came out, you could talk some sense into her."

"I might just have to do that," Ellen Cole said. "But first, I want to talk to Tinsley. This isn't a good time for me to leave the ranch, you know. If she'll listen to reason over the phone, I could save myself a trip.''

"It won't do any good,'' Delores warned. "You know how she is when she gets hold of something. Like a terrier!''

"You mean, stubborn as a mule!''

"As I said. Do you know what else she told me? She's even been writing poetry about the man! Ellen, I swear to you, this is serious!''

"LET'S GO. Swimming time.'' Alex threw a beach towel at Tinsley. "What're you so busy with over there?''

"Nothing.'' Tinsley quickly hid the poem in her files by striking two keys. It starred Alex and was reaching epic proportions. She'd die of embarrassment if he saw it. "Just messing around.'' She picked up the towel. Her suit was already on. "I'm ready,'' she announced.

Alex regarded her with cheerful suspicion. "You're lying to me, woman. You never just mess around. Not on the laziest day of your life!''

"You don't know that. I've only been around you a few weeks.''

"*Three* weeks, two days.'' He tossed her the suntan lotion. "Let's go.''

Rubbing the cream onto her face and shoulders, Tinsley followed him down the beach. She had come a long, long way in three weeks, two days, she reflected. She had a job, a cause she believed in, a lover and a best friend in Alex. And she had made great strides in conquering her fear of water.

But, something was not quite right and she had no idea what it was.

No more unpleasant or frightening incidents had happened. Jack was still on the mainland, but happily engaged in some profitable stud work for his owner.

Tinsley's thoughts turned to her own problem. She knew now that any woman who planned on spending her life with Alex Berringer was going to have to give him kids. He never said a word about it, but she knew. She knew by watching, listening and analyzing. This was a man to whom children meant the world. No woman who really loved him could deny him that.

But, for the present it didn't matter to them. They were just lovers, buddies and business associates. So that couldn't be what was bothering her.

Maybe it was his mother. Tinsley had met Susan Berringer a few days ago and taken an instant dislike to the woman. Which, she was sure, was cordially returned. Unlike Alex, his mother seemed cold, remote, critical—completely without the capacity to love. She couldn't fathom how such a man came from that woman.

It was a mystery, and mysteries *always* bothered her. So, maybe...

"Hey." Alex's arm went around her shoulders. He had dropped back to keep pace with her. "A penny for those gloomy thoughts."

"They aren't worth that kind of money." She smiled at him. "Now, if you started offering ten thousand dollars, you might have a sale."

"No. I have better things to spend my dough on." He turned serious. "Are you worried about today?"

She considered. "No, actually, I'm not. Janna and I are ready to hit the deep ocean together for the first time. Working with a four-year-old makes me brave." She laughed. "I couldn't stand to chicken out while she went right into the waves."

"Good." He hugged her to his side. "That's what I figured."

You know me too well, she thought, not unhappily.

Janna was waiting down the beach by the small cove Alex had chosen because the wave action was less than it was in the open areas. With the child were her mother and older brother, as well as a small group of well-wishers and little friends. Apparently the first deep water outing in the real ocean was a big deal. Even for an island child like Janna who had played on the beach and paddled around in the shallows much of her young life. Tinsley found herself wishing someone from her own family could be there. But that was foolishness, she realized. Alex represented her family now.

Wasn't that a kick!

Janna ran up and reached for a hug, which Tinsley willingly gave. The girl's tiny body felt warm and wiry in her arms. What would it be like, she wondered, to have such a hug from her own daughter? Then, she commanded herself to stop thinking that way.

Alex watched as Tinsley worked the crowd. She wasn't doing it consciously, but there was no better word for it. She greeted everyone, from the grandmother down to the nursing infant still in Janna's mother's arms, and she made each and every one of them love her.

Just as she had made him love her. It was her gift, given freely without any strings or chains attached. He no longer doubted his feelings, just where they might lead. "Okay, people," he said, finally, clapping his hands for attention. "Let's see if these two ladies are ready to graduate from the tidal pools to the real thing. Janna, Tinsley. Are you ready?"

Both nodded. Tinsley, resplendent as usual in her silver swimsuit, looked pale and tense. Janna was as eager as a puppy.

"You both know the drill. It's simple," Alex went on, walking out into the gentle surf. "Get out far enough so you can't touch, then swim." He regarded his two charges. "Because of the difference in your heights, I'll stay in between you both. If you get tired, just holler." *And if you panic, I'll be there before you can go under, Tinsley.*

Tinsley swallowed hard, smiled at Janna and entered the ocean. By her side, the child struggled to walk until she couldn't touch the bottom any more. Tinsley hesitated, wanting to help, but Janna struck out with a vigorous, enthusiastic dog paddle and was soon making her way with no problem. "Go on, Tinsley," she cried out, her grin wide. "Get with it!"

"Right." Tinsley walked farther. The pull of the waves against her body was disturbing. She was thankful they were in a sheltered area where the undertow was slight. She couldn't imagine fighting a real strong current. She walked farther.

Alex stood off to one side, watching. Janna was having no problems and was squealing with delight at the freedom she felt in the deeper water. She caught him looking and did a little dive, coming right back up to the surface and blowing water out of her mouth. She resembled a little otter.

Tinsley, on the other hand, resembled a reluctant Venus. She finally reached her depth and struck out, her hair, temporarily tamed into a ponytail, streaming wetly behind her. Alex held his breath.

She did fine!

So well, in fact, that he began to worry. She had mastered the basics of the flutter kick and dog paddle in the deeper pools, but now she was trying a sort of breaststroke, something he hadn't taught her. And, she was heading out to sea instead of parallel to the shore. "What are you doing?" he called, fear growing. "Tinsley, get back here!"

"I don't think I can," she cried. "How do you put this in reverse?"

Alex swore, trying not to let his fear for her show. He signaled one of the older boys to swim out and stay with Janna. He started after Tinsley. He reached her just in time to save her from drowning...

... in laughter.

"Had you going there, didn't I?" she asked, rolling onto her back and sculling her hands to stay afloat. As he had taught her. "Reverse!" She almost went under, snickering.

"If I weren't worried about your sanity, I'd show you reverse," Alex snarled. "Now, get your fanny back to shore."

"Don't be such a bad sport," she said, obeying his order. "I admit I'm showing off, but it's because you're such a great teacher." Her breaststroke was uneven, but strong.

"I didn't teach you that," he said, impressed in spite of himself. "Your technique stinks, but you have control. How did you pick that up?"

"I watched the older kids." She shrugged and almost went under. "I've never had much problem with physical things. My brain seems to translate what I see directly to my body, and it knows what to do."

"I can vouch for that."

She splashed him, and did go under for a moment. Laughing, Alex hauled her up, enjoying the touch of her body against his in the water. It was incredibly sensual. "You really aren't afraid anymore," he said, wonderingly.

"Nope." She rubbed water out of her eyes, using his body to support herself by wrapping her legs loosely, sexily around him. "Of course, I'm not exactly ready to swim the English Channel or go deep sea fishing, but I—"

She never finished the sentence. A muffled roar sounded, then a thunderous explosion of noise. Beyond the screen of trees, a fireball erupted into the sky. Debris flew darkly upward. Children screamed. Tinsley let out one yell and went under water. Alex grabbed her in the crook of his arm and stroked for shore, his mind refusing to accept what he had just seen and heard.

CHAPTER THIRTEEN

THE THUNDER of the explosion still ringing in her ears, Tinsley ran with Alex along the beach. After he had dragged her, sputtering and splashing, from the water, he ordered everyone to stay where they were and started sprinting for home. She disobeyed and followed, terrified for him and for what he would find.

They rounded the curve of land and saw, and Alex's cry of anguish was echoed by her own.

The house he loved so much was a smoking, fiery ruin. Alex ran forward; Tinsley followed more slowly, recognizing his right to be alone for the moment.

The house was totaled, only a few sections of wall and some twisted metal pipe still stood upright. Fires burned here and there. Smoke billowed up into the clear, sunny sky. The blast had been so powerful, it had dug a crater in the sandy ground. Alex stood as near as he could, his posture showing both deep sorrow and unmitigated rage. Tinsley looked away.

And saw the bottom of an overturned boat bobbing away from the damaged dock. Next to it, a body floated. "Alex," she yelled. "It's Timothy!"

Alex turned at her cry. Saw her racing down the now rickety dock. Saw her jump into the water and paddle her way awkwardly toward the overturned boat.

And the body.

The shock galvanized Alex—whose muscles had become frozen at the sight of his devastated home—into action, and he followed her. Running down the dock, he plunged into the water just as she latched onto Timothy and tried to drag him to shore. Her efforts were futile. Alex took them both in his arms and kicked until he felt sand beneath his feet. Tinsley touched down at the same time, and between them, they managed to get Timothy onto land. Blood trickled from the boatman's nostrils, but he wasn't breathing.

"Is he dead?" Tinsley cried. "Alex! Do something!"

Alex did. He bent over his friend and breathed life into Timothy's body. Tinsley placed her fingers on Timothy's throat to check for a heartbeat. Finding none, she began pushing on his chest, matching her rhythm to Alex's breathing. They worked together.

She heard sirens, was conscious of people gathering around, of anguished screaming and crying, the heat of the sun on her bare shoulders and back, the stink of the explosion and destruction. But none of that mattered. Her universe was centered on the man she and Alex were trying to bring back to life. She did not know she was also crying, tears running freely down her cheeks.

Alex saw her, loved her more at that moment than he thought possible. But he, too, was centered on Timothy. Then, a miracle. He felt the big man's body shiver, draw a breath, cough and choke. Alex nudged Tinsley aside and turned Timothy onto his side while the boatman struggled to clear his lungs. "Come on, Tim," he whispered harshly. "Don't check out on me now, man!"

Tinsley scrubbed at her own face, scratching her wet skin with her sandy hands. "He's going to live," she whispered, seeing life return to Timothy's grayish skin. Then, she said it louder. "He's going to live."

She heard voices around her, lifting up the words like a prayer. But they were all drowned out by the clatter of a helicopter and the roar of boats with sirens as the official rescuers arrived on the scene.

MUCH LATER, she was delivered to Delores's house in a Carleton Cay County squad car. One of Tottie's officers drove, since the sheriff was down at her headquarters, still interviewing Alex.

She shut her eyes for a moment, thinking of the despair she'd seen on his face. The despair at his own loss, and the fury at seeing his friend hurt. Tinsley still wore the silver swimsuit and now a blanket provided by the sheriff. Her feet were bare and bruised, her hair a wild tangle. Tremors of tension and shock shook her from time to time.

Old Jason met her at the door. "My brother called me from the island," he said, his expression full of emotion. "My Lord, child! Who did that thing?" He helped her inside, thanking the deputy with a nod and a kind word. "Come on. Got to get you in some warm clothes and give you some hot tea."

"I d-d-don't want tea, Jason. I want a stiff bourbon." Tinsley shrugged his hands away. "I'm all right. Really."

"Yes, indeed!" Silvie appeared, anger and sorrow drawn heavily on her face. "You're all right, for sure! That's why you're shaking like a little kitten. Come with me, child. Now!" She put her arm around Tinsley's waist and started leading her up the stairs. "Jason, you go make one of them toddies and don't spare the liquor, you hear."

"I hear." Jason disappeared.

"Where's Delores?" Tinsley asked as Silvie hustled her toward her bedroom. "I expected her to be all over me when I came home."

"She isn't here." Silvie's grim expression turned mellow for a moment. "Went out to lunch with that nice gentleman she met over at Alex's place. They've been seeing each other now and again."

"Joseph Meadows?"

"Mmm-hmm. It's a good thing for her. Now, you! You get undressed, honey." Silvie bustled into the bathroom and turned on the shower. "Take yourself a hot shower. Then come on down and drink that toddy. That'll fix you up just fine."

It did. Tinsley was feeling almost human again as she sat in the living room and sipped the potent mixture. In fact, she was beginning to relax enough to think about calling the sheriff's office and finding out about Alex when Delores ran in through the front door. Joseph Meadows trailed right behind her.

"Silvie! Jason!" Delores cried. "Silvie, have you heard from Tinsley? Is she all right? We heard on the radio that—"

"I'm right here." Tinsley set her cup down and stood up. "And I'm fine. Now," she added.

Delores rushed over and embraced her tightly. Tinsley returned the embrace, but pulled away immediately. "What did you hear on the radio?" she asked. "What're they saying?"

Delores sat down, sinking into her chair as if her legs could no longer hold her. "That there had been a terrible accident on the island. A huge explosion. That a home was destroyed and an unknown number of people were injured." She looked pale.

"We knew it had to be Alex's place," Joseph said, pulling a straight chair away from the wall and taking a seat on it near Delores. He looked as if he wanted to hold and pat her hand, but still wasn't sure enough of her to take the liberty. "The report said it was a big explosion, and his place is the biggest on the island."

Tinsley sat back down and nodded, tears filling her eyes at the memory. "It was his place," she said, looking at the floor. "Everything the man owns and has worked for is gone." She took a drink. "The only person injured, though, was Timothy, the boatman. It was bad. But I think he's going to live."

"Timothy? What was he doing in Alex's house?" Joseph looked concerned. "And why weren't you two there?"

Delores gasped and started to sniffle. "What a thing to say, Joseph!"

Joseph turned ruddy. "I mean, where were you that you weren't caught in the blast? Thank God, you weren't, of course."

"We were out swimming." Tinsley picked at a frayed seam on her jeans. "Just happened that today we were out much earlier than usual. If we'd been going by our regular schedule..."

"Oh!" Delores started crying. "I knew nothing good would ever come of your being with that man!"

"Delores," Tinsley said, warningly. "Don't do this."

"Why not?" Delores looked up, angry now. "I told you, didn't I? He's bad for you. He's no good! He's..." She sobbed, unable to finish her diatribe.

"Now, Delores..." Joseph reached over and patted her shoulder. "You shouldn't say..."

"Why not!" Delores snapped at him. "I know he's your friend, but he's wrong for my niece. I'm sorry someone was hurt, but I can't be sorry for Alex Berringer. Not when he..."

"He what?" Tinsley slammed her cup down and stood up. "What did he do besides give me a job, give me some new self-esteem by helping me learn to swim, and, yes, give me his love and trust?''

"Tinsley, the man is trouble. Nothing else. You were vulnerable, and he took advantage. Can't you see that, now?''

"No one took advantage of me! Alex *helped* me, for crying out loud. As for the explosion, how can you blame him? It's not his fault!'' Tinsley was shouting now. "It isn't! Someone is trying to kill him!''

"I don't believe it!'' Delores stood now, facing off with her niece. "The radio said it was an accident. Maybe a propane tank. Certainly not a deliberate assassination attempt! That's ridiculous!''

"Propane?'' Tinsley sank back down. "Is that what they're saying?''

"Yes, Tinsley.'' Joseph put his hand on Delores's and eased her back into her chair. "They indicated that maybe it was even Alex's carelessness, although they didn't use his name, of course. Just that the owner—''

"Oh, God.'' Tinsley covered her eyes. "All he wants to do is help kids. Help other people who need him. He is a *good* man! Why is this happening to him?'' She started to cry again.

No one else had anything to say.

Joseph left a few minutes later. He and Delores murmured to one another out in the foyer, but Tinsley didn't hear a word. Didn't hear the door close behind the man. Nor see her aunt come back and sit down. She could only think of Alex and what he must be suffering right now. It wasn't right! Wasn't fair. All a person could do was work with what you had and fight for what you wanted....

Fight....

She stood up. "I'm going out,'' she said. "I don't know when I'll be back, but don't worry about me, please.''

Delores sat still. "Tinsley, please don't."

"Don't what? I'm not in any danger. And I need to do something, or I'll go nuts!"

Delores leaned back and covered her eyes with her hand. "You are an adult. I can't stop you. Do what you want."

Tinsley pulled out of the drive onto the street with a move that sent the gravel flying. Clayton Berringer's house was quite far, but she reached it before her brain had time to warn her that this was not a great idea.

Clayton himself answered the door. He looked pale and was obviously shocked to see her. His mouth opened and closed like a fish's, but nothing came out.

"Where were you earlier this afternoon?" Tinsley asked, glaring at him. "Out in your boat? Or paying Alex another special visit?"

"You... you're not hurt?" He had an odd expression on his face. "I mean..."

"I know what you mean." Tinsley folded her arms so that she wouldn't be tempted to hit him. "Missed me again, Clay. Or was the drug you gave Jack actually meant to cause him to attack Alex?"

"I... I didn't..."

"Oh, sure. Where were you this afternoon?"

His eyes hardened. "Get off my porch. Get off my property. You're trespassing."

"Make me." She planted her feet, daring him. Knowing if he did get violent, she was quite capable of taking care of him. Her rage was enough to give her the edge, and she hadn't spent her youth on the ranch in the company of scrappy cowboys without learning a few fighting techniques. Far in the back of her mind, a voice warned her that she was acting badly, but she just didn't care. She was ready for a fight.

Clayton looked as if he were considering giving her one, but just then a car horn honked. His belligerent stance faded. Tinsley turned around.

Sheriff Reynolds had pulled into the driveway. Beside her was a gorgeous red-haired woman, wearing a business suit and a stern expression. In the back, in the squad car cage, was Alex. He stared out of the closed window at her, his face drawn and haggard.

Forgetting her quarrel with Clayton, Tinsley ran over to the car and beat her fist on the window. "What are you doing here?" she cried. "Alex, what's going on?" He just shook his head and looked away.

Tottie Reynolds got out. "Question ought to be, Tinsley Cole, what are *you* doing here? Thought we sent you home, girl." She looked angry.

Tinsley pointed at Alex. "What's he doing in the back seat? Is he under arrest?"

"Of course, he is," Clayton drawled, coming off the porch to stand by the squad car. His fingers caressed the door on the passenger side where the redhead sat. "Haven't you a grain of sense, Miss Cole? He bombed his own place. Blew it all to kingdom come, and almost took poor Timothy with it. Attempted manslaughter, I believe."

Tinsley simmered for about two seconds, then launched. Only Alex's arm around her waist kept her from committing assault and battery on Clayton Berringer right then and there. How Alex had gotten out of the car in time to grab her, she didn't know, but when she realized it was he who held her, she turned around and embraced him with all her strength.

"It's not true," she said, burying her face in the joining of his neck and shoulder. "Nothing they're saying about you is true. Don't you worry, though. I know this lawyer in Wyoming. Do you want me...?'' She started sobbing and couldn't continue.

"Tinsley, I'm not under arrest.'' Alex pulled her away from him. "I was just riding out here to witness Paula's interview of Clayton. That's all. Honey, I'm all right. We just came from the hospital.''

"Timothy?'' She wiped her face. "Is Timothy...? How is he?''

Alex frowned. "Not good. But he's a fighter. He has everything going for him, now.''

"He does since Alex arranged for one of the country's best trauma specialists to be flown in to handle the case,'' the red-haired woman in the business suit declared. "While we're all impressed, his largesse could be interpreted as an attempt to ease a guilty conscience.''

Tinsley turned, ready to strike out again, but Alex held her too tightly. Warningly. "Tinsley, this is Paula Dixon, our assistant D.A., Paula, Tinsley Cole. Tins, Paula is just doing her job, so simmer down.''

Neither woman made any attempt to shake hands.

The five of them went inside Clayton's house, Clayton and Paula Dixon leading the way. Tinsley hung back a bit. "Old girlfriend?'' she asked Alex in a whisper. "Didn't end well?''

He nodded. Looked embarrassed.

"Thought as much.'' She took a deep breath and told herself to act like an attorney, not a lover. It helped, somewhat. She was going to need everything she had to keep control, if Alex was actually charged with a crime.

The questioning was directed at Clayton, however, much to her relief. She knew her fuse was dangerously short, and the fact that Dixon was drop-dead gorgeous and groomed to perfection didn't lengthen that fuse. She thought of the woman with Alex and all kinds of jealous demons surfaced, full of life and full of venom. She felt dowdy, large and ungainly beside the petite D.A.

But, after a few minutes, her professional persona kicked in. She began to listen and to plan strategy, just as if she were in a courtroom, confronting a hostile witness. And Clayton was certainly hostility personified. The glances he shot at her were evidence enough.

"You say you were here all day, Clayton," Tottie stated, checking notes in a little spiral book she held. "But that no one else was with you."

"That's right." Clayton sat back on his sofa, his eyes half shut. Lazy-looking. Wary. "I have no alibi. But then, I don't need one, do I, Paula?"

The D.A. didn't answer. She just watched. Tinsley's estimation of her went up a notch. She might have been Alex's lover at one time, but now, she was all D.A.

Clayton moved on the sofa, adjusting his position nervously. He cleared his throat and folded his hands in his lap.

"You were out at Alex's place the morning his horse was poisoned, though," Tottie went on. "And you were alone once you left the front porch, supposedly to return to your boat."

"I did return." Clayton shifted again. "What's this got to do with the bomb? I had nothing to do with his damn horse. Ugly brute, anyway. Kick you soon as it would look..."

"Jack kicked you?" Alex asked. His voice was calm, quiet. "When was that, Clay?"

"I didn't say he kicked me." Clayton sat deeper in the cushions. "Just said he would, if he got a chance." His hands twitched. Unfolded.

"Did he have a chance?" This from the D.A.

Clayton regarded her for a moment. "I want a lawyer," he said, putting his hand over his lips.

"No one's accused you of anything, Clayton," Tinsley said, sensing opportunity. "Why do you need a lawyer?"

Clayton exploded. "Maybe I want to charge you with trespass and assault, bitch! Did you ever think of that?" He came halfway off the sofa toward her before he stopped himself.

Tinsley smiled. Mission accomplished.

Predictably, she was asked to leave after that. But Alex left with her. "I'm not under arrest," he said as they walked out the door. "Do you have a car?"

"Yes. I stole Delores's. It's over there." She gestured. "But, what . . . ?"

"Wait," he cautioned. "Not yet. I'll explain in a minute. You drive."

"I was planning to." She unlocked his door, then went around to the driver's side and got in. She didn't have time to think before she was encircled by his arms.

Alex's embrace was hard and hurt for a second, until she relaxed into it. He kissed her, and his ardor was greater than anything she had felt from him before. Not even in the high throes of sexual passion had he kissed like this!

And suddenly she knew he loved her. Her heart beat so fast she was sure he could hear it, and her breath caught in her throat with the realization. He *loved* her. The kiss lasted a moment more, then he let her go.

"Tinsley," he said, his gaze boring into her eyes, commanding her full attention. "That explosion was meant to kill us both. I saw the preliminary report from the bomb experts. It was set and timed. We were supposed to be blown up, killed at two this afternoon."

Tinsley forgot about love. She felt cold deep inside. "But, why? And why was Timothy there? Who knew our schedule? Who would want us both dead?"

He released her and returned to the passenger seat. He looked out the window. "I don't know any answers, yet. Particularly about Timothy. But, I think we'd better find them. And soon."

She started the engine. "Because whoever it was will try again?"

Alex didn't answer. He didn't need to.

She drove him to his mother's house at his request. Regretfully. They would sleep apart tonight for the first time in weeks. He explained he would rather not go through the hassle of trying to convince either Delores or Susan to let them stay at either home together. Tinsley agreed, wholeheartedly. She'd had her fight for the day. She didn't need another.

"I believe we're safe enough tonight," he said, not looking directly at her. "Whoever it is will need time to make other plans, now that this one failed. But tomorrow morning, pick me up as early as you can. Pack a bag for a long haul. We're going to keep moving."

"A moving target is less likely to get hit?"

"Exactly. We need to think and plan. We need some time and space to do that. I trust Tottie Reynolds and her staff, but they are limited and have many other problems besides ours. If we want to see the end of this, I think we need to get our hands dirty." He sat very still. "Tinsley, I..."

"Me, too."

Their hands touched, clasped and released. Nothing more needed to be said. Alex didn't look back as he got out of the car and went up the stone steps to his mother's home.

Tinsley drove back to Delores's, her heart light and heavy at the same time. To be in love and to be loved was wonderful, but it wasn't right, yet. With Alex and herself, the emotion was tied to fear. To danger. Once that negative was dealt with, what would they have? Could they live with her physical incompleteness? What lay ahead?

Maybe, nothing. Maybe...everything.

The sun set as she entered the driveway, and the lights from her aunt's home flooded the yard. Tinsley glanced at her watch and noted that she was still in time for dinner.

LIFE WAS FULL of surprises, Alex thought as he listened to his mother speak. They were seated in the den, sipping sherry before dinner. She had greeted him tenderly when he entered the house, almost scaring him with her emotion. First warmth he'd seen from her in years.

"I was terrified when I heard the report," she repeated. "To think you escaped only by chance." She touched her chest with her hand. "I don't think I could have survived losing you, too," she said, her voice so low, he wasn't sure he heard her correctly.

"I was supervising a swimming event," he said. "If it hadn't been Tinsley's big day in the ocean, we'd both have been in the house when it went."

Susan Berringer frowned. "Does that woman have enemies? Someone who might want her dead?"

"No, Mother." Alex lifted his glass. Took a sip of the sweet, nutty liquid. "Unless someone knows by hurting her, he hurts me."

"Do you love her, then?"

Alex looked up. No rancor in his mother's face. No...censure. "Yes, I do," he answered. "More than I can say."

Susan nodded, but she said nothing. Her features softened, however, and Alex noted that his mother looked younger. A tear fell down her cheek.

Alex sat, frozen. She hadn't cried when his father died. Not that he knew of, anyway. Another tear fell.

"Mother?" He half rose from his chair. "What's wrong?"

She held up her hand. "Nothing. I...I just am remembering what it was like to love." She blinked, causing more tears to fall. "It can bring great pain, Alex."

Tears filled his own eyes. "I know. But, the joy..."

"I don't know." She fumbled in a skirt pocket and brought out a handkerchief. "I can't honestly tell you the joy was worth the present pain. The constant feeling of loss." She pressed the cloth to her eyes. "You know, I still miss him so terribly sometimes my heart feels like it has been torn in two."

"Oh, Mom! Why didn't you ever say anything?" Alex got up and went over to her, but she held her hand out, pushing him back. "I would have..."

"What?" She spoke softly. "Comforted me? Son, you are the image of your father. Each time I saw you, it hurt. And as you grew to be a man, I could barely stand to have you near." She looked up at him. "I have a lot of sins to answer for, but my rejection of you is probably the greatest. You did nothing to deserve the way I've treated you."

Alex turned away. The wound was too raw, and he couldn't stand to have her see his tears.

In time, they both recovered their composure, but dinner and the rest of the evening at the Berringer mansion were spent in almost total silence. Reflective silence.

SILENCE WAS NOT a factor at the Bishop house. Nor was reflection. Delores met Tinsley at the door, a check for airline tickets in her hand. She waved it at her and followed her into the living room, uttering threats. It was entirely out of character, but Delores seemed possessed by anger and anxiety. Her niece would be on the next plane to Wyoming, she declared, or she'd know the reason why!

Tinsley started to tell her, then thought better of it. Delores did, after all, have her best interests at heart. She sat down and tried to speak reasonably.

But they fought. Reason became the first victim of the battle. Fought over safety, over Alex, over the future, and over love.

"I cannot believe you're being this stubborn," Delores shouted. "You were almost blown to smithereens! What more reason do you need to go home? To get away from whatever crazy person is responsible for that outrage!"

"I want to stop that crazy person," Tinsley declared. "Stop him once and for all, so Alex will be safe!"

"And then?" Delores circled around her chair and slapped her hands on the back of it. "What do you plan, Tinsley? Living with him? Marrying him? What?"

"I don't know. I just know I can't leave. I love him."

"Oh? Really?" Delores sat and glared. "And tell me, my dear niece, what do you really know of love? True love? The kind that lasts forever? Even beyond the grave."

Tinsley stared and thought. If Alex were dead, killed today as he was meant to be, would she still feel this way for him?

Yes! Yes, she would. The realization rocked her to her core.

"Tinsley?" Delores's ranting tone had gone. "Tinsley, I am so sorry. I didn't mean . . ."

"It's okay." Tinsley smiled, not really seeing her surroundings. "It's okay. Thanks, in fact. You just gave me an answer I've been looking for." She focused on her aunt. "Looking for all my life, I think."

Alex Berringer was the man she was meant to love. The problem of her barrenness would be one they would face together. Somehow, they would work that out. They were destined for one another, and she knew it.

The problem was, someone evil was trying to take him away from her.

And Tinsley was not about to let that happen.

CHAPTER FOURTEEN

THE NEXT MORNING, she drove over to the Berringer home as Alex had requested, but she did not have her belongings packed, as he had asked. She parked, got out, and strode up the stone steps to the door. She rang the bell and waited.

Alex answered the door. When he saw her, his expression underwent a number of interesting transformations. "Tinsley, darling," he said. "What . . . ? You . . ."

"May I come in?" she asked, moving past him to the foyer before he could invite her. "Get suited up, Alex. We have work to do," she said.

Alex stared. This was a new Tinsley Cole, visually. A stranger. An unknown. She was dressed up, for one thing. Had her hair back in a controlled, styled twist. Makeup on her face. "Tinsley?" he peered at her. "Is that really you?"

The old Tinsley, the familiar, beloved Tinsley broke through for a moment. She grinned. "Yeah. Ain't it a kick?" Then, she reverted. Became brisk and businesslike. "Come on, Alex. We can't afford to waste any time. Get yourself into some city clothes. We have work to do."

"Why, Miss Cole. Good morning." Susan Berringer came into the foyer. "Are you joining us for breakfast?"

Tinsley hesitated, then realized there was no hostility in the invitation. "Why, yes. That would be nice, if it's no trouble." Other matters would wait, she told herself. If his mother was willing to call a truce of any kind, it was worth it to accept.

"None at all." Susan's gaze passed over her, hovered, approved. "Please," she said, gesturing in the direction of the dining room.

"Thank you." Tinsley followed.

Alex stood alone for a moment, trying to digest what had just happened. Then, giving it up for the time being, he hurried to join the women.

Breakfast was over before he began to get a grip on events. Tinsley had been demure and decorous to the extreme, but she had also taken no guff from his mother. The two were sparring, he realized. Establishing parity, recognizing rights. Where Tinsley was behaving with real attention to conventional manners, his mother had relaxed her own. They almost reached common ground. That was encouraging for the future, he thought.

But Tinsley had her own plan for the future. After Susan excused herself, she leaned over the table and gave Alex an intense look. "We can't run," she said, her voice low and emotional. "If we do, we give them partial victory. We have to stand and fight."

Alex nodded, surprised but pleased. "I came to much the same conclusion last night. We're definitely on the same wavelength. But you..."

"But, nothing. Listen, Alex. I don't know if Clayton has the guts to have done the job yesterday or not. But I do know someone did. And we have to find out who."

"Agreed." He got up and went over to the sideboard. "More coffee?"

"No. I'm swimming already. This is my second breakfast. Say, what got into your mother, anyhow? She was really nice this morning."

He shrugged, unwilling to speak of it. "You have a plan of attack?"

"Sort of." She tapped her finger on the dark, glossy tabletop. "I think we need to leak news of our engagement plans."

Alex sloshed coffee into the saucer. "What?" He felt as if he'd been hit with a sledgehammer.

"The way I see it, is this." She leaned forward again. "There was no reason to try taking me out, unless whoever is after you is afraid you plan to marry me. Why blow the house, if not to get me? There was a lot to risk in that. More people around. Like Timothy. Why not wait until you were alone out on the ocean? I'm the new ingredient in the stew. If we had kids, that would cut Clayton out of the inheritance he wants and..."

"Tinsley, slow down. You still think Clay is the culprit?"

"Not necessarily directly. Though I haven't given up on him entirely." She rested her chin on her hand. She exuded confidence. Intelligence. Purpose.

Alex sat down. He took a deep breath. "Talk to me," he said. "Tell me what you're thinking."

She began. And he listened.

THE MAN STOOD by his office window, staring out at the morning, seeing none of the beauty of the South Carolina day. Alex Berringer and his Wyoming whore still lived and breathed and were likely breeding right at this moment! Matters were desperate enough, but if they produced a child, even illegitimate, his hopes and plans were lost forever. His agent was a fool, a bungler, a failure. If he showed his pathetic face around here, he was likely to get it kicked down to his heels! He was definitely fired, in any event.

There was still a concern. Why hadn't the idiot come around to collect what he must believe was his due? It didn't fit with the man's grasping personality. But, then... Better in the final analysis if he disappeared forever. One less line to be traced back to the source. Himself.

Time to take the job on personally, he told himself. To do a job right, do it by oneself. That was a rule he should have remembered. He shrugged, feeling the movement of his aging muscles under his shirt.

But he had to be realistic. Direct physical violence was beyond his abilities these days. He picked up the telephone receiver, controlling the trembling in his hands with difficulty. There were, however, other ways to do harm to an enemy. Other methods to gain objectives. Many other ways.

"So, HERE'S WHAT we plan to do," Alex told Joseph as they lunched together in a small downtown restaurant decorated to look like an English pub. "We won't wait until Tinsley gets her bar exam passed to open a practice. I'll open my own, with her as secretary-assistant. When she passes, we go into partnership. Get married. Maybe start a family. Anyway, I've given up on the island. My heart's not in it, now. Too much terror." The lie sounded false to his ears, and he was positive Joseph wouldn't buy a bit of it. Further, he hated using his old friend like this. But they were using everyone they knew, weren't they? Why should Joseph be exempt?

"Lad, you must be joking." Joseph set his fork down. "I can't believe you'd give up your dreams just because of an... accident."

"It was no accident."

"So you say." Joseph looked away. "Are you doing this because of Tinsley? If so, you're making a mistake. She's not one to run from a fight, and she won't respect you if you do."

"Wait. Wait. First, you seem to think the explosion was accidental. Then, you accuse me of turning tail. Joseph, what's really on your mind."

The older man thought a moment. "I wish I could say for sure. I don't feel I know you anymore, though we've been friends for years. You seem . . . secretive. Cagey. As if you have something to hide from me. From a great many people. It doesn't become you, Alex. Not one bit."

"Damn." Alex looked down at his uneaten food. "I ought to have known better than try and pull one over on you."

"Want to spill?"

"Yes, but I need to have my partner present. Not any reflection on you, of course. But I owe it to her."

"I assume the beauteous Miss Cole is this partner." Joseph now looked amused and at ease.

Alex smiled. "Sure is."

They caught up with Tinsley as she came out of the county courthouse. One look at her, and Alex knew trouble was brewing. Her blue eyes were almost literally shooting sparks.

"Some idiot lost my application," she fumed, giving him a perfunctory hug and kiss. "I don't believe it!" She turned to Joseph. "Hello, Joe," she said. "Alex fill you in over lunch?"

"Oh, I would say so." Joseph chuckled and took his pipe from his pocket. "Now, if the two of you don't mind, I'd like to hear the truth for a change."

Tinsley blushed. "What?" She looked at Alex.

"He isn't buying our story, darling. And I think we should trust him." He touched her cheek. "I have for years, after all."

She eyed Joseph. "I trust my aunt," she said. "But I'm lying like a rug to her. Why should you be the privileged one?"

"My, Alex." Joseph hit his pipe bowl against his palm. "You do have a scrapper here. Hope you're strong enough for her, if any part of your fairy tale actually happens to be true."

"What's true," Tinsley said before Alex could reply, "is that we are trying to set traps. Flush out whoever's been at the bottom of Alex's troubles."

"I see."

"Let's not do any more seeing right here on the street," Alex advised. "Tinsley, where're you parked?"

They drove out of town and down along the coast road, Tinsley at the wheel, Alex in back and Joseph in the front passenger seat. Joseph listened as Tinsley talked, with Alex adding details now and then.

"Unless Alex is the target of a maniac, which I doubt, whoever has caused his troubles has a clear motive for doing so," Tinsley explained.

"You have to accept our belief that all my bad luck has been deliberately arranged," Alex added. "If you don't, we have nothing more to discuss."

"You have had more than your share," Joseph said, his tone reflective. "All right. I accept your premise."

"It's more than a premise." Tinsley slowed as another car came toward them on the two-lane road. Memories of her accident flared in her mind, then passed. "And the point of it all is his island. Someone wants Alex's island badly enough to kill him for it."

"That's a bit extreme, don't you think?"

"Extreme? You weren't there when the house went up," she replied.

"But Timothy was." Alex said this, and his tone was strange. As if he were considering something.

Tinsley waited, but he didn't say anything else, so she went on. "What we need to do is figure out who on the long list of people wanting to buy the place is desperate and ruthless enough to kill for it."

Silence followed this statement.

After a while, Joseph cleared his throat. "You two have taken on quite a job."

"We have no choice," Alex said. "Not if we don't want to spend the rest of our lives looking over our shoulders. And turning the place into a virtual fortress, when we rebuild. I won't live like that."

"So. You aren't leaving your island?"

"Of course not."

"I didn't think you would." Joseph leaned over the seat and slapped Alex on the leg. "Good for you." He sat back down. "And for you," he said to Tinsley. "Now, what can I do to help?"

Tinsley looked back at Alex. Alex nodded. So, she told Joseph. He listened, laughed, sobered, argued, then agreed to the plan.

Later, after they dropped the older man off at his car, they went over to the hospital to check on Timothy's condition. The boatman was in a coma.

"I don't know what to tell you," Dr. Liipford told Alex. "Mr. Blane is a strong man. He could come out of it at any time. He could stay like this for years. With head injuries, it's quite impossible to predict."

"Head injury?" Tinsley's interest perked.

The doctor put his hands on his chest. "Yes, your friend sustained a severe blow to the head, resulting in..."

"He wasn't blown up?" Alex asked, thoughtfully. "Then how did the boat get overturned?"

"Not by the explosion, apparently," the doctor said. "There's no evidence of any other wounds or burn injuries. It looks as though someone hit him."

"Makes sense," Tinsley added. "The dock should have been even more damaged, if the blast had overturned the boat. I don't know why we didn't see it right away."

"Too caught up in saving the man's life, I suppose," Dr. Liipford said, conversationally. "I hope he does recover, of course. But you've certainly got a can of worms for yourselves if he doesn't."

Tinsley stiffened. "What do you mean?"

The doctor reddened, realizing he'd said more than he should. "Just that an insurance investigator was asking me some rather pointed questions today. About your relationship to Mr. Blane, and why he might have been in the wrong place at the wrong time. Seen something he shouldn't have, perhaps. Like, perhaps, the person or persons who caused the calamity. Taken a clip on the head for his curiosity, perhaps...."

Tinsley swore and grabbed Alex's arm. "Let's get out of here," she said. Alex went with her, calling a thanks to the doctor as he did so.

Out in the afternoon sunlight, Tinsley looked grim. "I don't like the pattern I'm seeing develop here, Alex," she said. "I think we need to do some serious damage control."

"I don't follow you."

She held up her hand. "First," she said, pointing to one finger, "my application to take the bar exam has mysteriously disappeared. Since all my information was vaporized along with my computer, it'll take me some time and trouble to get it back together and in submittable form again."

Alex nodded.

She raised another finger. "Second, even Joseph was inclined at first to believe the explosion was accidental. Not a deliberate murder attempt. I didn't hear any news reports, but Delores told me yesterday, it was being billed as a possible propane explosion. Carelessness."

"Oh, Lord."

"Exactly. Now, we have Timothy. Not a victim of the blast, but of a blow to the head. And his boat? Was there any damage to it? I bet not. That old scow would have overturned if you looked at it the wrong way. Easy enough for a strong man to scuttle it, after bashing the owner. Alex, Timothy saw something and was almost killed because of it."

"If he comes to..."

"We can't count on that." Her mind raced. "In fact, I think we had better hope for now that he doesn't. Oh, Alex. If Timothy seems to be getting better, the bad guy's liable to try killing him again."

"Get in the car. We need to talk to Tottie."

JOSEPH MEADOWS set down the receiver of his telephone, after having a conversation with his investment advisor, and smiled to himself. The bait was out, and he could count on his advisor flashing it all over the countryside. Now all that remained was to play the part assigned him and wait to see who bit. He hated that this was necessary because his friends were in danger, but he had to admit to himself he was having more fun than he could remember in a long time. Lord, but he loved to fish!

He also rather enjoyed Delores Bishop's company and decided it really wasn't too soon to start that part of the game plan. Tinsley might not approve of his making that move so soon, but she was not his boss, just his coconspirator. And he had other motives besides their strategy in mind. He really liked Delores, no two ways about it. Tinsley didn't seem to realize that yet, but she would. He picked up the phone and dialed her aunt's number.

But Delores proved a more difficult catch than he had hoped. "I'd really adore to have dinner with you tonight, Joseph," she said, her tone sincere. "But my sister's flying in from Wyoming, and I must meet her at the airport. It's rather a sudden visit. Unplanned, until Tinsley got into so much...trouble. Jason's getting ready to drive me there right now."

Joseph waited and hoped for an invitation to ride along. When none came, he tossed out a lure. "I hope she's here to talk your niece out of her unwise association with Alex Berringer."

Silence for a moment. Then, "I thought you were his friend."

"Well, I certainly thought so myself. We've fished together for years. But I can't stomach the idea that he blew up his own place just for the insurance. And when that boatman was injured..."

"The insurance?"

"Yes, haven't you heard? The place is heavily insured, my dear. Far more, I believe, than it is...was worth. A great temptation to anyone. And you know young Berringer has little money sense."

"I didn't, but..."

"It fits. He's not a responsible person. That island ought to be placed in the hands of someone who knows its value, if you ask me. But, enough of such unpleasant talk. I do hope to meet your sister while she's visiting." Hint, hint.

Success! "Why, of course! That would be so delightful. How about dinner tomorrow night? Here."

"I would be honored." When he finally hung up, Joseph did feel pangs of guilt at deceiving such a nice lady. But, he reasoned, she would forgive him once she understood. After all, it was her niece whose future happiness was at stake. Alex Berringer, Joseph reflected, was a damn lucky man. He only hoped the lad realized it. He was a fool, if he didn't, and while he wasn't always centered down on planet Earth like regular folks, Joseph Meadows had never seen Alex be foolish.

"THAT'S A DAMN-FOOL notion if I ever heard one!" Tottie Reynolds waved a hand at Alex and Tinsley. "You have no proof. Nothing for me to go on. Why you even bothered coming here, I don't know."

"Because you know me. What I believe in, and what I do." Alex glanced at Tinsley, warning her to keep her temper under wraps. "Tottie, have I ever lied to you or harmed anyone deliberately in my life?"

The sheriff didn't answer. She sat back in her chair and regarded Alex thoughtfully.

He plunged on. "All I ask...all we ask, is that you consider what we've said. Timothy needs guarding, around the clock. I'll pay out of my own pocket for the extra expense to the office."

"You don't do that." Tottie looked angry. "That's like buying the police."

"Hell it is!" Tinsley broke loose. "We can hire private, if we want. We're trying to stay as far within the boundaries as possible. But Timothy Blane's life is more important than any rules! I can make one call and have as many gunmen out here as—"

"This *ain't* the OK Corral, Missy!" Tottie leaned forward and slapped her desk. "No hired help, you understand me?"

"That man is in danger." Tinsley met her glare directly. "Are you going to wait until he's dead to do something?"

"No!"

"Good." Tinsley sat back. "Thanks."

Tottie sat back too, her expression showing she realized she had lost that round. "But I won't take a dime from you, Alex. That clear?"

"As daylight."

Tottie nodded, satisfied. "Now, then. What else have you two got in mind for me?" she asked. "And don't look innocent, because I know you aren't through."

"Well . . ." Tinsley began.

"We weren't going to use . . . ah, ask you to do the next part," Alex said. "This was more in Paula's bailiwick."

"I'll call her up." Tottie reached for the phone. "Come election time next year," she said, dialing, "I don't want folks asking, 'How come you didn't know what that Berringer boy was up to, Sheriff?'" She sat back, waiting. "Don't cut me out of the loop, you two," she warned. "Or I'll have your hides on my wall."

Both Tinsley and Alex voiced wide-eyed denial. Then, they smiled at each other. Tottie was in!

Paula Dixon took a little more work. The assistant D.A. wasn't bothered so much by her past relationship with Alex, Tinsley decided, as she was by the political implications of throwing in with them. If they were guilty, she would have egg all over her political face and lose any chance of advancement forever. Tinsley tried reason, listing the reasons why Alex would have no motive for blowing up his home, including the fact that his financial situation was good. He certainly didn't need the insurance money.

"Some people think you're a little crazy," Dixon said. Her gaze rested on Alex. "You know, you don't have a reputation for being exactly normal, Al," she added.

Alex reddened. "I can't help what folks think or say about me. I just live life the way I choose."

"Not necessarily a popular attitude."

"She's right, Alex," Tinsley interjected. "But, Paula, that doesn't make him a criminal. Just sort of a social misfit."

"Say...!" Alex looked indignant.

"Hush." Tinsley told him. When he quieted, she went on. "Here's all we're asking you to do, Paula. Just keep the focus on Alex. We want whoever is really responsible to relax. We want it to look like Alex's luck has run out. The bad guys know he is innocent, but what they don't know is whether he has enough cash to ride out a trial. After all, his money is all tied up in investments and trust funds. We want them to think he needs to sell the island."

"You're sure that's the prize in this?" Tottie asked. "Why?"

"Not positive. But pretty darn sure." Tinsley frowned. "We can't know exactly, until we get evidence. That's where I come in. You're both public officials, and you can't take the time to do the research needed to prove Alex innocent. All you can do is act on evidence of guilt. I intend to get that for you."

"How?" Dixon regarded her with new interest. "And why? This isn't necessary, you know. We haven't made any decision in my office to file any charges."

"But, I expect you will, because whoever is behind it isn't done, yet." Tinsley reached over and touched Alex's arm. "There will be more things happening. More reasons for Alex to seem guilty. Or at least unreliable. Maybe, even crazy..."

"That's already started." Paula looked down. "We had two anonymous calls this morning, claiming Alex had talked about blowing up the whole island before he would let developers touch it. That if it was going to be spoiled, it should be destroyed, first." She sounded uneasy. "A reporter called, too. With the same kind of questions."

"What!" Alex came out of his chair. "I can't believe it! I'd never..."

"I know that," Paula said, regarding him with a hint of affection. "Al, you wouldn't hurt a fly, if it landed on you and bit you. But you don't play by the rules around here, and you have made a number of people very uncomfortable over the years, because—"

"Because he's a decent man." Tinsley said, softly. "That's real hard for the undecent to swallow, isn't it?" She looked at Dixon, and the woman nodded, understanding.

The four of them talked a little longer. Paula agreed to do what she could without compromising her office or stepping in beyond her depth. But, she warned them both to be careful. "You aren't professionals," she said. "According to the reports I've gotten, the bomb was rigged so that it is very difficult to prove it wasn't a propane explosion. A good lawyer could make a mess out of an attempt to prove you were a victim and not a careless or deliberately willful perpetrator. That was the work of a pro. And Timothy..."

"We've covered that," Tottie said, filling her in.

When the sheriff was finished, Paula turned once more to Alex and Tinsley. "So," she said. "While we're busy protecting Mr. Blane and blowing informational smoke

about you, what're you two going to be doing? I expect to
be told, now. No lies, please.''

"I can't lie, because I don't know what we're going to
be looking for," Alex said. "We just intend to do a great
deal of paper-sifting. Someone's left evidence of this
somewhere. We're going to hunt for it.''

Tinsley nodded agreement. No need to say anything
more, she thought. What the law didn't know wouldn't
hurt them or anyone else, including Alex and herself.

"And when you find evidence?" Tottie asked.

"Directly to you." Alex held up his hand. "I swear it."

Dixon looked at Reynolds. Then, they both sighed.
"Okay," the D.A. said. "But you keep Annie Oakly here
under control, or..."

"Don't worry about me," Tinsley said. "I talk a hard
game, but I really do play by the rules.''

"Why am I not reassured?" Tottie muttered, looking
worried.

But Paula Dixon just smiled.

It was late afternoon when they left town and drove
down the coast to the deep harbor where Alex said he kept
his big sailboat and some of his belongings. Tinsley was
at the wheel, Alex seemed to be dozing in the passenger
seat.

But he wasn't asleep. "Have I told you how terrific you
look today?" he asked. "Or was I too busy being
stunned?"

She smiled. "No, and I don't know."

"Well, you look terrific."

"Thanks. Takes a little longer in the morning, and I
don't usually see the point in bothering. But, I knew I was
going to do battle today, so on went the war paint..."

"You know, it's not your fight, Tins.''

She steadied the car on the road as another vehicle came toward them. "Why the hell not?"

"You walked in on the middle of it. Took a number, and got involved, but all you need to do to get out is buy a plane ticket home."

She glared over at him. His eyes were shut and he looked relaxed. Until she noticed his hands. They were clenched on his thighs. "Delores already tried that," she said, softly. "Waved the damn thing in my face last night. I told her I wasn't leaving."

"Why? Bottom line. Total honesty, please."

"I love you."

He said nothing, but as she stole another glance, she saw his hands had relaxed. His lips turned in a shadow of a smile. A few minutes later, Alex was snoring softly. The lines of tension on his face were almost completely erased.

CHAPTER FIFTEEN

"SHE WAS BUILT IN 1922," Alex said proudly. "I found her dry-docked and falling apart. Rotting, really. Rebuilt her and refinished her. I bet I scoured every ship grave-yard on the East coast to find original parts."

Tinsley ran a hand along a section of smooth, gleam-ing teak. "Well, you did a wonderful job. This is a beau-tiful boat."

Alex smiled and patted a glowing brass fitting. "Thanks. Come on below while I get my stuff. I've even got some of my business papers here, so you can look through them while I get organized."

"Sounds good to me." Tinsley followed, her mind clicking. The first thing she had noticed was that she had no fear being on the water in this boat. For some reason, her phobia didn't trigger. Maybe it was the weeks of swimming lessons. Maybe it was necessity.

Maybe it was the love she'd already confessed.

Whatever the reason, it was a good feeling not to be terrified as she felt the motion of the water underneath her feet.

The second matter that occurred to her was that Alex kept his boat far enough down the coast so it was in the state of Georgia. Registered there, too, he'd told her. So, anyone checking his files in South Carolina might miss it, even though it was in his records as property.

Also, he explained he hadn't used it for a long time for sightseeing cruises. Those he had essentially abandoned when his work on the island became the driving force in his professional and personal life. The coast cruises were something he might take up again, he said, but not for a long time. Certainly not until the current disaster was cleared up.

So people might have forgotten he had this boat.

Tinsley stopped musing once she was down the stairs and into what Alex referred to as the living quarters. "This is a palace!" she declared. She moved through the tiny, but well-appointed galley and looked into the captain's quarters. "A miniature mansion! Where in the world did you get the crystal chandelier?"

"Boston." He encircled her with his arms. His breath was warm and stimulating on her cheek. "It's vintage, but the bed's new. Want to try it out?"

She answered by kissing him fervently.

He undressed her with an almost reverent touch. Tinsley shivered with erotic anticipation as he removed first her skirt, then her blouse and laid them carefully on a built-in wooden clothes rack. But he didn't go immediately to the hook on her bra. Instead, he held her at arms length and regarded her, thoughtfully. Tinsley waited, aching with desire, but respecting his mood.

"I wonder," he said, finally, "if you have any idea how much you move me." He shook his head, forbidding her to answer. "No, don't talk. I think, in my heart, this is beyond words. There is no way to describe it, Tinsley. Do I like you? Certainly. Lust for you? Obviously. Love you?" He pulled her close and gently kissed her lips. "I would, without hesitation, die for you."

"That shouldn't be necessary," she said, fighting tears now, along with her passionate feelings. "We're going to make sure of that!'' She wrapped her arms around his neck and twined her leg between his. He seemed to fight something inside himself for a moment, then he brought his lips down on hers in a kiss that was both painful and ecstatically fulfilling for both of them.

Talk ceased.

Afterwards, he slept for a while, and she lay beside him, thinking. His loving had been different. Better, actually. More...loving. Something had happened to make him...different.

She could not, for the life of her, decide what it was, though. The puzzle gnawed at her too much for her to sleep. So, Tinsley got up and dressed, careful not to disturb her lover.

The sun was setting, but there was still enough reddish light coming in the porthole for her to sit at his little ship's desk and go through his papers. When it got too dark, she reached over and switched on the tiny lamp hooked to the top of the desk. The rocking motion of the vessel increased slightly, and she assumed the tide was coming in.

It didn't bother her. She felt comfortable and quite safe.

Until she found the proposal.

It was several years old and tucked behind some other papers in an accordion file folder. Is she hadn't been set on going through every scrap of material, she probably wouldn't have bothered glancing at it. But when she did, her blood froze.

''What is it?'' Alex put his hands on her shoulders. ''Find something?''

Tinsley yelped, then settled. ''You startled me. When did you wake up?''

''I've been awake for a while. Watching you.'' He leaned over her. ''What's this?''

"Alex do you remember this?" She held the proposal up. "It's a definite lead."

"Let me see." He took the papers and held them near the light. "No, I... Oh, yeah. This is that old deal Sanford Taylor was trying to put together years ago. I'd just moved out to the island, and he assumed I wouldn't stay long." He dropped the papers back onto the desk. "Hungry?" he asked, stroking her neck.

She batted his hand away. "Alex, quit it. Think. When did he withdraw this proposal? It's pretty detailed." She flipped pages. "See? He even has bids on connecting the water lines and sewer to the mainland. Taking the phone system off electricity and cabling it, so you could have access to lots of different services. Including cable TV."

Alex sat down on the side of the bed. "I don't remember. Think this is important?" He rubbed his chin and looked serious for the first time.

"It might be. How anxious was Taylor to have you sell out?"

"Pretty damn anxious at the time." He rubbed his chin again. "But I haven't heard much out of him since then. I did tell you he's in a cartel now. They stopped exerting pressure when I made it crystal clear I was on the island for good. Now and then, I still get feelers, though, as I told you. Sure, they'd jump at the chance to buy, but—"

"I need all their names. Access to tax records..." She turned and looked at him, thinking. She touched her own hair. "How long would it take you to grow out that beard?" she asked.

"Huh?"

She smiled at him. "Let me explain. I have an idea. One that might fit nicely into our other plan. And make it safer," she added, seriously. "I think we need to put safety up at the front of our priorities, now."

THE PHONE RANG and Delores lunged for it, not waiting for Silvie to answer. "It must be Tinsley," she told her sister. "I can't imagine why she didn't come home or call before this."

Ellen Cole sat, her coffee cup balanced on her lap. "I can," she said. "Tinsley walks to her own beat these days." Ellen and Delores were relaxing and talking, waiting for Tinsley to show up and be surprised that her mother was visiting. Delores had strongly suggested that they keep Ellen's presence a secret until Tinsley actually walked into the house. Otherwise, she might stay away in order to avoid a confrontation, Delores declared.

But the call wasn't from the missing Tinsley. "Why, hello, Sanford," Delores said. She mouthed a negative to Ellen. "No, I've no idea where either Alex or Tinsley are. Yes, I'm sure. No. But I'll let them know. Goodbye." She hung up. "That was odd."

Ellen waited.

"I don't understand why Sanford Taylor would be looking for Alex." Delores picked nervously at the sleeve of her dress. "He doesn't even like the boy."

"Who does?" Ellen took the cue. Alex Berringer and his alleged poor character was the main reason she had made the long journey back to her childhood home. That and, of course, Tinsley's close call when Alex's home had been destroyed. "You told me even his old friend, that Mr. Meadows, has deserted his cause."

"Well, I wouldn't exactly put it that way. But Joseph did say he was disillusioned by the rumors that..."

"Rumors?"

"Why, yes. I've heard more than a few myself since—"

"Delores, why don't you start from the beginning?" Ellen set her cup down on the side table. Tinsley was her only child, and she was determined, if she could, to help her girl through this. The last time, with Brad, she had been entirely taken in by the man and his supposedly honorable intentions. Not this time! "I think I need to hear this from the very first. And don't leave out one single detail, please."

Delores nodded and began.

THE MOON WAS RISING when Tinsley drove back toward Carleton Cay. She drove fast, her feelings mixed. She had presented her excellent idea to Alex and encountered a stone wall. He had not agreed they should go into hiding by taking his sailboat out and disappearing for a while. He had argued for working on a quick, open settlement to the problem. None of her hiding-and-searching scheme. There was more, too.

He didn't trust her to be able to handle living at sea. And he didn't want to accept her darker fears about Sanford Taylor's involvement in their troubles. Her belief that the man was personally behind the death attempts seemed farfetched, he said. He didn't give her credit for clear analytical or reliable instinctive thinking. That had hurt her pride. Her heart, she knew, belonged to him, no matter how angry she got. And she was angry now.

He was being a stubborn jerk, generally. But, damn it, all his objections involved thinking of other people, not himself. What an idiot!

Too bad she loved him!

She glanced at his profile, visible by the dim dashboard lights. He was as angry as she was, that was easy to see. "Aside from all the other people who count on me, I can't do it to my mother, Tinsley," he said, repeating his main argument. "It's that simple. If we disappear, she'll believe the worst. She will surely think I've drowned like my father."

"Better that than have you go to jail for insurance fraud."

He shook his head. "It won't happen."

"Maybe not. But are you willing to bet on it? Someone's spreading rumors about you and putting barriers in my professional path. I bet my bottom dollar it's Taylor. Okay, maybe he didn't actually plant the bomb, but I bet he was directly involved. At the very least, we..." Her voice trailed off.

"What's the matter?"

"I don't know, but see those headlights in front of us? They seem to be moving around on the road."

"Slow down."

She gripped the wheel, her hands suddenly slick and slippery with sweat. Horrible memories flooded back, almost paralyzing her. "Alex, it's like just before my accident. I'm going to stop. Let you drive."

"Okay. Pull up over there. It's a long drop down to the beach. The sandy shoulder's no place to— Watch out! He's running right at us!"

Tinsley fought for control. This was no time to panic. The oncoming car raised its headlights, blinding her. She sensed it swerving at the last moment to avoid a head-on collision, and she swerved harder, so that the bumpers barely scraped.

But they were off the road, listing dangerously. The right-hand tires caught in the sand on the shoulder, and the automobile started to tip. She screamed, heard Alex yell at her to ride it out, and the night went upside down, right side up, then black.

A LITTLE WHILE later, in an elegant old home on the best residential street in Carleton Cay, a phone rang. The owner of the home answered the phone curtly. It was too late for any business calls, and he wasn't expecting anything social. When he heard the voice, he very nearly hung up. But some instinct kept him on the line. He listened, his hand tightening on the receiver. Finally, he said, "You're sure?" Then, "Yes, I know where to send the money. I'll see to it in the morning."

He hung up, a twinge of regret twisting inside him. But it lasted only a moment. They were dead. Both of them, the other man claimed, though he admitted he hadn't actually seen the bodies. No one could have survived the flaming car wreck. Too bad about that. But, the money! There would be gracious plenty of it now. More than enough! When his wife querulously asked what the call was about, he told her it was nothing.

Nothing at all.

THE FIRST THING she saw when she woke was the shadow play of fire dancing on the rocks near where she lay. Tinsley sat up, rubbing the bump on her head. "Alex?" she said, her voice gravelly. If he was hurt or worse, she would die! "Where are you? Alex, please . . ."

"Right here, love." He was by her side immediately. "Don't move. Are you . . . ?"

"I've got a headache, but I'm fine." She looked at him. Blood ran down the side of his face. "You're cut!"

"Just a scratch. Don't let the blood bother you. Tinsley, we were deliberately run off the road. You were right. Whoever it is will just keep trying. Whether or not it's actually Taylor now makes no difference. If we stick around to prove it openly, we're in deadly danger. We've got to disappear."

"The car? Delores's car?"

"Is burning. I hauled you out just before it went up. Whoever did this watched. I got us behind these boulders where we can't be seen from the road. But I could see the car waiting up on the road. When the fire started, he drove away."

"No attempt to help? You're certain it was all deliberate?"

"Hell, yes. And if he'd gone for help, it would have been here by now. Hear any sirens?"

"No."

"Can you walk?"

"Sure." She stood up. "But . . ."

"But, nothing. Tinsley, if I ever doubt your instincts again, please remind me of this. I can't believe I didn't see this coming. My mother would be a whole lot worse off if I actually died, rather than just pretending to for a while. I'm too much of a dreamer, and I need your practical, down-to-earth turn of mind." He brushed her hair with his hand. "My darling, I'm only half a human being without you. You complete me."

In spite of the earlier terror and in spite of the pain in her head, Tinsley smiled. "You won't make me turn over a car next time you pull your stubborn act on me?"

"I promise. No, I swear!"

"Then, let's disappear. We'll call Tottie and explain some of it, so she won't tear out her hair, when she finds out we've tricked her, but she has to swear silence. We'll have to be a mystery for a time, agreed?"

He showed no reluctance now. "Agreed!" There was a hard look in his eyes and on his face that she had not seen before.

And, she realized, she approved of it.

"THERE WERE NO BODIES in the wreckage, Mrs. Bishop," Sheriff Reynolds said. "We found traces of blood in the sand behind some rocks. The type matches with Alex's. But no bodies. Maybe..."

"Maybe they drowned," Susan Berringer said, her voice hollow and whiny at the same time. "Just like his father did, and..."

"Susan," Ellen Cole said. "Shut up. They didn't drown. If Tinsley were dead, I'd know it." She spoke harshly, but went over to the other woman and put her arm around her thin shoulders. "They've gone somewhere, but they're all right." She knew it, deep in her heart, but it still tore at her to think of her child maybe hurt and lost somewhere. And with a man who was far less than the sort she'd want for Tinsley under dangerous circumstances. Under any circumstances! If Susan's weak spirit was any guide, her son was a real loser!

"We're watching the tides," Tottie said, nodding encouragement. "If they did end up in the water, they'll show up eventually. But, like Ellen here, I don't feel death in this." She looked at the two mothers, the aunt, and longed to say more, to relieve their fears, but didn't dare. Too much was at stake. They'd understand eventually. Hopefully.

"Why?" Delores had her hands clasped tightly together. "My car is wrecked and burned. No trace of either of them. Why shouldn't we fear the worst?"

"Because of Alex and Tinsley." Tottie tapped the desktop with a pencil, wondering how best to reassure these three frightened women. "The two of them are like cats," she finally said. "Always ending up on their feet. Nine lives, and all that." She looked at Mrs. Berringer. There were still things she herself didn't know. All she'd gotten was a brief message from Alex that he and Tinsley were not dead and that she was to keep in contact with them at a special number where an answering machine would be set up. He'd hung up before she could ask a thing. She had no idea where the two had actually gone. Maybe his mother could help. "Do you have any idea where he might have gone, if he didn't want anyone to know where he was?"

Susan just shook her head, sadly. "My son and I have been estranged for years. He has his own life, and I know nothing of it."

Tottie's pencil tapped faster. "Okay. But if you think of anything…anything at all, please don't hesitate to call me. Night or day, understand."

Susan nodded. Tears filled her eyes and spilled. When she left the office, however, Delores and Ellen were on either side, speaking comfortingly and supporting her.

Tottie watched until they left the building. Then, she picked up her phone and dialed a number. The recording machine answered, as she had been told it would. She left her message, telling how the relatives had handled the news and she then hung up, feeling very used. Sort of angry, too.

But more than a little bit relieved. They could have really died in that wreck. And she would have been powerless to do anything about it. Now there was a chance to get the bad guys. Tottie smiled to herself, thinking that with Alex and Tinsley teamed up, it was a damn good chance!

TWO WEEKS LATER, a young couple from Florida bought a small house in Columbia, the South Carolina state capital. Access was easiest here to the public records involving land purchases and holding companies. The place was dirt-cheap and they paid in cash, telling the realtor they wanted a fixer-upper. He believed them, told them what a bargain they'd gotten, and grinned wolfishly to himself at his cleverness in unloading that cracker box.

The point of buying was to keep their activities totally secret. Even a rental held risks of the owner snooping. Tinsley swept dust out of the tiny bedroom and coughed. "I saw two large roaches," she declared. "And where there are two, there are two million. Did you buy a bug bomb, Max?"

They had money. While they sailed, Alex had raided an offshore bank account he kept, he said, for emergencies. This certainly qualified. She wiped sweat off her tanned forehead. Her short brown hair had reddish highlights, but no hint of blond. The color rinse and haircut were a sacrifice, but worth it. She doubted her own mother would recognize her without a close look. To the rest of the world, they were Max and Tess Vale. For as long as it took.

"That I did, Tess." Alex produced the item and grinned, his teeth white against his black beard and sun-darkened skin. "Shall we go commit bugicide?"

"By all means. I won't be happy setting up a computer, much less a bed, until the place is ours instead of theirs."

"That may take awhile," he warned.

"Do your best." She put her arms around him and kissed his neck, wondering as usual, at the love she felt for him. And whether the feelings would last once the adventure and threat was over.

While the insecticide did its work, they took a walk around the neighborhood. Establishing their bona fides, Alex said. "We're newlyweds," he stated, speaking as if he were trying to memorize the new persona. "Perpetual students, living on shoestrings, but so in love with each other and with our research that we don't care."

"Ha." She put an arm around his waist. "I'd never be so impractical. Love and poverty are a difficult mix."

"True. But others have done it, and done it with dignity. When they had no other choice."

She thought of his home. "You miss the island, don' you?"

"Yes."

"You'll go back."

"I know."

Walking silently, she vowed she would do everything possible to get him back there. No matter what it cost her, she'd help get Alex back to where he belonged.

Whether he would want her there with him forever or not.

She devoted the next few days to smoking out lines of inquiry to follow, while Alex made house-fixing motions. He carried out boxes of debris, and told her that this was so no one would notice when he carried in the computer components. Tinsley wondered if the neighbors really cared.

But she did wander down to the nearest computer store and nosed around, trying to decide what kind of software would help her detective work. After a few visits, she got to be buddies with one of the sales clerks, a thin boy, barely out of high school. His name, his tag declared, was Jeremy.

"Just what is it you want the system to do, ma'am?" Jeremy asked. "General computing? Word processing? Accounting. Spreadsheets? What?"

Tinsley laughed, relaxed enough to be honest. The kid was just being polite. He didn't really care about anything but making a sale. "Actually, I want to break into the records of a rich guy and prove he's into crooked land deals . . ."

"Hush!" Jeremy put his hand up to her face. "Not so loud, ma'am." He looked around. They were alone—it was nearly closing time. "You kidding me?"

"Sure. Just kidding. I wouldn't try anything illegal. After all, I—"

"No. Really. If you're serious, I think I could help." His narrow face had an earnest expression.

Tinsley regarded the boy. "You mean it, don't you."

He nodded.

"You do this often?"

He turned a bright shade of red. His yellow hair even seemed to glow orange. "No, ma'am. I never have. Not as long as I've worked here. I'm trying to earn enough to pay for tuition. You can get kind of desperate, you know. And what you said about crooked land deals? My folks were wiped out by one ten years ago down in Texas. My daddy committed suicide over it." He blushed deeper, clearly still feeling sorrow over his parent's situation.

Tinsley regarded him for a moment. She thought of the parallel with Alex and his father. "Jeremy, how much do you pull in an hour working here?"

He told her. And told her his full name was Jeremy Dunlap.

"Okay, Jeremy. What you're making here, I'll triple. Maybe more. I'll wait for you to close up. I want you to talk to my friend."

But Alex wasn't buying. "No, no, no. Look, Jeremy. I appreciate your expertise as a hacker, even your motivation, but I can't condone illegal activity. If you can help us within the boundaries of the law, that's one thing, but..."

Jeremy looked at Tinsley. "Is this guy for real?" he asked. "For serious?"

She nodded. "Last of his kind, Jeremy. Now, given the strictures, can you help?"

Jeremy considered. "I think I can. But you got to give me an idea what you're really after." He blushed again. "And why."

Tinsley looked at Alex. He looked at her, then at Jeremy. And nodded. So they told him. When he'd heard the whole story, Jeremy whooped and did a war dance around the small living room. "I never got a shot at the guys who did my dad," he declared. "But this is gonna be almost as good! When do I start?"

"Now," Alex said. "Actually, fifteen minutes ago. When we took you into our confidence."

Jeremy sobered and nodded. He realized then, Tinsley knew, how serious this really was.

It took exactly ten days for the three of them to gather the necessary information. With Jeremy's help, Alex set up a computer to help garner and to store the data. Tinsley scouted the public records, spending long hours bent over legal documents, translating the legal language into plain English. It was exhausting work. But in ten days, they had him.

Sanford Taylor. There was no question.

"Geez, this guy is dirty right through," Jeremy commented, after assembling the details into a readable report. "A real, live stinker. I can't believe no one's gotten on to him before."

"He's a retired banker," Alex said. "No reason to suspect him. Doesn't live above his means. Not until you look under the rocks, of course." He thought about it. Taylor was badly overinvested in land all around the area. But his financial dilemma was cleverly covered by indirect dealings, holding companies, front men, and the like. How to get him in the open was the question.

"This all goes to Paula," Tinsley said. "She's got to run it through the system. But even then, if Taylor stonewalls, she can't actually prove he managed your 'accidents' or our car wreck. That still could have been hit-and-run. All we have here is a picture of a man obsessed with owning your island. That's no crime."

"No, it isn't," Alex agreed.

"You're gonna have to scare him, some way," Jeremy said. "Or get him to admit it on tape. Send in a wire like they do in the movies."

Alex smiled. It was a wicked expression, and one that almost startled Tinsley. He did have a touch of nastiness in him, after all, she realized. "Joseph," he said, "will be our wire." He turned to her. "But you, my love, will be the scariest thing Sanford Taylor has ever in his long life encountered."

"Huh?" She frowned. "What are you talking about?

"Poetry, my dear," Alex said, striking a pose and speaking in a close parody of Sanford Taylor's style. "You will haunt him with your verse. After all, he thinks we're dead, doesn't he?" He paused. "First, of course, we've got to let our families know we're all right. Now the danger's off us and on him. We can afford to be resurrected, don't you think?" He explained, in detail.

Tinsley couldn't say a thing at first. Then she started laughing. And laughed until the tears flowed.

A cleansing flow.

CHAPTER SIXTEEN

ONE WEEK LATER, Alex's plans and schemes began to bear fruit.

"Have you heard anything from them, yet?" Tottie asked Paula Dixon. They were in Paula's office, waiting for a fax to come in. A fax they had been told to expect by an anonymous phone caller. The voice hadn't been recognizable nor the locale traceable. Tottie's expert had pinpointed it as belonging to an adolescent male, but the call had been too short to effectively place beyond the fact that it was within state. Not much help there.

"Not a peep," Paula admitted, her frustration showing in the worry lines on her pale forehead. "That Alex Berringer. He's playing games, isn't he?"

"I don't think so." Tottie walked over to the window and stared out. "His mom suddenly stopped walking around like a skinny ghost. She's over to Bishop's place all the time, now. Cheerful enough, from the look of her. And Tinsley's mom flew home the other day. She wouldn't have done that if she was still waiting for her kid's body to float in."

"They've been in contact with them, then, do you think?"

"Bet your life."

"Damn. But not with us."

"Not yet." Tottie gestured toward the fax machine. "Maybe this is the payload."

"Damn."

Tottie turned around. "You're still kinda fond of Alex, aren't you, Paula? Come on, just between us girls?"

The assistant D.A. laughed. "I always will be, Sheriff. But I can't stand the guy, either. He's too... I don't know. I never really felt comfortable with him. Like I was with a person from another planet or something. Off in some cerebral outer space. Believe me, Tinsley Cole is welcome to him, if she can take it."

Tottie nodded. "They're two of a kind. I think she can."

Paula agreed. "If she's put up with all this insanity, she can sure take the good times. I wish them both the best."

Just then, the fax machine started clacking. The two women watched it, as if it were a living thing. When the message was done, Tottie grabbed the paper. She scanned it, started to laugh, and said, "Well, I'll be damned! I will be damned."

Paula snatched the paper and read. Her reaction was similar. But she said with affection, "That sly, sly fox. Can you believe it? I always knew if Alex used his brains for something practical, he'd be downright dangerous." She set the papers down on her desk. "But we can't use any of this."

"Not without a confession." Tottie folded her arms across her chest. "Now, why do I have the feeling he knows that, too?"

"He does. Count on it."

"So does she. And they both know the law."

"Let's just hope they stay within it."

"Yeah. Let's hope." Tottie tapped the papers. "So, Sanford Taylor's the king rat, huh? The mastermind be-hind all Alex's troubles." She slapped the papers. "I'd give a lot to put cuffs on the smug bird. I've known what he's like since I was a little kid. Bad News Banker. Fore-close on you, soon as look at you. Loves the whole power trip. He *likes* making folks miserable, you know.'' She thought again for a moment. "Say, let's take ourselves over to the hospital for a little talk to Timothy again. See if he can recall anything more than he already has. All we need's one detail. One link. One.''

"Let's go,'' Paula said. "If Alex can't manage, it's go-ing to be up to us.'' She gathered up her briefcase and purse. "But, just between you and me, I think he can do it. With Tinsley's help, that is.''

SANFORD TAYLOR'S hands shook as he read the latest in-stallment of the epic poem, *Tailor's Raiders*. This was the fourth scurrilous verse in as many days that had ap-peared on his front door, nailed there without postmark or signature.

After the first time, he'd posted a guard, one of his most trusted house servants, but the man hadn't watched closely enough, or he'd been in league with the mysteri-ous writer. Now he was fired and wouldn't find work in the area ever again, if Sanford had anything to say about it. The notes continued to appear every morning, no clue as to how they got on the door.

He knew exactly where they came from, however. The Cole bitch was still alive.

Easy enough to recognize her crude style in the poetry. He remembered his instinctive dislike of her the first time he'd met her at the Literary Society meeting. Yes, it was easy enough to see she was still at work, undermining his present and future plans. Not dead, as he'd been told. And, her work had been frighteningly successful. Easy to understand from the poetry. Hard to believe the amount of pure, factual information she included in each verse.

She knew about his land deals, and his plans for Ber-ringer's Island. And she was letting him know through these ugly missives. Would the blackmail note come at the end of the poem?

Or was she after something other than money? No indication whether Berringer had lived through the car wreck, even though she obviously had. She might be out for revenge, if she'd really been in love with the man. In love? Unlikely. In lust, maybe. After the Berringer money, no doubt. Planned on getting at it by marriage, perhaps. If Alex was dead, would she go after Clayton? Who would know?

Why, Delores Bishop, of course. She was not only emotionally involved, she was so socially aware that she would certainly be sensitive to any gossip in the community. He put down the page and picked up the phone. He should have been cultivating the silly woman long before this, anyway. She was a conduit.

And Joseph Meadows had been sniffing around her, as well. Meadows was known to be an old crony of Alex. Perhaps the two of them could be persuaded to drop some information. Some clue about where the Cole girl was.

Some clue he could put to use. For, if this drivel was ever published, he was doomed. No matter the accusations were veiled in a period poem with a slight name change here and there to disguise the present-day reality. No one in the land development business on the East coast could fail to see him in it. No one.

And, then, no one would likely do business with him. He shuddered, then forced a smile as his wife walked past the study. Checking him out; he had been behaving strangely, lately, she kept saying. He waved at her, indicating the telephone. Sweat trickled down his side as he waited for her reaction. She nodded and moved on. And

Delores Bishop answered her phone. Sanford continued to smile as he spoke.

"HE'S TAKEN the bait in a big way, lad," Joseph told Alex as the two of them hunched over mugs of beer in a small waterfront tavern in an unsavory section of Charleston, a full day after Sanford's hasty, nervous call to Delores. It was a place no one who knew either of them would ever expect to find them.

Alex nodded, his attention on his drink.

"He's been picking at poor Delores like she was the vault at Fort Knox," Joseph added. "Me, he's inviting to invest in his future plans for your place. Downright pushy about it. Can you believe that? We're to have dinner tonight, and he's going to make a detailed investment proposal, I think."

"I can indeed believe every word you say." Alex drank some beer. "The man has no morality. I don't believe he understands the concept."

"You may be right. But he isn't a killer. At least not with his own hands."

"I didn't think he was. There's someone else out there who did the actual deeds. Think Timothy is going to be able to help?"

"Maybe. The local law isn't exactly taking me into her confidence, if you get my drift. Not that she's not entirely on your team, lad. She and that D.A. Two of your biggest fans, I'd say. Just you give 'em what they need, and they'll pin old Sandy right to his own wall."

"We know. We're working on it." Another drink of beer. "How's my mother?"

"Like a prisoner freed. I've never seen a woman change so much in a few weeks' time. Since she learned you were alive, she's gotten ten years younger, I swear though she's careful to keep up the act of grieving mother when she's in public.''

Alex smiled, his heart warming at the news. ''Just remind her we're not through yet,'' he said. ''We still have bad guys to catch.''

''Aye, Captain.'' Joseph saluted. ''I'll remember.''

''Do you also remember what you've got to try getting on tape tonight? All we need is an admission of involvement in illegal tactics to get my island. No particulars. We've got proof enough of them. He just has to confess he was aware. Any more, and he might regret what he said. If he cuts and runs, we may never nail him.''

''I think I can manage.'' Joseph slapped Alex's arm. ''Trust me, laddie. I have a very important stake in this affair, you know. I intend to catch the garter at your wedding.''

Alex raised his eyebrows and grinned, but didn't reply. In the tradition they both knew, the man who caught the bride's garter at a friend's wedding was the next man who would marry.

Interesting. Alex wondered if Delores was aware of Joseph's line of thought.

Or, if Tinsley was, what would her response be? They hadn't spoken seriously of their own futures. He knew he needed to deal with that issue. But not just yet. Not until all the dust settled. Then, he would deal. In Hearts!

JOSEPH HELD Delores's hand tightly, willing reassurance to her. ''No, I didn't tell the lad what I intended, my dear. Or that so many others were involved, as well. He would have forbidden me to do it. Somehow, he would have managed to thwart my plan in order to save us from any danger.''

"Oh, I am so afraid for you!" Delores's eyes filled with tears. "If you're hurt, I'll never forgive myself."

"And why's that? After all, I am a grown man, able to make my own decisions about my health and safety."

"But, this isn't your fight. Nor the others. Joseph, you—"

"It is my fight, Delores. *Our* fight. I am Alex's good friend. He's helped others for years. Now it's time to pay him back, at least in part. He asked for help. We're giving it to him." Joseph paused, smiling at her. "Just giving him a little more than he wanted, that's all." He squeezed her hand, tightly again. "You know your part?"

"Of course. At ten, I call the restaurant and ask to speak to you. If you come to the phone, we don't talk. I hang up and call Sheriff Reynolds immediately. It means you've been successful."

"Good." Joseph released her hand. "Now, how about a kiss for luck?"

Delores stared at him, then smiled. Then complied with enthusiasm.

SANFORD TAYLOR shifted uneasily in his chair. The restaurant was surprisingly empty tonight, but that ought to have made him happy. Less likelihood he and Meadows would be overheard. Instead, he was nervous.

So was Meadows. He tried not to show it, but the constant fussing with the pipe, the glances around, the disjointed sentences gave the man away. Well, perhaps it was to be expected. The deal he was offering would set Meadows back a sizable amount of cash until the dividends came in. Maybe he was just nervous about the money.

Maybe.

The restaurant staff seemed different also, but he hadn't been to this particular place in a long time. The maître d' was a young man. The waiter was slightly clumsy, but he was polite and apologetic when he made an error. Well, it didn't matter. What mattered was getting Meadows to buy in.

"You must understand my reluctance, Sanford," Meadows was saying. "Without proof Alex wants or wanted to divest himself of the island, I don't see how you can offer shares in any future development."

"Actually, you are quite right, my dear Joseph." Sanford took a sip of wine and set his glass down. "One reason why I wanted to talk to you was to find out if you had any information about that."

"I don't understand."

"Young Berringer has disappeared. There was an accident. You know his girlfriend's aunt's automobile was found wrecked by the ocean."

"Of course, I know about that. Delores is worried sick. But, I still don't see . . ."

"Bear with me. Suppose Alex is dead? Oh, don't look so shocked. It is likely, you know. His father, and all."

"You mean . . . ?"

"A suicide, of course. It does run in families. Bad blood or some such thing."

"But the woman . . ."

"A pact, perhaps. Or perhaps she's just gone home. Has Delores heard from her?"

"Not that I know of." Joseph tried to eat, but found he had no appetite. He forced himself to play the part. "But, then, Ms. Cole is selfish to the extreme, from what I've seen of her. Probably wouldn't think of her aunt's feelings. You know."

"I certainly do. I was not at all favorably impressed the first time I met her. And I've heard . . . Well, unsavory things since."

Joseph bent over his food. He needed to disguise hi
expression. "Let's say," he said, "that Alex is gone
When could the deal on the island be closed? I don't car
to tie my money up for too long."

Sanford Taylor smiled. He explained that Clayton ha
already signed an agreement. "It will slide right into ou
hands, once Alex is declared legally...out of the picture
But, there is one problem. Unless we have proof, the es
tate will languish for years."

"Seven? I believe that's standard."

Sanford nodded. "But, if we had a witness, w
wouldn't need more...exact physical proof."

"You mean Tinsley? But she's disappeared, too."

"Yes. And no." Sanford debated once more, as he ha
done over and over since he had decided to take the risl
of bringing Meadows in. "I believe she is still aliv
and..."

"Well, isn't Alex with her, then?"

"I don't know. If he is, why doesn't he come for
ward?"

Joseph put down his fork and leaned forward. "San
ford, are you on to something the rest of us don't know?'
He lowered his voice to a conspiratorial level. "Because
if you are, I'd like to know. It just might influence m
decision."

"You were Alex's friend?"

"*Were* is the operative word. When I learned he prob
ably blew up his own place for the insurance, it was th
last straw. I'd been thinking for a long time that hi
goody-goody pose was all a sham. I am now only con
cerned with my own interests. My future and sufficien
finances to afford to live it the way *I* choose. I have n
loyalty left for him, anyway, if that's what you're ask
ing."

It was. With those assurances, the dam broke. The blatant hint of greed did the trick. Sanford also leaned forward. "If Alex is still alive, he won't be the moment he raises his head. If the Cole girl wants a piece of the action in order to keep her quiet, that's all right with me. There'll be enough to go around, and then some."

Joseph sat back, saying nothing, feeling the tape running, letting his face register fake confusion, skepticism and greed. Mostly, greed.

Sanford went on, almost babbling, as if he were relieved at last to unload his burden. "You're wrong in some of your assumptions. I have a man working for me," he said. "One who doesn't balk at doing some rather difficult things. Do you understand?"

"No."

"Do you really think Alex blew up his own place? After all the effort he put into it?" Sanford looked around. No one stood nearby. "Come on, Joseph. He was parked out there for the rest of his damn life! It was the only way to move him! Now do you understand?"

Joseph made himself smile. "I think I do." He set his napkin alongside his plate. "And I must say, I do see how you could be motivated to do it. I confess, I do truly understand. You are still in contact with this...person? The one who blew up Alex's home?"

"Not exactly. I paid him off for taking care of them in the car wreck, but..."

"But there were no bodies."

"So, he still owes me. He's been paid, but..." Sanford stopped, suddenly aware he'd said too much.

"Well." Joseph tried not to look triumphant. "This is far more interesting than I dreamed it would be. Sanford, you are a clever man. And courageous. I admire

you. Not just anyone would dare involve themselves wit
a hired killer, no matter what the stakes."

Taylor's face darkened. "He was a bum!" he spat ou
"A dilettante."

"The killer?"

"No. Of course not. Though he is hardly a man of hig
ideals or station. Or ability. He's failed to do the job agai
and again. No, I meant Alex Berringer. I hated his fa
ther, and I hated him."

"Why?" Joseph prayed the tape was still running. The
hadn't figured it would take this long.

"He never earned his money, that's why. Inherited
and has squandered it ever since. His father refused t
invest when I was president of the bank. Kept his funds i
another institution, mind. Like a slap in my face! I..." H
reddened more. "I'm saying far too much about my ow
feelings."

"That's fine."

"But how I feel has nothing to do with—"

"Mr. Meadows." The waiter came over to their table
moving carefully, so as to alert them before he was withi
earshot. "There's a phone call for you. Can you take i
sir?"

"Yes." Joseph stood up, relief flooding him. The cha
rade was almost finished. "I certainly can. Sanfor
please excuse the interruption. I'll be right back."

Sanford Taylor murmured something, but Josep
didn't catch it. He moved away toward the phone, pa
ting the tape recorder microphone nested in his tie tack
He was thinking of hearing Delores's voice and didn'
notice the sudden movement behind him. When he did,
was too late to do anything about it.

Nor, thanks to Alex's friends, was it necessary. San
ford Taylor, a steak knife in his hand, was writhing on th

floor in the grip of the young maître d', Clara Sinclair's son, Nash. Nash was gaining control of the much older man when Clara appeared from the kitchen, a fury brandishing a frying pan. With a whoop of anger, she banged Taylor on the head, putting a swift and slightly musical end to his struggles with her son.

The few other patrons stood up, clearly not upset at the events, and Joseph smiled. They were all, each and every one, Alex's friends. White and black, poor, rich and in between. He and Nash had made certain that no outsider had been allowed into the restaurant in case the situation turned uglier than anticipated. He saw that Nash and Clara were in control of the unconscious Sanford Taylor, and he took the phone.

"Hello, dear," he said. "Everything's just fine. Slight change of plans. Taylor just tried to skewer me with a steak knife. No, no. I'm not hurt. Please, though, do call the cops. I'm afraid Alex's friends were a little too enthusiastic in moving to his defense." He hung up while Delores was trying to find out what he meant by that last comment. And while they waited for Sheriff Reynolds, he played the tape loudly for the assembly. They were an appreciative audience, to say the least.

TWENTY-FOUR HOURS later, Alex and Tinsley met with the sheriff. Tottie filled them in on what she knew, so far.

"So, Timothy is much better. He confirmed there was a stranger around your house that afternoon, even though he didn't see him when he was attacked. Whoever it was came up on Timothy from behind, when he rode out to investigate," Tottie said. "It has to be the same guy, and Timothy can identify him as a trespasser, at the very least."

They were meeting on Alex's big sailboat. "The i
truder was a man Timothy says he'd seen before out in
boat in the channel. Maybe watching you and your plac
but he can't be positive about that."

Alex considered. "We won't be sure we're safe until v
get that man," he said. "Taylor hired him to do a job.
isn't done yet." His tone was bleak.

"I won't stay in hiding the rest of my life just on th
account," Tinsley stated. "Nor will I continue to wear n
hair this color."

"It looks cute," Tottie said, teasing. "But what I r
ally like is the big guy's face fuzz. I didn't know you ha
it in you, Alex." She tried to lighten the atmospher
though she did agree with Alex's pessimism. These tw
were still in real danger, and she wasn't about to let ther
out of her sight until she felt secure about their safet
Trouble was, she had no idea how to see to that.

"Thanks." Alex was not in the mood for jokir
around. He didn't see through Tottie's facade to the co
cerned law officer beneath. No one but him seemed t
sense impending danger. Professional assassins did n
like to leave loose ends, especially when their employe
were babbling their heads off to D.A.s. Paula had r
ported that Sanford Taylor had broken down entirel
once he was made aware of the tape and the other ev
dence against him. Of course, the attack on Joseph woul
net him prison time all by itself. Alex sent up anothe
prayer of thanksgiving that his old friend had not bee
injured.

And that, to his own amazement, so many folks ha
rallied to his cause. He was, honestly, surprised at that.

But it wasn't time to run around congratulating him
self or anyone else, yet. He sat back, listening to Tinsle
and Tottie and thinking. Worrying, actually. He foun

himself distracted by Tinsley. Her moves, her voice, her kaleidoscope of animated expressions—all had wound their ways into his heart. He loved her passionately, intellectually, physically, spiritually... Completely.

And it was almost time he told her so. Whatever else happened, she deserved to hear him say the words. He was sure she already knew the feelings he had for her, but words were important. So was timing. She needed especially to know that her inability to have children didn't matter to him. There were so many other kids around to love, it didn't seem to matter anymore that he and Tinsley wouldn't have their own.

He was pondering this when a slight sound from the upper deck caught his attention. At first, he thought it was only a sea gull, foraging for scraps. Then, he realized the sound was too furtive. It had his attention. His entire attention. He listened some more. Then he moved.

Tinsley was aware when Alex left the galley. She had just refilled his cup of coffee, turned her back to do the same for Tottie, and he was gone. Like a ghost. She smiled at the sheriff. "This boat is really his home," she said. "He's in his own element here, more so even than he was on the island. The two weeks we sailed around I could see it. Thank goodness I'm no longer spooked by the water. I'm still not crazy about it, but at least I don't panic at the idea of going swimming."

"I'll say." Tottie took a drink of coffee. "Tell me if I'm being too nosy, but do you two have plans for the future?"

Tinsley shrugged. "Well, we haven't really talked about it."

Tottie smiled. "Some things, you don't need to talk about." She looked around. "Say, where'd he go?"

"I don't know. One minute, he was here. The next, he wasn't." She listened. Nothing.

"Keep talking." Tottie rose, unsnapping her holster flap and putting her hand on her gun. "I'm going to see what—" A loud crash from above cut off her words. More bumps, crashes and curses followed. Then, Alex' voice was distinguishable as he yelled in fury.

Tinsley's heart seemed to skip a beat in her fear for him. She'd never heard that particular tone from him before. She grabbed for a weapon, putting her hand on the first utensil that came to hand, and ran up the stairs. Tottie, behind her, called for her to wait.

But Alex was in trouble. She wasn't waiting for anyone! She emerged on deck, her senses tingling, ready for a fight.

The fight raged, but she wasn't able to get near it. Alex and a strange man rolled around on the deck, struggling for control of a knife. Blood stained the left side of Alex's shirt. The other man was uninjured, but clearly not getting the best of the battle. A look of desperation twisted his features.

Alex Berringer looked ferocious, like an unleashed avenging angel. Her man was fighting for more than the moment, she realized intuitively. He was doing battle for everything that had been done to try destroying his life. *Their* lives. He was protecting her! And doing it very well indeed.

Tinsley hesitated. Tottie came up beside her. "What the hell . . . ?" the sheriff said. Then, "What do you figure to do with that?"

Tinsley looked at her hand. She carried an oversized stirring spoon. "Nothing," she said, tossing the spoon aside. "And don't you use the gun, either!"

"Wasn't planning on it, unless I had to." Tottie Reynolds holstered her gun and took the handcuffs off her utility belt. "And it doesn't look like I'm gonna need anything but these babies," she added, grinning. "Good for you, Alex!" she yelled as Alex delivered a blow to his opponent that made the knife fly through the air and splash harmlessly into the water.

But then, things got out of hand. Tinsley watched in astonishment and horror as Alex continued to fight, dragging the stranger across the deck as if he planned on throwing him overboard as well. The man was screaming in terror that he couldn't swim. Alex didn't seem to hear. He swore at the man. "You'll never have a chance to hurt her again!" he exclaimed, his voice full of dark promise.

Tinsley cried out, calling Alex's name. He stopped to look up at her. "Alex, stop it," she yelled. "He's done, can't you see?" The fury on Alex's face slowly changed to surprise and confusion. Then Tottie moved in, taking advantage of the lull.

Moments later, the stranger was cuffed and begging Tottie to take him to jail. Anything to get him away from Alex!

Sheriff Tottie Reynolds complied.

Tinsley rushed into Alex's embrace and held him tightly. His body was shaking, and she thought she heard him whisper the words, "I was going to kill him." Regardless of what he said, there was so much pain in his tone that it nearly broke her heart.

"I love you," he said, more clearly. "I love you, and I brought you into a nightmare!"

"It's over, Alex," she said, hoping to calm him. "It's all right."

He held her so close, the breath went out of her for moment. He groaned, then spoke. "No, it isn't. He to me he was going to get me out of the way first, then ta his time with you. Tinsley, I was not going to stop until was dead!"

CHAPTER SEVENTEEN

"So, TIMOTHY BLANE has positively identified Grant as the man at your house and probably the one who attacked him just before the explosion. Unless Grant admits it outright, of course, we can't prove he ran you two off the road, or if he was involved with Clayton in the incidents with your horse, but that doesn't really matter. If nothing else, Tottie witnessed him fighting with you while he was armed and you weren't," the assistant D.A. said to Alex. Paula Dixon looked singularly triumphant.

So did the sheriff. Tottie Reynolds slapped her palms together. "With Taylor's confession, we now have a clear case. He will identify Grant. No loose ends. I love it! Both of them will be going to prison for a long, long time."

"Now we have to get to Clayton's case," Paula said. "Alex, the move is yours, you know."

Alex, who sat at the head of the dining room table in his mother's house, regarded Paula thoughtfully. He said nothing, and his face showed little of his friends' enthusiasm. In fact, his face showed little of anything but strain from the events of the last few days.

Tinsley studied him. Almost two days after the capture and arrest of the man named Steve Grant—the hired killer—all danger was past. This should have been a time of great rejoicing, but Alex wasn't celebrating.

In fact, he seemed unhappier than she had ever seen him. She had a good idea why. There were two reasons.

They had learned that Clayton had been responsible for giving the drug to Jack Tar the day the animal went berserk in his stall. But Clayton had never worked with Grant, nor had he known of Grant or his evil activities. He apparently wasn't even aware how much harm the drug would do; he was just concerned with harassing Alex. And he had not been the one who had shot at Jack on the beach. That was Grant's doing, though unfortunately there was no evidence.

Still, Clayton had intended to do harm to his cousin's horse, if not Alex, himself. Alex couldn't argue with the proof in the form of a purchase record and Clayton's tearful confession to Paula Dixon. When confronted by the angry D.A., Clayton had admitted to doing the prank, as he referred to it. Alex had been betrayed by his cousin.

Worse, though, for him: he'd been betrayed by himself. The latter was the most painful and damaging to Alex's sense of who he was.

Until now, Tinsley had no idea how much his peaceful, nonconfrontational existence meant to him. Although he had not mentioned it again, she knew he had been quite ready and willing to kill Steve Grant.

They had to talk, she realized. She had to get him to talk to her or he was going to brood himself into some real problems.

"Clayton has shown signs he is really repentant," Alex said, his tone soft and weary. "His complete confession for one; his willingness to make reparations in whatever form I demand, for another. Though it grates me to my soul, he is my cousin and I'm inclined to give him another chance. I do know from other examples in my life that if I bear him a grudge, I'll harm myself more than him in the long term. So I won't press charges."

Tinsley said nothing. Just listened to her lover.

His expression darkened. "It's enough for me to know that Grant and Taylor are going to pay for the rest of their lives."

"Don't be an idiot, Alex," Susan Berringer stated, her expression and voice harsh. "Miss Dixon told us all about it before you and Tinsley got here. Clayton bought that drug he gave to your horse. The evidence is clear. He tried to harm you deliberately. Don't you dare protect him from the consequences of his actions. He deserves punishment. It doesn't matter that he's family."

"He's a weak man, Mother," Alex said, not looking at her. "He needs help, not punishment. He only meant to scare me. Not to hurt anyone." He paused. "I'm not going to negotiate on this. I'm very sure of myself."

Susan humphed. She folded her thin arms across her chest. Earlier, she had expressed tremendous pride in her son's accomplishments. She approved of his fury at the two other men. Now, she was angry with him again. Angry at him for being true to his forgiving nature, Tinsley realized.

"Well, it's your choice," Paula declared, clearly also unhappy with his decision. "I hope you aren't making a mistake, though. He really hates you, you know."

"No, I don't know that." Alex stood up and walked over to the huge sideboard. He poured himself another cup of coffee. His fourth or fifth. Tinsley had lost count. She saw his hands shaking as he held the cup, and she was sure it wasn't all from the overdose of caffeine.

He spoke again. "I think he desires what he believes my money would bring to him more than he hates me or anyone else." His broad shoulders seemed squarer, his back straighter. "If I thought it would help him, I'd give it to him, but as he is, it would only destroy him."

"There are those who are more deserving of your gen erosity by a long shot," Delores said. "And you've seer to it they've received what they needed." She reached over and took Joseph's hand in hers. "Many of them came to your assistance when you needed it, too."

"Don't think I intend to let Clayton off without mak ing certain he pays in some way for what he's done," Alex said, his back to the group. "But I refuse to let any of you tell me how to manage that. I have my own plans." His voice held a strong note of determination and assurance. Of deep and thoughtful conviction.

"Alex." Tinsley stood up. "Let's take a walk."

"I don't—" he began.

"You need some fresh air," she said, putting her hand on his elbow. "*I* need some air. Come on."

He looked at her, touched her face, then nodded. "All right."

"We'll be back in a while," she told the others. No one said a word.

Outside, even though it was still just late May, summer gripped the air. Stifling heat and blanketing humidity. Tinsley gasped for breath and felt the sweat break out over her body. Alex didn't seem to notice either the heat or her reaction to it. He jammed his hands in his jeans pockets and walked. She saw no sign of perspiration on his face. It was as if he were too cold inside to react to the weather outside.

After they had gone about two blocks, he spoke. "I wanted to marry you," he said. "After you admitted you loved me, and we made love on my boat, I decided. I wanted you to be my wife. I wanted to be your hus band."

"Why the past tense?" She was suddenly as cold as she had ever been in a Wyoming winter. Sweat turned clammy on her skin.

"I could have killed a man. I would have, if Tottie hadn't stopped me. If you hadn't distracted me. I had murder on my mind."

"Yeah, I guess you were coming close there for a moment."

Alex stopped. They were within sight of the stone wall where he had found the little lizard for her the first time they had taken a walk together. "A moment was too much," he said. "I can't ever trust myself again. Life's too precious, Tins. No matter whose it is, it isn't up to me or anyone else to destroy it. And I would have." He looked at her. "Because that would have made you safer."

"You see something wrong with that?"

The pain in his eyes was so strong, she almost winced.

"I guess you do," she said.

He started walking again. "I have to answer yes and no to that. Given my motives, I know I'd do it again without hesitation. But, it's tearing at me inside."

She started to interrupt, but he held up a hand. "Let me explain why," he said. "When I recovered after my father died, part of my healing process was that I swore I'd do nothing to harm another person," he said. "It had nothing to do directly with my dad's death or with the way I behaved before. I believe it was a response to the pain I felt. Not logical, perhaps, but it made a difference in how I was able to deal with life. It's been almost a religion with me since then. Kept me focused. Do you understand?"

"Maybe." She thought for a moment. Then: "Sure, I do." She paced beside him, not touching, but so close she felt the heat from his skin. "And I understand you failed for a moment in your own estimation. That makes you nothing less than human."

He didn't respond.

"Alex, damn it!"

He shook his head, kept walking, not looking at her. "You deserve a better man than me, Tinsley. I have too many flaws. The fight for the island hasn't ended with Sanford Taylor. There always will be greedy people wanting what I have, what I want to preserve. And there will always be other people I'll care for more than life itself and—"

"And you're afraid you'll get violent again?"

He didn't say anything.

"Well, if you do, you'd better be sure I'm around to hit you over the head and save you from yourself," she said. "Besides, it kind of gives me a feeling of security, knowing that you hate violence but are willing and able to fight when you have to."

"I appreciate what you're saying. But, it's more than that I'm worried about." He stopped and pressed his hand to his forehead. "I've been thinking, and I don't like what I'm concluding."

"Which is?"

"I believe my whole family is... You deserve better than us, Tinsley. As I said, we have what I believe is traditionally called 'tainted blood.' A quick glance around the old family tree shows rot clean through."

"Ha!" She still felt cold, but she was beginning to see the cause of his emotional turmoil. "That's a good one!"

"I'm serious. My father, for whatever reason, died young, leaving a bitter widow and a shattered child. Maybe it was suicide, I don't know. I'll never know for sure, and that's a fact."

"No, you don't know. And that's something you have
live..."

"Listen to me!" He stopped again, turned and grabbed
r shoulders. "What you don't know is that Clayton's
rents were on board the boat when it went down. If my
ther did commit suicide, he killed his brother and sis-
r-in-law as well. My paternal grandmother raised Clay,
d it was not a happy household. She and Clayton were
nstantly at odds until the day she died."

"Oh." Tinsley put her hand to her mouth. "So, that's
hy Clayton feels you owe him."

"Look at us, Tinsley," Alex said, ignoring her com-
ent. "Aren't we a sorry bunch? Face the reality. Who
e we Berringers? Who am I? A recluse, who salves his
cial conscience with self-serving philanthropy. My
other? A woman so blinded by her pain, she can't freely
ve the son she was left with. My cousin? A young man
 greedy he's willing to harm an innocent animal to get
 his own cousin. And—"

"Stop it!" She stepped back, wanting very much to slap
s face. "I said I loved you, and I meant it. I still love
u, and I mean it. And, regardless of anything that
appens, I know I will always love you. Furthermore, I
now you love me." She took a deep breath. "Deal with
at reality, for a change!"

"If we have children, they might have the weaknesses
at runs—"

"Well, you aren't likely to by me, remember? I'm not
appy about it, but that's the way it is, and I'm living with
. If I can do it, so can you."

Pain twisted his features. "My God, I do love you," he
hispered. "How can I feel this way? Nothing's ever hurt
e as much."

"Alex, Alex, Alex." She turned around, so sh
wouldn't be tempted to laugh, or cry or hit him. "Yo
sound like a bad Southern novel. Love does hurt. Som
times."

"Does my love hurt you?"

"Yes." She hugged herself. "Sometimes. When I thin
of not being able to have your children, it hurts. When
think of not being able to help you with your pain,
hurts. When I think you might reject me out of som
warped view of doing me good, I nearly scream! We're
team, Alex. We've proved that under fire. If you push m
away, I'm liable to tear in two."

"Oh, God."

"I mean it." She turned around. "Every word."

"I've lost so much," he said, reaching to touch her fa
again. His hand shook. "I don't have any idea how lor
it'll take to rebuild. To drop back to square one on all m
projects and start over from the beginning. Are you r
ally willing to share that struggle with me? To take th
risks living life with me might bring?"

"I am." She held out her arms, encompassing him an
his life. "The struggle and the risks and anything else th
comes along. Compared to what we've been through, it
be easy." She smiled at him. "I guess you could say, it
my job. I've finally found out what I was meant to do i
this life, and you, Alex Berringer, are it. *We're* it."

He frowned, then smiled. Then frowned again. "Tin
ley, we *have* been through a lot and I still see many oth
battles ahead."

"So? That's the way life is. One of the things we hav
to face is that we probably won't have any children of ou
own. Can you honestly tell me it won't make a diffe
ence?"

"Yes," he said, firmly. "But that doesn't mean I won't help you as much as I can. We won't give up hope until we've exhausted every medical measure there is."

"Oh, Alex." She was nearly speechless. If she was barren, it no longer mattered. She believed him in a way she hadn't dreamed possible. To have this kind of trust in another person was almost incomprehensible to her.

"I will love you forever, regardless," he said, solemnly. "For all of my sentient existence. I have no doubts about it."

Laughter filled her and sputtered over, even though she clapped her hand across her mouth to prevent it. "All of your sentient existence? Will you please quit being such a professor! Only you would put undying love that way!"

"Too pedantic for you?" For the first time in days, a smile tugged at the corners of his mouth.

"Yes," she said. "But that's okay. I can deal with it. And so can you." Then she hooked her arm around his neck and kissed him.

Alex felt the touch of her lips on his and his soul spun. Never mind that they had made love over and over and were familiar with one another's bodies and needs. Never mind he knew her weaknesses as well as her strengths. Never mind she annoyed him at times, drove him to distraction at others. Good and bad, he loved her. All of her. She roused him to an ecstasy of mind, body and spirit he knew no other human could ever give him.

All of this, he realized in a flash. And he knew that no matter how guilty he felt about dragging her into his life, he could never live without her.

"There," she said, letting him go and smiling at him. "That ought to answer any questions you have.

"It does," Alex replied, his voice husky with emotion. "When you kiss me, I just don't have any more ques-

tions." He touched her cheek. "I love you. I have n
choice," he said, his tone so tender it was almost a cares
itself.

"Then, let's get married."

"Hey, isn't that my line?"

"Only if you had beat me to it." She grinned. A decid
edly wicked expression. "Out West, we gals don't wait fo
a man to get around to business, if we think the time ha
come. I'm no magnolia blossom, willing to sit and twid
dle my thumbs, hoping my guy'll make up his mind even
tually."

"No." Alex regarded her, laughter showing in his eyes
"A magnolia, you *ain't*. That's for certain."

"So, let's get on with it," she said. "How soon...?"

"Hold up." Alex slipped his arm across her shoulders
"*Soon* is not a word one applies to a Berringer marriage
my dearest love. If you are willing to take me, you have t
take the whole package, including the pomp and circum
stance."

"Oh, shoot."

"Besides," he said, more seriously, guiding her back t
walking at his side. "Before we get into wedding plans,
have to set myself at ease about a few other things an
people."

Tinsley reached up and touched his hand where it reste
on her shoulder. "I know," she said. "I understand."

Alex felt the reality of that curl like a warm han
around his heart. She did understand him.

They walked for a while longer, looking for the littl
lizard, but not finding it. "Maybe it just showed up t
give us good luck that first day," Alex commented. "Eve
with all that has happened, we've had the best of it."

Tinsley felt a lump in her throat. He had lost so much
but he could still say that. "Too bad we can't spread i

around, some," she said, just making conversation to cover up her emotions. Crying was not what he needed to see right now. "Share the wealth, sort of."

"Hmm," said Alex.

She looked at him and recognized his expression. Alex was thinking. His next words proved her right.

"Let's get back to the house," he said, "before the party breaks up. I have an idea I want to try out." He moved away from her, his pace increasing.

Then he stopped. He leaned back against the wall, a pensive look on his face. "No, wait. I'm not telling anyone else about this. Just you and me, for now. What do you think," he said, "of yoking Jeremy Dunlap and Clayton together for a while? Making them a team? Under close supervision, of course."

Tinsley stared at him. "What? What in the world are you talking about?"

"Just this." He gestured for her to come closer. She did. He went on. "I know Clay. He's a dreamer. Of bad dreams, perhaps, but nevertheless he's a sort of visionary."

"Like you?"

He blinked, then nodded. "Yes. But he lacks the stuff to put his ideas into action."

"Which you do not."

"Not usually," he admitted, skipping over the compliment. "And as we both have seen, young Jeremy is a man of action. Not always legal or well thought out, but a doer of deeds. Right?"

"Yes, but—"

"Listen to me, Tins." He put his hand on her shoulder, but his gaze was somewhere beyond both of them. "After all Jeremy did for us, do you think it's right just to throw a few dollars at him and let him go back to working in that store? Maybe slipping back into illegal behavior?

"It was hardly a few dollars, Alex. But I see what you're saying."

"Clayton needs to do penance. He's enough like me that I'm sure about this. We have old-fashioned souls, we Berringers. Penance is a satisfactory way of exorcising guilt, and Clayton won't get a fresh start on his life until he does that."

"I'll take your word for it."

"No, don't." He gazed at her. "I'm asking for your opinion. Jeremy is more like you, I think. What will this do for him? Get him out of his spiral down into white-collar crime?"

"Alex, don't you think you're overstating..." She let the words trail off, remembering how Jeremy had calmly offered to use his computer knowledge to get information illegally. "No, I guess you aren't. What do you have in mind for the two of them to do?"

He smiled. "You'll see," he told her. "If you have a sense I'm on to something good, that's enough for me. I need to think about it a bit more before I have the details worked out. Just trust me until then, please." He leaned back against the stone wall again, pulled her to him and kissed her.

Tinsley decided *that* was good enough for her. She could wait and trust. He would do the right thing, she was sure of it. When she opened her eyes, she saw the tail of a little lizard flicking over the top of the wall. A good sign, she decided.

Shortly thereafter, they returned to his mother's house. Tottie and Paula had left, but Delores, Susan and Joseph were sitting down to lunch. Sandwich makings were set out on the sideboard. Delores spoke first. "My goodness, Alex. What in the world happened to you? The weight of the world's off your shoulders for a change. You look like a new man. What's caused this?"

He grinned. "Oh, nothing really," he said. "Tinsley just asked me to marry her. That's all."

"Oh, my!" exclaimed Susan. Her thin face first paled, then turned rosy. "*She* asked *you?*"

"It's the way we Western types do it, Mrs. Berringer," Tinsley said, helping herself to the food and taking a seat by her future mother-in-law. "Alex wasn't exactly dragging his feet, but he wasn't bolting out of the stall, either. So, I did the only sensible thing. I popped the question myself."

"I see." Susan Berringer took a gulp of her iced tea. "Or perhaps I don't," she said, regarding Tinsley. "But I don't suppose that matters."

"I'd prefer if it did." Alex took a seat next to Tinsley. "Mother, I want us to matter to each other again," he said. "I know we haven't for a long time—"

"Alex!" Susan went pale again. White as her napkin. "This is hardly the time or place to—"

"Well, I disagree with you," he said. "Tinsley is going to be my wife and your daughter-in-law. Delores will be kin by marriage, and Joseph is my friend."

Delores started to stand. "We can leave if—"

"Sit." Tinsley's voice was firm. "Sit down, now, please. Listen to Alex."

Delores sat down.

Joseph had a strange look on his face. He put his hand on the back of Delores's chair.

"We have far too often let propriety and politeness dig the gulf between us deeper, Mother," Alex said. "'Now is not the time.' Or, 'I don't wish to discuss that at present.' When you do that, or I do that, we never do get back to it, do we?" His tone was warm and kind, but his gaze was direct and unrelenting. "Well, do we?"

"No." Susan looked down at her plate. "I suppose we do not." A tear slid slowly down her white cheek. "I . . . get very confused inside about how I feel sometimes. And I try to turn away from that."

"I won't let you do that anymore," he said, his voice gentle. "Because I do love you, Momma."

Susan Berringer put her face in her hands and began to weep. Tinsley felt tears running down her cheeks. Delores lifted her napkin to her eyes. Joseph cleared his throat several times.

Alex got up and went over to his mother. They embraced and cried together for the first time in over twenty years. Happily.

THE NEXT MORNING, Alex began to put his plan for Clayton and Jeremy Dunlap into action. Convinced he knew exactly what he was doing, Tinsley let him set the stage and the pace. They had talked about it late into the night, and she approved of his ideas, after making a few amendments of her own. It was, she realized, a pattern of behavior they had established from the beginning. A pattern she hoped would last a lifetime.

"So, Clay." Alex sat back in his chair and put his fingertips together, studying his cousin over the steeple of his hands. "Do you agree to the terms?"

"Do I have a choice?"

Tinsley watched. She stood behind Alex's chair, one hand on the back of it. They were all in the den, and he was seated behind the desk that had belonged to his father. The whole room had been his father's, and because Susan had kept it untouched and shrine-like, it was still a very masculine room. Dark wood. Brass ornaments. Old English hunt paintings on the wall. And the desk.

It was huge, oak and suited Alex to a *T.* He had dressed for this interview in a gray suit, complete with vest and red tie. Power dressing. He was shaved, his beard gone, and his hair groomed to perfection, as well. He *looked* like a lawyer, she thought. A successful one with all the authority of that position. And his mom had been tickled to see him so decked out! Although Susan was making determined progress in accepting her unconventional son the way he was, she still did love it when he broke his own mold and followed convention.

And, Tinsley had to admit, she kind of liked it herself, as long as it wasn't a permanent condition.

Alex regarded his cousin. "Of course, you have a choice," he said. "I'm not pressing charges, as you well know. Although I hate what you did, I am not holding a thing over your head. This has to be a free decision on your part, or I won't accept it."

Clayton still looked skeptical. From the chair by his side, Jeremy spoke up. "I'm game," the young man announced. "It sure beats the heck out of any other job I could get. And, like you said, it's legal. Maybe even good."

"Good?" Clayton turned and looked at Jeremy closely for the first time since they'd been introduced about thirty minutes ago. "What do you mean, *good?*"

"Well." Jeremy frowned, then smiled. "See, if you work for Alex, here, you're at the front line of what he's doing. Right? I mean, anyone who gets to manage his data files'll get to see firsthand what he's working on or for."

Clayton looked puzzled. "But, it's just glorified clerking, isn't it? How much good is that? And who cares?"

Alex stood up and walked past Tinsley. His hand brushed her arm for a second. "Maybe no one else," he said. "No one outside this room, anyway. But I care. I want Tinsley free to write her own material. Her poetry. If you don't take over her job, she'll be right back at it the moment I can rebuild out on the island and get new computer equipment." He went over to one of the windows flanking the desk and looked out. "So, what do you say? Will you go to work for me?" he asked, staring through the glass at the yard beyond.

Tinsley saw by the lines of his profile that he was tensely waiting for Clayton's response. When it came, she was as surprised as Alex was.

Clayton groaned, a heartbreaking sound.

"Geez, man." Jeremy grabbed his arm. "What's wrong? You all right?"

"They all love you!" Clayton declared, standing and pointing at Alex. "You've spent your damn money and your precious time and brain helping them, and they've repaid you by loving you. You just have no idea how much, do you?" Tears ran down his face.

"Clay, what...?" Alex looked amazed and worried.

"I'll work for you! I'm not sure I like it but I know when I'm beaten. You're a good man, just like they all say. I'm not. Maybe I'll learn from you." Clayton sat down, his tears gone, but his expression bleak. "God knows, I need to learn something from someone. I just never thought it'd be you. You've lived the right way. What I've seen out on the island proves that. No doubt about it."

"What are you talking about? What's going on out there?"

"You don't know?" Clayton looked astonished. "You mean, you didn't ask anyone to do it?"

"I have absolutely no idea what you're talking about."

"Well, I'll be..." Clayton sat back, his features softening in awe. "I think I believe you, Cousin Al. And I'm here to tell you, if anyone had told me, I wouldn't have. You know nothing about it. That's the damnedest thing I've ever heard. Yes, I'll work for you. On any terms you want." He looked at Tinsley. The respect in his eyes was genuine. "Take this man out to his home," he said. "He deserves to see what's being done out there. Do it now!"

CHAPTER EIGHTEEN

LESS THAN AN HOUR LATER, they were on the way to the island. Neither of them had any idea what to expect. Neither of them changed out of their good clothes. They were, simply, too anxious.

The channel was as smooth as glass. Tinsley handled the boat with no difficulty, though her palms had started to sweat when Alex asked her to take the helm. She had done so with reluctance, but seeing how tense he was, she did it for him. She was sure her emotions were nothing compared to those seething in her lover. The tense, taut lines of his body reflected his feelings. He was edgy and nervous to the extreme. Neither of them knew what to expect, and Clayton had done nothing to enlighten them. Just take Alex there, he'd told her. Let him see for himself. Let him see...

See what? Tinsley wondered.

There had been something in Clayton's expression. Something in the tone of his voice.... In the way his attitude had suddenly changed about working for Alex. Something that made her think this was going to be a good thing, in spite of her natural distrust of her cousin-in-law-to-be.

Well, in a second now, they would know the truth. She took a deep breath as they rounded the side of the island. That breath became a cry of joy that burst from her heart and soul.

But it was nothing compared to the shout Alex raised. He stood up, rocking the boat dangerously. He braced his feet and lifted up his arms. His red tie fluttered in the wind like a banner of triumph.

The home he had left in smoking ruins weeks ago was almost rebuilt. People swarmed over it, tools in their hands. When one man spotted Alex, a series of greetings and shouts sounded across the water. The workers and helpers stopped what they were doing and ran down to the beach, waving and yelling, delightedly.

Calling on skills she'd learned during the time they'd spent on Alex's sailboat, Tinsley steered carefully, making allowances for Alex's precarious position in the bow. She was able to recognize young Samuel, Clara and many others. Her heart was so full, she almost couldn't catch her breath, but she managed to remain in control.

That was far more than Alex could do. As Tinsley slowed and began to guide the boat in toward the dock, he yelled again, kicked off his shoes and dived overboard. He swam ashore heedless of his clothing, and began embracing his friends.

His friends welcomed him with happy tears and a joy equal to his own.

Tinsley docked the boat and watched the reunion for a moment. Then she saw Timothy limping down the pier toward her. She ran to him and gave him a hug. "You look wonderful!" she said. "I didn't even know you were out of the hospital."

Timothy grinned. "Doctor wanted me to stay for a bit longer, but I was lonesome for home. I knew when I was all right to leave, no matter what they say. I heal better here on my land. Near enough to my ocean to see and hear it. They tell me I owe you for being alive. You went in after me when I was drowning. Think I know how hard it was for you to do that. I got to say my thanks to you.''

Tinsley blushed. "I... You're welcome. Alex actually saved you. I just jumped in after you. We both could have drowned, since I didn't have the slightest idea what to do once I grabbed you.''

"Maybe so." Timothy regarded her. "But it took courage. Remember I saw you first time you went out here. I know how scared you were." He eyed the boat. "Looks to me like you learned some lessons since then.''

"I don't know," she said, gesturing over at the crowd around Alex. They began walking toward the group. "I'm marrying the guy. Isn't that crazy? How much have I really learned?''

"A whole lot," Timothy said, his smile widening. "I'd say that, if you asked.''

She was about to reply when a small shape came rushing toward Tinsley, calling her name and squealing with delight. Tinsley went down to her knees, heedless of her skirt and hose and held out her arms. "Janna!" she cried, embracing the little girl. "Janna, I did miss you, honey!''

Janna hugged her tightly, almost knocking her over in her enthusiasm. "Me, too," she said. "Me, too!" Then she pulled back and stared. "What happened to your head?" she asked, her eyes wide.

Tinsley touched her short, brown hair and laughed. She'd forgotten about her disguise. "Don't worry, darling," she said, reassuring the child. "It'll grow back blond in time for the wedding, I'm sure." She stood up and walked forward, carrying Janna on her hip.

Alex came over to her. "Look at what they did for me," he said, his expression even more awestruck than Clayton's had been. "I can't believe it." His green eyes shone with a kind of light she had seen only a few times before.

"Believe it, man," Timothy said. "I ain't exactly been in any shape to help out, but I've been supervising, you might say. You had some structure problems with the original building. This place is a whole lot better built than the old one was."

"Timothy was in the engineers corps when he was in the service," Alex explained. "So whatever he says about structure, I trust." He put his arm around Tinsley's shoulders. He looked at the house. "This is a better home for us, that I do believe."

"Because of the love that went into it," she said, looking at him. "Listen, Alex, I don't care what you said about Berringer pomp-and-circumstance marriages. There's only one place we ought to hold the ceremony, don't you think?"

Alex looked at her. "You read my mind."

"No. Just your heart."

Alex's expression was almost beatific. "Come on," he said. "Let's get the tour. Then, we need to make some plans. Did you know we have a church here on the island? Timothy's brother is the minister, even though he fishes for a living."

Tinsley felt a strange emotion rise in her mind and heart. "Really?" she replied. "I guess I should have known. People living here need a place to worship, don't they? It would be a problem sometimes to get to the mainland just to attend..." She stopped walking and stared around.

"What's the matter?" Alex started to take Janna from her. He was plainly worried. "Delayed reaction from steering the boat?"

"No. No," Tinsley said, keeping the child. She gazed at her lover. "I just realized something very basic and important."

"What's that?" He frowned.

"Why, simply that I've come home."

Alex's smile was brighter than the sunlight.

THEIR DECISION caused the expected uproar. Susan and Delores each had a fit, insisting that a wedding held out on a beach in front of an unfinished dwelling was hardly suitable for two people of Tinsley's and Alex's ages and stations in life.

"You simply cannot get married outdoors, away from any proper church. You will seem like throwbacks to the flower children weddings of the sixties," Delores declared. "What are you planning to wear? Sarongs and leis? Or, perhaps, nothing at all?"

Alex took charge. "I'll wear proper formal attire, I swear. And I understand the fears you and my mother share. But I'm going to ask you to trust Tinsley and me for a change. We know what we're doing."

"You won't be embarrassed," Tinsley assured them. "I promise."

Delores looked at Susan. "Do you trust them?" she asked. She was still bristling for a fight, Tinsley could tell.

But Alex's mother was not. "Not as far as I can throw them," Susan replied. Then, she sighed and smiled. "But, I suppose, we have little choice. They are, after all, adults."

"So rumor has it," Delores responded. But she was trying not to smile, too. The dramatic events of the last few months had mellowed her, Tinsley reflected. The events and her developing friendship-romance with Joseph. Only time would tell, but she was willing to bet that Delores and Joseph would eventually look into some sort of permanent arrangement themselves.

But she doubted they would get married the way she
and Alex were going to. This was going to be unique.
Theirs alone.

Even if she had to break her promise about embarrassing her aunt and future mother-in-law.

HER PARENTS, Ellen and Ted Cole, flew in for the wedding two weeks later. It was now summer. June, the tra-
ditional month of brides and marriages. Alex and Tinsley
drove down to Savannah to pick up her family.

Alex wasn't quite sure what to expect. Ellen, no real
surprise, was a younger version of Delores, though a bit
more relaxed, with a wind-tanned face and short blond
hair. She had the same aristocratic features and delicate
build as her older sister. In her beauty, he saw Tinsley's
beauty. Ted Cole, however, was a shock.

He was a man as big in looks and nature as the land
from which he came. He was well over six feet and built
like a fighting bull. Alex figured he must have the strength
of a dozen cowhands. But his thin lips turned in a wide,
friendly smile, and Alex saw the man's daughter in the
humorous light in Ted Cole's blue eyes. It was certainly
from her father that Tinsley got her size, irreverent attitude and remarkable strength.

"So, you're the guy she's taken on," Ted said, pump-
ing Alex's hand up and down. "Well, son, congratula-
tions. And good luck. You're likely to need it, now and
then."

"Dad, for goodness sake!" From Tinsley.

"Ted, please!" From Ellen.

"I know, sir," replied Alex, matching the handshake
grip with little effort. "I've already discovered that."

Ted threw back his head and laughed loudly, a rich, free
kind of sound. "I guess you have," he said. "I heard the

story from just about everybody but you, I guess. R
minds me of my great-granddaddy when he was fighti
them damn imported gunslingers for his land back in...'

"Daddy! Alex doesn't want to hear Cole family le
ends right now," Tinsley declared.

"Okay." Ted fixed his future son-in-law with a stea
gaze. "Don't call me 'sir.' I ain't been that since I was
the Marines."

Alex got a strange expression on his face. "All rig!
How about 'Dad,' then?"

"Sounds great to me!" Ted Cole grinned again a
embraced Alex.

"I REALLY DON'T NEED to ask if you're sure about this
Ellen said, when she and Tinsley were finally left alone f
a while. "I can see it clear as daylight on your face. A
his." She laughed and put a hand over her eyes. "It's s
of funny, you know."

"How?" Tinsley set down her glass of tea. They we
having a cool drink out on the porch. Evening had com
but Alex and Ted were still out at the island, checking
last minute details. Delores, Susan and Silvie were in tl
kitchen, working frantically on food for the party. T
three were sure they would never have enough. The
plies to the invitations had almost all been affirmativ
Several hundred people, at the very least, were likely to
there. "How funny, I mean," she added.

"Just that you've made it full circle, now," Ellen sai
"I left here for Wyoming. You've left Wyoming for..."

"For Alex. It wouldn't matter if he lived on the moo
I know that for a fact. I guess I've found what I've be
looking for all my life."

"I can tell." Ellen sighed and rocked in her cane chai
"You remind me of when your father and I were first

love." She looked up. "You do know it won't be easy, don't you? I mean, being from such different backgrounds. Different worlds, really."

"I watched you and Dad, Mom," Tinsley replied. "You haven't always liked each other. I know that. But you've always loved the ranch. That gave you focus. Something to hold on to when it wasn't so good between you."

Ellen was silent for a long time. Then, "You were wrong, Tins. I hated that damn ranch more often than I care to say. But I've always loved your father. Even when I hated him worse than the ranch!"

"You're kidding!"

"No, I'm not." Her mother smiled. "And don't worry. You'll be the same about your husband. The island is important, but it is just a piece of land. A partner to share joys and sorrows with you for the rest of your life, is far more important."

"Oh." Tinsley sat back and thought about it. Then, she smiled, too. "I guess I still don't know it all, do I?"

"No," said Ellen. "Not yet. But, neither do I."

THE MORNING of the wedding was rainy and beyond redemption, Tinsley was sure. She woke up for the last time in her room in Delores's house and ran over to the window. The silver sheeting of water on the glass dragged a groan of anguish from her. So much for the grand outdoor event, she thought. They'd have to crowd everyone they could into the tiny church, and that would leave so many folks out. Most of them probably wouldn't even bother to come because of the weather. Alex was going to be really disappointed.

So was she. She pulled on a robe and made her way downstairs for coffee. The idea of breakfast made her

slightly ill, but she would make the effort. Silvie was al
ready at work.

"You looking kind of gloomy for a girl who's gonna ge
married this afternoon," Silvie commented, handing
Tinsley a mug of steaming coffee. "You worried?"

"Look outside." Tinsley sipped, made a face. "The
tell me I ought not to."

"You ought not to." Silvie set a plate of eggs, bacon
grits and toast in front of her. "Eat."

"I can't." Tinsley pushed the plate away. "All of Al
ex's plans are spoiled by this rain."

"I'm gonna spoil you, if you don't eat breakfast," Sil
vie stated. "And don't you go predicting weather, girl
'Cause what you don't know about it around here woul
fill a great big book."

Tinsley felt a spark of hope. "You mean . . . ?"

"It'll clear." Silvie turned back to the stove. "Hav
some faith."

Tinsley looked at the food. Then at Silvie. Then out
side. "Okay," she said, "I will." She set to the breakfa
with her usual appetite.

ALEX WOKE to the smell of bacon frying and the sound c
sea gulls squawking. He crawled out of his sleeping ba
and greeted Timothy. "Going to be a good day," he saic
glancing out the window of his friend's home at the quie
sea. The far horizon was clear, even though rain fell i
sheets on Timothy's roof, making a musical sound.

"Your best day yet," Timothy said, grinning and tur
ing the bacon. "Coffee's in the pot."

Alex yawned. "Thanks," he said, and poured himse
a cup. "Now, what have I managed to forget?" he askec
sitting down to the plain, wooden table. "There's got
be something."

Timothy scratched his head. "Don't know. Marrying ain't exactly what I call myself an expert in. You better ask Clara. Her or one of the other old gals. They remember about presents and stuff like that... What's the matter?"

Alex slapped his forehead. "I remembered. What I forgot. I *knew* there was something!" He looked at his wristwatch. "Can you get me over to the mainland, Tim? I've got to find myself a jeweler."

"Lord! Don't say you forgot the ring, man!"

"No." Alex grabbed a handful of bacon and ate. "But did forget something almost as important."

As Silvie had promised, the sky began to clear by ten o'clock, but all morning Tinsley found herself anxious. It didn't help to have Silvie, Ellen, Delores and even Susan Berringer fussing over her hair, her gown, her makeup and her pearl jewelry. Only her father provided a small island of comfort and tranquility in what had disintegrated into a sea of feminine furor.

"I like your man, Tins," her dad said, in one of their quiet moments. "He's going to be fine for you."

"Thanks, Dad." She moved over carefully to kiss him. The bridal gown was all but immobilizing her. "I think so, too." She looked at her father. "Are you disappointed I won't be coming back to Wyoming?"

Ted Cole grinned, sun-squint lines radiating away from his blue eyes. "Not coming back? Who said that? Not Alex."

"But, he—"

"Honey, he ain't limiting your lives, and that's one of the main reasons I like the man. Why, he's so proud of your cowboy poetry writin', he could just bust, you know.

I don't think it's likely he'll keep you tied up out here when your audience is mostly back in the West.''

Tinsley considered this. ''I didn't realize he—''

''Tinsley!'' Delores ran into the bedroom. ''Tinsley, did you remember to get a groom's gift! I just thought of it, myself.''

''Yes.'' Tinsley went over to the small writing desk. She opened a drawer and took out a thin package. ''Here is my groom's gift, Delores. I believe you'll approve.''

Her aunt took the wrapped package. ''What in the world is it?''

''My first published collection of poems. It's dedicated to you, since it was your doing that brought Alex and I together in the first place.'' She reached into the drawer again. ''I have another copy for you.''

''I bless the day you came to live in this house,'' Delores said, hugging Tinsley close, but carefully. ''Your life has changed, and so has mine.''

''Are you and Joseph . . . ?''

''Not yet, but we're talking about it.'' Delores touched a handkerchief to her eyes. ''It's hard to think of marrying another man. But I know Frank would want me to be happy.''

''Frank would approve of your Joseph,'' Ted Cole said. He was standing quietly out of the way, but now he came over to give Delores a hug. ''I know it.''

''He sure would, but we don't have time to talk about that now,'' Ellen said, entering the room and tapping her wristwatch. ''Come on, everyone. Jason and Silvie are already down in the limo.'' She came over to Tinsley. ''Are you ready, kid?'' she asked.

''As I'll ever be!'' Tinsley touched the veil covering her short, blond hair. The brown rinse had grown out, and she had cut it off. For this momentous occasion in her life, she

nted to look as much like herself as possible. "Let's do
"

IE TRIP OUT to the island was made in relative luxury,
nsidering the way she had journeyed there the first time.
• her amazement, Clayton had come through with a
nnection that provided the bride's wedding party with
special yacht. Tinsley moved from her protected place
hind the cabin to peer at the island where a crowd on the
ach waited for her. A crowd that did not include the
oom. Where in the world was Alex?

"I don't see him," Joseph said, moving over to stand
side her. "Wasn't he supposed to sail out to meet us in
e new boat?"

"Yes." Tinsley felt queasy. "I don't see any sign of an-
her boat, do you?"

"No. But..."

"Where is he?" Delores asked. "Tinsley, this isn't
nny, if that's what you hoped it would be."

"I don't know. He..." She broke off, listening. "Do
u hear that?"

Ted Cole looked skyward. "Sounds like a helicopter."

Tinsley put her hand up to shade her eyes. "Oh, my.
hat's exactly what it is. And this is not what we in-
nded." She started to laugh as she saw Alex seated in the
assenger seat of Bob Duncan's 'copter. He was wearing
formal wedding suit, including the top hat. He grinned
own at her and waved. Tinsley, heedless of the damage
e wind and helicopter rotor downdraft did to her hair
d gown, waved back, enthusiastically.

"Hey," Jeremy shouted from the stern. "Timothy's out
re with your boat, Tinsley! He says you're to get on
oard while Alex lands on the beach."

"Oh, dear." Delores put her face in her hands. ".
those plans... Her gown! Her hair!"

"Now, now. My dear." Joseph consoled her with
arm around her shoulders. "Surely, you didn't exp
these two to go along with the program as outlined,
you?"

"I suppose not." Delores looked at Joseph and smil
"It would be out of character for them, after all, would
it."

"It would," Joseph agreed.

The wedding was a disorganized celebration after th
but it did take place in spite of the confusion, the sand a
the general hilarity. The guests all seemed to take the a
borne arrival of the groom and the seaborne arrival of
bride as part of the planned procedure. The minist
Toby Blane, Timothy's brother, managed to control
amused response to the wind-blown, sandy, dishevel
couple as they stood before him until he made the dec
ration that they were husband and wife. Then, the R
erend Blane smiled as the bride and groom kissed w
enthusiasm.

"I must explain," Alex said quietly to her as they sto
in line to receive greetings and good wishes from th
guests. "The reason I was late and had to use Bob's he
copter was—"

"It doesn't matter." She kissed him. "I know you h
good cause, whatever it was. What was it?"

"Curious?" Alex smiled.

"You know it!"

"Later, then." He grinned. "Trust me."

She smiled back at him. "I can do that," she said.

Later, she was glad she had. As the sun set and the pa
continued to roll on without them, Alex led her to t
section of his yard where the horse corral and paddo

still stood. They had been relatively unharmed by the bomb blast. Tinsley lifted her wide skirts as they crossed the ground. "Delores would have a fit," she said, "if she could see me in this muddy... Oh, Alex!"

"Your bride's present," he said, gesturing.

Jack Tar whinnied and bobbed his big, black head at her. The mare by his side did the same. Tinsley ran forward, heedless of her gown. "She's beautiful!" she declared. "Oh, Alex, what's her name?"

"Trouble." He came up to the fence as Tinsley reached out and touched the mare's velvety nose. "Just like her mate, I figure."

"No. Really. How should I call her?" Tinsley scratched the horse's ears. Jack Tar tried to shove the mare aside in order to get the attention for himself, but she held her ground, baring her teeth at the stallion. Then she made a low, murmuring noise and presented her nose again to Tinsley for stroking. "Oh," Tinsley cooed. "You are a lovely one."

"Her name's Poetic Lady," Alex said, his voice a caress. "Jack was in love, and I thought it appropriate she join our family."

Tinsley turned to look at her husband. "So you were late because you and Bob brought her over this morning? That's why you showed up in the helicopter?"

"No." Alex touched her cheek with a finger. "No. Lady's been here a few days. I went over because I forgot to pick up this." He handed her a long jewelry box. "Open it," he said.

Tinsley took the box and, curious beyond measure, opened it. On the black velvet bed lay a necklace. The pendant was gold with diamonds. "ILT?" she asked. "It's beautiful, Alex, but what does it mean?"

"Well." He took the necklace and placed it around he[r]
neck. "You see, I was setting up the computer for Jer[-]
emy and Clayton the other day, and I remembered how
you broke into my original system so easily. Althoug[h]
things certainly seem to be going well with the two o[f]
them, they are far from the most trustworthy of employ[-]
ees, as we both know. So..."

"So, you've encrypted files. Just like you did befor[e]
when you didn't want me finding out stuff."

"Exactly." He gazed at her. "Do you have any ide[a]
how beautiful you are to me?"

"Alex, is this the code?" She touched the necklace.
"What does it mean?"

"Why, it's the same code I used before. The one you
couldn't have broken, no matter how hard you tried. Because you didn't know."

"Didn't know what?"

"What it stands for."

"And that is?"

"I Love Tinsley. Corny, maybe. But it's sincere. You
see, I knew it was a true condition of my heart well before I was ready to admit to you I even wanted to get you
in bed."

"Son of a gun." She stared at him. Touched the necklace reverently.

"I suppose it seems sort of corny still, but..."

"Alex, I love you." She held his hand to her heart.
"Let's go for a ride."

"Like this?" He indicated her gown and his suit.

"Yes. Why not? We've already broken convention, and
everyone from the stuffiest old-guarder to the youngest
kid is having a blast. I want to try out my new horse."

"Delores is going to have my liver for lunch," he said,
mournfully. "On a skewer. So will your mother and

mine." Then, he picked Tinsley up in his arms. "So, I might as well die happy."

Tinsley wrapped her arms around his neck. "How do you plan to do that?"

"I'm going to get hay all over your gown." Alex kissed her. "Before we take the horses out on the beach, I am going to take my bride in the hayloft!"

She hugged him and snuggled as close as she could.

It wasn't too long before she was snuggling even closer, a condition Tinsley Berringer knew was going to be a major part of the rest of her life.

And Alex? Alex knew he had never been complete before. Now he knew he would never be incomplete again.

EPILOGUE

THE POET WILL READ from her work, the sign read. The lettering was crude and hastily drawn, but seeing it, Tinsley Berringer smiled. How different this was from the first time she'd seen those words almost three years ago, carefully lined and set up on a fancy easel at the Carleton Cay Literary Society meeting. This sign was hanging from the bulletin board in the high school gym in her old home town of Advance, Wyoming. How very different everything was!

She glanced down at her notes. They outlined her career as one of America's top female cowboy poets. Certainly, she was one of the most prolific. But one of the best? She still had trouble believing that.

But it was true, if one could judge her ability by the size of the crowd that came out to listen, even in this small community. She looked up from her notes to smile out at the audience. Many smiled, but Tinsley's eyes sought and found the people she was looking for.

The beloved faces! Tinsley felt her eyes stinging a little, but she didn't mind. Crying for sheer happiness was something she didn't fight at all these days. It happened just too darn often for her to put up a fuss. She touched a fingertip to the corners of her eyes and then heard her name as she was introduced. She stood to the hearty applause and yells of approval and, waving, walked up to the podium, carrying her book.

Alex Berringer managed to balance baby Ted in his lap, while he applauded his wife. Little Ted beamed in contentment.

Tinsley began to speak. "I learned that this collection of my latest poems were going to be published on the same day I learned I was expecting my son. Believe me, it was a day of miracles."

She gave Alex a tender look and continued. "When the publishing company wanted me to do a tour to promote the book, I said no. I couldn't leave my family to do this."

The audience moaned in disappointment.

"But," Tinsley added, "here I am." She gestured at her family. "And here they are."

The applause was deafening.

"Which just goes to show you anything's possible," she stated, smiling at Alex and the baby.

"Now, I'm going to tell you all a story." Tinsley opened the book. "This is a poem, and an adventure and a love story." She caught her husband's eyes once more.

She started to read. The epic was set in the old West. Alex closed his eyes, listened to the beloved voice and remembered every event, every word.

HARLEQUIN SUPERROMANCE®

HARLEQUIN SUPERROMANCE WANTS TO INTRODUCE YOU TO A DARING NEW CONCEPT IN ROMANCE...

WOMEN WHO DARE!
Bright, bold, beautiful...
Brave and caring, strong and passionate...
They're unique women who know their
own minds and will dare anything...
for love!

One title per month in 1993, written by popular Superromance
authors, will highlight our special heroines as they face unusual,
challenging and sometimes dangerous situations.

Don't miss our first exciting title:
#533 DANIEL AND THE LION by Margot Dalton
Available in January wherever Harlequin Superromance
novels are sold.

WWD-J

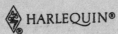

HARLEQUIN®

my Valentine

1993

The most romantic day of the year is here! Escape into the exquisite world of love with MY VALENTINE 1993. What better way to celebrate Valentine's Day than with this very romantic, sensuous collection of four original short stories, written by some of Harlequin's most popular authors.

ANNE STUART
JUDITH ARNOLD
ANNE McALLISTER
LINDA RANDALL WISDOM

THIS VALENTINE'S DAY, DISCOVER ROMANCE
WITH MY VALENTINE 1993

Available in February wherever Harlequin Books are sold.   VAL93

ROMANCE IS A YEARLONG EVENT!

Celebrate the most romantic day of the year with MY VALENTINE! (February)

CRYSTAL CREEK
When you come for a visit Texas-style, you won't want to leave! (March)

Celebrate the joy, excitement and adjustment that comes with being JUST MARRIED! (April)

Go back in time and discover the West as it was meant to be . . . UNTAMED— Maverick Hearts! (July)

LINGERING SHADOWS
New York Times bestselling author Penny Jordan brings you her latest blockbuster. Don't miss it! (August)

BACK BY POPULAR DEMAND!!!
Calloway Corners, involving stories of four sisters coping with family, business and romance! (September)

FRIENDS, FAMILIES, LOVERS
Join us for these heartwarming love stories that evoke memories of family and friends. (October)

Capture the magic and romance of Christmas past with HARLEQUIN HISTORICAL CHRISTMAS STORIES! (November)

WATCH FOR FURTHER DETAILS IN ALL HARLEQUIN BOOKS!

CALEND